WHO GETS THE APARTMENT?

"Rigolosi, a completely fresh voice in the mystery genre, writes with gusto…Don't miss this book."

—*Library Journal*

"Highly recommended for suspense fans and community libraries catering to them."

—*Midwest Book Review*

"Very clever and unique.…Rigolosi keep[s] his readers on edge with his easy-to-read narrative, lovable characters, and intriguing plot.…Rigolosi is poised to accomplish something in which few authors have succeeded—turning watchers of television into readers of books."

—Norm Goldman, BookPleasures.com

CIRCLE OF ASSASSINS

"This unusual crime novel will leave mystery buffs wanting more."

—*Library Journal*

"Part Martin Amis novella, part Minette Walters mystery, and part Magritte painting, *Circle of Assassins* offers readers a 360-degree view of crime, following not only the murderers and their victims, but also friends and family in the aftermath of the crimes. I don't think I've read such an ambitious and effective genre novel in years."

—*SpineTingler* Magazine

more…

ANDROGYNOUS MURDER HOUSE PARTY

Tales from the Back Page #3

Steven Rigolosi

Ransom Note Press

Publisher's Note: This is a work of fiction. Names, characters, places, and incidents either are the product of the author's imagination or are used fictionally, and any resemblance to actual persons, living or dead, events, or locales is entirely coincidental.

Requests for permissions to make copies of any part of the work should be e-mailed to editorial@ransomnotepress.com.

www.ransomnotepress.com

First U.S. edition

Library of Congress Cataloging-in-Publication Data

Rigolosi, Steven A.
  Androgynous murder house party / by Steven Rigolosi. — 1st U.S. ed.
    p. cm. — (Tales from the back page ; #3)
  ISBN-13: 978-0-9773787-6-0 (pbk.)
  ISBN-10: 0-9773787-6-4 (pbk.)
  1. Interpersonal relations—Fiction. 2. Parties—Fiction. 3. Murder—
Investigation—Fiction. 4. Snobs and snobbishness—Fiction. 5. Androgyny
(Psychology)—Fiction. 6. Manhattan (New York, N.Y.)—Fiction. I. Title.
  PS3618.I43A83 2009
  813'.6—dc22
                              2008030721

Published in the United States and Canada by
Ransom Note Press, Ridgewood, NJ

10 9 8 7 6 5 4 3 2 1

Printed in the United States of America

ISBN: 978-0-9773787-6-0

Ransom Note Press, LLC
P.O. Box 419
Ridgewood, NJ 07451

This book is dedicated to two great ladies:

Mary Ann O'Donnell
for 25 years of advice and friendship

and

Norah Lofts
(1904–1983)
for early encouragement and inspiration

Part One

A GATHERING ON LONG ISLAND

RENT EVERYTHING!

Looking to throw a party with flair, verve, pizzazz? Why not rent a belly dancer, a cotton candy machine, a fortune teller, a 1950s jukebox, or a mime? From tame alligators to dancing zebras, we have everything you need to make your get-together memorable. Call us at 212-555-9090, or visit our Website at **www.partyrentables.com** for the full list of rentables. You'll be glad you did!

1

One loves one's friends, one really does. But to be forced to entertain them for an entire weekend? To plaster a smile on one's face so tightly for three days that one practically gives oneself a facelift? To suffer through the lingering effects of long-ago misunderstandings that have never been satisfactorily resolved? This, surely, is asking too much of one?

Yes, it *is* asking too much. And yet that is exactly what Lee did—phoning me up and suggesting none too subtly that a weekend getaway could be just what the doctor ordered. Apparently, Lee and assorted others had been chatting, and the subject of my house on Long Island cropped up, and before anyone knew it, plans were being made to invite our entire circle to _____ for the upcoming holiday weekend. The rub being, of course, that the gathering needed my blessing to come to fruition.

The tender young thing who does my manicures was gently applying a protective glaze when the phone rang. At that very moment, I was wondering whether I should place my hand on that untamed youth in a way that would make my interest obvious, as the two of us have always had a physical chemistry that we must stop struggling against, at some point.

I fear I became slightly grumpy as a result of the ringing phone's interruption of what was looking to be at least a *liaison dangereuse,* if not an *affaire de coeur*; as the manicurist is a dear thing, but quite vapid and certainly not one to keep around one's manse for longer than, say, a season, and preferably the season in which the fewest clothes are worn.

"Who is this calling?" I barked truculently into the receiver. I fear I have the habit of broadcasting my state of mind quite blatantly, as I have found that inhibiting one's thoughts leads to all manner of gastric distress.

"'Tis I," responded Lee, in that ambiguous manner that is so hard to gauge; one can never tell whether Lee is speaking seriously, or whether fun is being had at one's expense. "Am I interrupting anything dreadfully important?"

"Not at all," replied I, shortly yet graciously, as I have always felt it incumbent upon me to demonstrate a certain amount of *noblesse oblige*. "The child who does my manicures is just finishing up. Hold the line a moment, would you?"

I reached into the pocket of my robe and paid the urchin, adding an ample gratuity. The creature is always on time and always efficient, and therefore deserves the money; and, due to extreme mindlessness, is certainly fated to end up in an abusive relationship, so why not help the child enjoy life a bit more now? As the manicurist left, I gave those well sculpted buttocks a small pat, a liberty well within my rights, given the tip I'd bestowed.

"We had the most fabulous idea," Lee continued, as I listened, grimacing. The combination of "we" and "most fabulous idea" could only mean that Lee *et alia* had cooked up a scheme sure to involve me in its serpentine machinations. "Wouldn't it be simply irresistible to have a gathering at the house in _____ over the weekend?"

"You can't possibly be serious, Lee," I gasped. "The weekend is a mere four days away. To get the house opened, have it cleaned and staffed, and have all the foods and spirits ordered would take at least a month. I simply cannot believe you are suggesting such foolishness."

"Oh, be a sport, Robin. I'll help with the arrangements, and I'll even come out early to help set up. I still have my key, so I can see to matters if I arrive before you do. It'll be tons of fun. Besides, the gang hasn't been together for a while, and we miss you."

This is the problem with longtime dear friends; they know your weaknesses and how to exploit them. Lee knows that I am, at heart, a romantic, and that I can neither abide nor resist sentimentality. Thus, in less time than it takes dime-store nail polish to dry on the fingernails of a Times Square hooker, I'd agreed to the gathering and was planning the guest list with Lee, who'd determined whom to invite long before calling me.

There'd be few surprises among the guests; they would be the same group of posers, dilettantes, and frauds who've been boring me senseless for the past decade or more. Of course, one or two would ask to bring a current lover or flavor of the month, and we'd have some good-natured fun with that person, in a manner that Lee once likened to George and Martha's treatment of Sunny in *Who's Afraid of Virginia Woolf?* This was an observation, not a judgment, since it went without saying that anyone fool enough to traipse into a gathering of long-time friends deserves that sort of trial by fire.

"I think we have everyone," I said, ticking off names. "Except for Michael and Michael. Did we exclude them deliberately?"

"Perhaps unconsciously. But even if they were invited, I doubt they'd come. They're in the middle of a huge…thing. It seems that Michael was jogging in Washington Square Park when he bumped into—of all people—Michael…I know, I know, I am as surprised as you are…The two were having an uncomfortable chat when suddenly Michael arrived on the scene with Michael. Well, Michael had a wild idea, and the four of them went back to Michael's loft, and…well, you can guess what happened. Of course, word got back to Michael, and he flipped! Meanwhile, it turns out that Michael's roommate, Michael, was an ex of Michael's from way back, and much old sludge was dredged up, with the result that Michael and Michael are now not speaking."

"Oh dear," I sighed. "I'd best just send them a written invitation through the U.S. Postal Service a few days before we leave for _____. The weekend will be over before they even get it."

We divided up the tasks, with Lee calling the guests to proffer the formal invite and me making the arrangements to get the house opened and ready.

Within seconds of hanging up the phone, I felt a migraine aura forming in front of my left eye. Why was Lee always able to talk me into these mad schemes? Our relationship had ended long ago, but I suppose a bit of the magic remained. And perhaps some of the bitterness.

2

Dr. Rosenthal called in the prescriptions I would need to make it through the weekend. As is my wont, I put my guests' needs first and asked the good doctor to order plenty of extras of everything. For there was no question that certain guests would arrive undermedicated, and the extra supply was going to be necessary if the rest of us were to avoid scenes of a disagreeable nature.

I have certain requirements that must be met regardless of my location. Whether in Algeria or Australia, Zanzibar or Zimbabwe, I must have my freshly squeezed Valencia oranges each morning, along with a ripe mango from the produce dealer I use in Brooklyn. Cut flowers are also a must, daily. The correct brands of shampoo, conditioner, facial cleanser, body wash, skin cream, toothpaste, mousse, and styling gel are as essential when away as at home—perhaps even more so, given the stresses that are an ineluctable result of being plucked from your comfortable apartment on Manhattan's Upper West Side and being dropped into a overlarge, over-drafty Tudor in _____.

It will thus come as no surprise that I sacrificed much sleep over the following days to ensure that I would be well appointed for my upcoming *pilgrimage*. So, after stocking up on the oranges and mangoes, as well as the coffees that I simply must brew each morning if I am to not be a complete brute; and after visiting many independent apothecaries around town in my quest for fresh tubes, jars, and bottles of my health and beauty needs, and coping with many incompetent salespeople whose levels of intelligence indicated the likelihood that they ingested more cosmetics than they sold; and after fighting with my florist, who complained bitterly about having to deliver flowers "all the way out to Long Island" despite the business I bring to his shop, which is always struggling as a result of his being more willing to chase a piece of ass than a sale; and after valiantly seeking out a new feather pillow in a well-known Park Avenue linens store, where the inept sales clerks would have been better utilized in a sweatshop making bedclothes—after nearly two days of these activities, I had finally attended to my own needs and could begin the quest for those items, conveniences, or inanities that would put my guests at ease, since making one's guests feel comfortable and welcome is, after all, the essence of hospitality.

Lee would be simply unbearable if a certain brand of pistachio were not provided, or if any of those pistachios were not split open in such a way as to allow easy access to the nut. Not wanting to worry about this when I arrived at the house,

I spent several hours in the apartment separating the correct pistachios from the incorrect ones, discarding those that would have infuriated Lee. During the years of our relationship, Lee had been ever vigilant for small reasons to fly off the handle, and, after years of suffering through those bouts of temper, I was unwilling to provide any excuse for such behavior this upcoming weekend.

Alex would, of course, demand satin sheets in that difficult-to-find hue somewhere between aquamarine and teal, and would complain the entire weekend if such creature comforts were not available. So back I went to Park Avenue to find the sheets, once again entering the world of female sales clerks whose attitudes were as big as their buttocks, and male sales clerks whose egos were inversely proportional to the unimpressive bulges in their off-the-rack H&M slacks.

J insisted on particular aperitifs and dessert wines from the northeast corner of Italy and the southwest corner of Switzerland, while Chris refused to go near any libations from either region, demanding the heavier and more syrupy spirits of the former Ottoman Empire—all with the result that I spent nearly half a day chasing down the potables that would help J and Chris accomplish the task they find most daunting in life: the maintenance of an emotional equilibrium between a disturbing euphoria and a pugilistic contentiousness.

Law, too, would be there—or had, at least, accepted the invitation. To satisfy the needs of that difficult but sensual individual, I purchased a dozen packages of clove cigarettes, as well as some other exotic treats for which Law had expressed a preference in the years of our acquaintance. Perhaps this weekend Law and I would indulge our unspoken and mutual passion, as we sometimes do; though such consummation, I knew, would have to come from a carefully staged series of events made to look spontaneous; and whether I would have the energy to engage in the hunt, and whether I would think it worthwhile to do so, remained to be seen.

Having returned utterly exhausted from my errands, I finished my after-dinner sorbet and retired early, setting the alarm for four a.m. I would, of course, need the morning to get the house in _____ prepared, though I'd given the caretakers strict orders regarding what needed to be done. If I were lucky, the daft old couple would have followed 80% of my instructions, and I'd have a few hours to myself before the horde descended. But if the old coots were in one of their more difficult or ignorant moods, I'd need the whole morning to put the house into a semblance of order. So, best to leave Manhattan early, to be on the safe side.

As soon as my head hit the pillow, a wave of exhaustion washed over me: the type of exhaustion felt by battle-weary soldiers, or medical students who've worked three-day shifts in a hospital, or Olympic athletes who've practiced for sixteen hours. Honestly, I loved my friends more than life itself, but they were going to be the death of me.

3

Oh yes, the Long Island "Expressway." I'd had powerful fantasies that leaving at six in the morning would have allowed me to whisk my way briskly across that *outré* outer borough of Queens. Alas, it was not meant to be.

I'd managed to get out of *La Città* rather quickly, which made having to share the Midtown Tunnel with foul-mouthed truck drivers (who'd probably just had sex with diner waitresses) and swarthy purveyors of illegal substances (most likely on their way to LaGuardia or JFK to pick up the week's shipment of crack cocaine) more tolerable than it otherwise would have been. But the moment the tunnel spilled me into Queens, traffic came to a dead standstill. As was only to be expected, Buicks, Saturns, and other working class coupes began cutting one another off to advance six inches at a time. I saw someone in the car to my left giving me the eye, as it were, but I was in no condition for a sexual romp, having taken less than the usual amount of time with my toilet, and not feeling as though I looked my best. But isn't this always the way? One is always at one's most unexpectedly sensual when one is most natural.

When we'd moved no more than two miles in half of an hour, I gave up the valiant fight and popped two of the 'peach pills' so kindly provided by Dr. Rosenthal. They kicked in after fifteen minutes, just as the traffic jam began to dislodge itself. On the horizon I saw the cause of the horrific delay; it appeared that a gap-toothed yokel wearing some sort of "sports" clothing had smashed into the rear bumper of a car driven by a young woman with a large lipsticked mouth whose hair was teased higher than the cruising altitude of a 747. Yet the boy did have a certain slimy sensuality, and the size of the young lady's mouth did hint at the many items it could comfortably accommodate. I found it interesting that at one stage of my life—the stage during which I'd been with Lee—I would have preferred one of those young people now standing in the left lane of the L.I.E., dodging the bullets shot by motorists made irritable by the delay; but now, after a reversal of sexuality that stunned some and was seen as inevitable by others, my eyes lingered much longer on the other; which, I suppose, only made the delays behind me last that much longer, though if I'd needed to wait so long to get to that point, surely it was only fair that those behind me do the same.

I pulled into the once-lovely hamlet of _____ at 10 a.m., already an hour behind schedule. As the "season" had not yet started, my passage through the town was unimpeded by large-thighed women from the Upper East Side in search of organic grapes or ill-behaved children frolicking in the streets as their *au pairs* searched every storefront for a man who would marry, and thus bestow U.S. citizenship upon, them.

The caretakers, whose names I always forget but who are paid quite well for their services nonetheless, had arrived even earlier than I. The house's many windows were open, as were those of the guest cottage. The male caretaker, who smells like mold, helped me carry in my many shopping bags and valises, and the female caretaker, who smells like swamp water, helped load the icebox and the cabinets. Of course she attempted to place the several fine burgundies I'd purchased into the refrigerator, but one did need to practice at being patient, because the guests would be arriving soon enough, and one needed as much practice in patience as one could get before their various grand, swooping entrances.

I unpacked several of the bags and unloaded their contents on the dining room table, which my great-grandfather had brought to the States from England more than a century earlier. Dividing the goodies into various piles, I dispatched the male caretaker to bring the pistachios to Lee's room and the satin sheets to Alex's. I sent the female caretaker to the guest cottage with the inebriants I'd selected for J and Chris, who were now officially a couple after several years of an approach-and-retreat game that had maddened all within a ten-mile radius (including Lee, who had, I was certain, dallied with J at one point). I thought they'd enjoy the privacy of the cottage, and placing them there meant I would see less of them than if they'd stayed in the main house. Clearly a desirable scenario for all concerned.

The needs of my guests attended to, it was time to arrange my own bedroom, as I am used to having every personal item in a specific location, and it would be unfair to my guests if I were to arrive grumpy at breakfast the next morning due to a misplaced bottle of scent or a lost tin of deodorant.

The useless caretakers were nowhere to be found—a not unexpected occurrence with domestics, whose laziness and sense of entitlement are so well documented—so I was forced to carry my personal valise all the way up the stairs to my *chambre*. I was not surprised to find that the door to the master bedroom had not been unlocked, for surely it is too much to expect the caretakers to have prepared the homeowner's room first? I could feel the onset of a migraine, or perhaps a cluster headache, as I returned to the study on the main floor and retrieved the master set of keys. I didn't recall locking the bedroom when I was last at the house, which only added fuel to the fire of my migraine or cluster, because the logical conclusion could only be that the spiteful caretakers had purposely locked that door to cause me as much inconvenience as possible.

I had just unlocked the door, and was turning the knob, when I heard the female caretaker re-enter the dining room and say, "Robin? Excuse me, Robin?" An unwanted interruption by a servant is bad enough, but this was all the more crazymaking because I have told the caretakers more than once that we are not on a first-name basis.

The door to the bedroom swung open just as I looked over the balustrade to inquire what the nervy hag wanted. From behind me I heard a loud crash and the sound of breaking glass.

The male caretaker ran out of one of the guest rooms—Lee's—as the female caretaker ran up the stairs, as impatient for information as the housewives who subscribe to *The National Enquirer*.

"My God! What happened?" asked the harridan.

I poked my head into the master bedroom. The crystal chandelier that my mother had hung there nearly half a century earlier had somehow crashed to the place on the floor where I would have been standing if I'd entered the room. Normally I do not share personal information with hired help, but I was caught off guard and thus poured out my heartbreak to the caretakers, telling them that the chandelier had been handcrafted by Parisian artisans at the command of my father, who'd ordered it as a birthday gift for Mother.

"I think you should stop complaining and start being thankful that it didn't land on you," said the vicious harpy, who clearly enjoyed the adding of insult to injury.

"If you'd just opened up the master bedroom for fresh air like you did with all the other rooms, this could have been avoided," I shot back, all too anxious to share some of the pain I felt for the loss of the priceless chandelier.

The male caretaker spoke up. "We only did what you asked." He sounded as defensive as a once-muscular man whose pecs have turned into breasts and has that fact commented upon by a younger rival.

"Please stop speaking nonsense," I said, as the migraine/cluster reached epic proportions. "You know that opening up the bedrooms is always part of your duties when preparing the house."

"And we would have," the wretch responded, "if you hadn't specifically told us not to."

"Have you gone mad?" I demanded.

"Did you or did you not leave a message telling us that you wanted to get your bedroom ready yourself, and that it should stay locked until you got here?"

"I did no such thing."

"Well, someone did, because we got a message saying exactly that."

So now this Julius and Ethel Rosenberg-type couple were lying to save their own skins. My head was pounding dreadfully; I couldn't engage in the conversation a moment longer, so I ordered the female caretaker to clean up the mess while I retired to another room for a much-needed nap.

As I entered the guest room soon to be occupied by Alex, a thought occurred to me. I turned to the slattern and asked, "Why did you call me from downstairs, just before I entered my *chambre*?"

The bandersnatch replied, "Because you ran over my bicycle with your car when you pulled up to the house."

And wasn't that typical of the female caretaker, to be worried about a mass-produced piece of metal and rubber when an irreplaceable handcrafted chandelier had just come crashing down? Never in my life have I encountered such self-centeredness.

4

It goes without saying that I was unable to rest; the stresses of a house soon to be full of horrid guests, combined with the loss of a lighting fixture with ample sentimental and monetary value, banished sleep.

Thus, after tossing and turning for nearly an hour, chased by the demons that haunt any host who has any concern whatsoever that the houseguests will enjoy themselves, I returned to the first floor to continue preparations. The caretakers had halfheartedly swept up the master suite and made a weak attempt at finishing some other tasks, undoubtedly feeling guilty about the loss of the chandelier (the value of which I was considering deducting from their fees) and therefore slacking somewhat less in their duties, as if such an attempt to curry my favor were not embarrassingly transparent.

Around two o'clock I watched through the kitchen window as a large truck pulled into the driveway. In preparation for the evening's meal, I was busily shredding crabs I'd had flown in from a small town in Maine at considerable expense.

Before going to greet the truck, I wiped my hands, which were already beginning to swell due to my moderate allergy to *les fruits de mer*—more proof, I maintain, that I put my guests' needs above my own, as both Lee and Alex had specifically requested the crabcakes. (J and Chris would, of course, eat anything placed before them, given their underdeveloped palates and penchant for wolfing down their food like pigs denied their slop. As for Law and me—there are those who believe that crabs are an aphrodisiac, and should I decide to pursue the seduction I'd been pondering, the crabs might be one way to begin paving a path between my bedroom and Law's.)

The truck was from the party rental company I'd seen advertised in the back pages of *The Clarion*, that ill-written rag for socially ambitious Upper West Siders. The well-built young man driving the truck set up the tables and chairs I'd ordered for the back patio, as the last time I'd been to the house I'd noticed that my recently purchased outdoor table had a small crack, undoubtedly due to the shoddy craftsmanship of those companies that mass-produce outdoor furniture for clock punchers who live in the low-end suburbs and who like to grill with their shirts off, proudly displaying their hairy beer bellies to the neighbors' wives, whom they have most likely bedded. I hadn't had time to purchase a new patio set, not having expected freeloaders at the house until later in the season, and I certainly was not going to give Lee—whose eye for detail was as sharp as that of a thieving prostitute looking for men to drug and rob, and whose tongue was as acidic as the wines at the Ninth Avenue bars—any ammunition to use against me.

After setting up the table, umbrella, and chairs, the driver—who really was quite fetching in that way of ostensibly "straight" men who go to the gym frequently and wear tight shirts to show off their biceps, telling themselves that such dress will attract women, while choosing not to notice that the attention they are garnering is coming mostly from other men—proceeded to set up a croquet playing field in the further reaches of the property. I oriented myself so that I could enjoy the view as he bent down to drive in the stakes, feeling a certain admiration for a person who was so clearly of no higher than average intelligence and who was content with his lot in life. One might even say that I felt envy for the fellow; how liberating it must be to live life so un-self-consciously, never entertaining thoughts of anything remotely philosophical or spiritual; never feeling compelled to get the best seats at cultural events; never eating anything other than beef and chicken. Yes, I admired the man's simplicity almost as much as I admired his buttocks.

"Ya ready for the birds?" he asked after setting up the croquet field, and I couldn't help but wonder if the attraction was mutual—there is a certain brand of man who likes someone older, and this particular man, whose nametag said "Bud," might just have been that type. But if Bud and I were to dally, he might still be present when the guests arrived, and eagle-eyed Lee would certainly read the situation properly and exact revenge for it the entire weekend.

"Yes, indeed," said I, avoiding temptation by simultaneously avoiding eye contact.

Bud walked into the truck and returned with three cages full of peacocks. He opened the cages and the birds emerged slowly and regally, taking over the property in much the same way that carbuncles slowly but surely take over the buttocks of adult film stars. Bud also dumped an unopened bag of feed on the patio, telling me that if I fed the peacocks every 24 hours, they'd be no bother.

"Do I have to worry about them flying away?" I asked, fearful that I was now responsible for the welfare of a dozen peacocks in addition to that of five emotionally unpredictable houseguests.

"Nah, they're lazy birds, they won't go anywhere. Just keep 'em fed and they'll be happy. I'll be back to pick 'em up on Monday."

I signed the paperwork and surveyed the flock. The peacocks did add a lovely touch; I'd been wanting to have the majestic birds on the property ever since I'd seen an English film whose title I cannot recall. Renting before buying seemed a good idea.

As I watched, two of the peacocks defecated amounts that were really rather shocking for birds their size. This was one occurrence I hadn't counted on. I had a moment of panic until I remembered that I have caretakers for exactly this reason.

5

No sooner had I breathed this sigh of relief than a public cab painted a noxious shade of vomit green pulled up. Out stepped Lee, who I must admit was looking as delectable as a bowl of pork rinds would look to construction workers who've just beaten their common-law wives for losing the TV's remote control.

"Robin!" Lee exclaimed, as if surprised to see me.

"Hello, dear," I responded. We embraced awkwardly, as has been our style for the several decades of our acquaintance. The embraces hadn't been any less awkward when we were together, partially because Lee was always very concerned that clothing remain unrumpled and hair remain unmussed; and partly because I have long felt that embracing is an overrated activity that can cause scoliosis, slipped disks, and other conditions that can make the aging process even more of a challenge than it already is.

"Why do you look as though you've seen a ghost?" I asked. For, upon closer inspection, I noticed that Lee's complexion was quite pale, which called unflattering attention to those blubbery yet lizard-like lips that have always been Lee's most unappealing (physical) quality.

Lee recovered quickly. "Oh, dear. Is it that obvious? I'm sure you can intuit what the problem is."

"Pat?"

"Yes, but the less we speak of it, the better. I'm at the end of my rope."

"But it just started. Has it gone sour already?"

Lee raised a hand to ward off further questions. "Please, Robin, this is not a good time. I still need several days to process recent events. I'm sure we'll discuss them before the weekend is over, but not now, *s'il vous plaît*. Suffice it to say that the past has come back to haunt me in a most unexpected way."

When not in the mood to discuss something, there is no one in the world more effective than Lee at blocking any attempt at communication—yet another issue we'd had during the tenure of our romantic relationship, and one that, combined with Lee's unfortunate tendency to embezzle my money and several small peccadilloes on my part not worth mentioning, had led to our ultimate break-up.

"Far be it from me to force confidences before they are ready to be shared," I responded jocosely. "I've put you in the room at the far end of the corridor, just for a change of pace."

"Who will be sojourning next to me?"

"You, then Alex next door, then Law, then I in my usual room."

"Ah." Lee sounded pleased. "And, remind me, is there a communicating door between my room and Alex's?"

I could not help but smile inwardly; here was Lee in the throes of a hideous something with Pat, yet conspiring, perhaps, to bed Alex. If gossip is to be believed, and I find that it usually is, Lee and Alex had engaged in quite a rapturous few weeks several years ago, exchanging erotic *billets doux* and generally making fools of themselves by denying the *liaison* to those who knew them best, and who knew exactly what was going on.

Or, might it have been that Lee, who is well aware that I occasionally experience just the tiniest streak of jealousy, asked the question *re* the communicating door solely to arouse that sleeping beast in me? If this were indeed the case, my options were limited to one: Play along and maintain the *sang froid* for which I am so well known.

"Yes, there is," I said mischievously, grinning, grinding my rear molars to dust, "and you may wish to ensure that it remains unlocked, in the event that you and Alex wish to play a moonlight sonata."

"I don't know what you're implying," Lee shot back. "It is sometimes fun to drink coffee and share confidences with one's friends late at night. If your one-track mind assumes activities beyond that, well, that is more of a reflection on you than it is on me."

"The caretakers will bring up your luggage," I replied coldly, looking at the twelve suitcases Lee had brought for the three-day weekend. I then exited the scene (slowly, deliberately, without any indicator of emotion) to check on the peacocks.

Over the next several hours, the remaining guests trickled in. First came J and Chris, who, as I believe I have mentioned, are capable of only two emotional states, intense love and intense hatred for each other, and who appeared to be deeply enmeshed in the latter. Chris was, as usual, wearing clothing one or two sizes too small, and as always I had to avert my eyes from J's hair, which had once again been dyed a color not seen in nature, and concentrate instead on J's form, which was overadorned with the usual odd pieces of jewelry that are sometimes a source of mockery among J's detractors. This distinctly strange couple I summarily dispatched to the guest house, the better to accuse each other in private of infidelities and other real or imagined slights. Alex arrived next, in a Chevrolet Cavalier that I insisted be hidden inside the barn/garage so as not to set the neighbors' tongues wagging. No sooner had the auto been stowed than Alex ran off in search of Lee, leaving me to wonder if Lee and Alex hadn't orchestrated this entire weekend as an excuse to be together; which, if gossip is to be believed, was exactly what they did the last time they carried on.

Last to arrive was Law, whose face seemed to indicate a legacy of tears from earlier in the day or, perhaps, the previous evening. As always, the flaxen-haired Law was cool, elegant, noncommittal; and off the dear creature went to freshen up for dinner, which I was busily preparing with no aid from anyone, which is only to be expected when one is surrounded by selfish people.

6

There are those who wonder why life sometimes becomes too much for me to bear. But: I ask you to place yourself in the following situation. Assume that, solely for your guests' gustatory pleasure, you have planned a simple but elegant meal for the first evening of everyone's stay: freshly prepared *pâté de fois gras* and tapenade, followed by a tossed salad with a light raspberry vinaigrette dressing, followed by saffron-infused crabcakes, and ending with a Linzer tart that you'd had the foresight to purchase in advance, all while knowing that you would be passing the torte off as your own creation, the better, perhaps, to ensure the accolades that are your due.

An unassuming meal that, for any other chef in the world, would have been easy to execute. But as I began to prepare the first and second courses, I was assaulted by the inferior quality of the products I'd procured. The goose livers were fatty and smelled worse than the armpits of a sailor, and were clearly useless unless I wished to give my guests trichinosis. Trying to stem a rising tide of bitterness and "Why me"-ism (two emotional states I make a habit of avoiding), I decided to focus my energies on the second course. I'd planned a salad of radicchio and arugula, and had purchased those items from the immigrant produce merchant in Brooklyn, who, it seemed, on the day of his radicchio delivery had been too busy thinking about how to hide the rats and cockroaches in his establishment from the health inspector to ensure that his produce met certain standards of acceptability—which it did not; my horror upon viewing the gamy salad greens heightened all the more because, like a buff young man whose clothes cover a body made pimply through steroid usage, the radicchio looked so pleasing on the outside.

The icing on the cake (if you'll forgive the pun, as mental exhaustion sometimes causes me to revert to clichés and other hackneyed expressions, which it is my normal practice to eschew) was unpacking the Linzer to find that the golden-brown crisscrosses of the crust had somehow been damaged during the trip from Manhattan, making the face of the tart resemble the countenance of a female televangelist whose make-up has been smeared beyond repair by the oral gratification she has just bestowed upon the cameraman.

This final discovery nearly sent me over the edge; and it was only with the aid of several of the 'apricot pills' prescribed by Dr. Rosenthal that I was able to regain any semblance of equilibrium or composure; and to my guests' occasional insincere queries whether I needed any help in the kitchen, I replied in the negative, as I have long suspected that nothing brings Lee, and possibly Alex, J, and Chris, more joy than to be a spectator of my suffering. Which pleasure, of course, I was unwilling to impart.

I scanned the countertop, averting my eyes from the unacceptable livers and sweeping away the hacked radicchio with one swoop of my chopping knife. This would not stand; a trip to the market was in order.

The guests were outdoors, lounging about idly like trailer-park denizens awaiting their welfare checks and the payoffs of their latest insurance scams. Lee and Alex were engaged in a lively *tête-à-tête*; eating pistachios and sitting quite close to each other, I noticed, their knees almost touching. One could not have imagined a better study in contrasts: blustery, chunky, hazel-eyed Lee and prematurely gray, slender-as-a-stick Alex. J and Chris were lazily playing cards, each more concerned with quaffing syrupy-sweet libations and delivering witty ripostes (as if they possessed the IQ's required to engage in such mental gymnastics) than with winning the game. Observing from a distance, one couldn't help but notice Chris occasionally stealing a glimpse at Law, who sat off to the side, smoking a clove cigarette, reading a magazine, and looking freshly scrubbed and radiant, as always. One also could not avoid noticing how oblivious J was to the subtext of the situation.

"I'm off to market," I said jejunely as I passed the five slugs sipping the spirits I'd chased all over Manhattan.

"Oh?" Law intoned, listlessly.

"Yes, I need a few last-minute items. Would anyone like to come with? Lee? Law?"

Both nearly jumped out of their skins.

"Oh, dear, I simply am not up for the ride," said Lee. "Plus I'm not loving my hair today. I couldn't bear to be seen in public." And I supposed I could not blame Lee, whose uncontrollably frizzy reddish hair looked more like a bird's nest than usual.

"Robin, I *would*," sighed Law, "but I'm just so exhausted from the trip out here. You don't mind terribly, do you?"

"Not at all," I replied; the trick of dealing with these people, whose sole goal was to drive one to the brink of madness, being the ability to lightly, freely, pleasantly dismiss their behavior as of no consequence, and having no lasting effects on one's psyche.

As I walked towards the car, I noticed all five guests moving off the patio and through the door into the kitchen. Perhaps they saw an opportunity to comb the house for antiques and heirlooms that would fit snugly into their weekenders?

I started the car and was about to put it in reverse when I realized that, in my haste to get away from that hateful radicchio, I'd forgotten my wallet. I knew the local greengrocer vaguely, a small, ratlike man whose inflated self-esteem was matched only by his inflated prices. Perhaps he'd sell me new goose livers and radicchio on credit; but I was loath to ask a favor of the rodentlike creature. So back I went into the house to retrieve some filthy lucre.

I'd just retrieved my wallet from the kitchen nook in which I hide it (the better to prevent petty thefts from caretakers and other passersby/guests who might be short on cash—which, due to their extravagant lifestyles and lack of consistent employment, most of my current houseguests frequently are) when I heard what can only be described as an explosion. The force of the blast shattered one of the kitchen windows.

In the backyard, what remained of my Saab was a smoldering wreck. My guests came running onto the scene and stopped dead when they saw me standing there, holding my wallet. Their faces betrayed at least two emotions: shock at the blast, and concern that their clothes might get dirty.

"Good heavens!" Lee exclaimed. "What's happened?"

I certainly had no idea, and said as much. "But I'm still standing, thankfully."

"Yes, thankfully," the shrimpish J said while the much taller, and gawkier, Chris nodded in agreement. The others remained silent, looking as horrified as the town whore who reads bathroom graffiti complimenting her skills.

"This is all too nerve-wracking," I said, once again experiencing those flashing lights that signal the onset of migraine. "First, the chandelier; now this."

"You must get some rest, Robin," said Law, kindly—the only person present, I believe, who was truly grateful that my heart was still beating.

I slowly trudged up to the bedroom as Lee placed a call to the caretakers to come and "do something about" the smoking wreck and shattered window. As I shut the door behind me and threw myself onto the bed, the lights of the migraine aura lit up my eyelids like the flashing metal fillings of grubby children whose mothers have let them eat too much candy; and before I knew it, my body gave out and I was asleep.

I awoke two hours later, feeling marginally refreshed and able to put the afternoon's events behind me. For how upset, really, can one become over an inevitable truth of the Modern Age—*viz.*, that machines can and do malfunction with regularity, and that innocent people are sometimes hurt as a result? To become upset would be to allow the world to triumph; and allowing the universe such an easy victory was not a course I particularly wanted to follow; not while life was so good, with my closest friends gathered around me.

I went downstairs in search of liquid refreshment. Alex and Lee were sitting in the kitchen sipping from a bottle of my most expensive Bordeaux, their backs to the dining room door.

"Well, I've tried twice," Lee said, sounding as pent-up as an overweight teenager in a miniskirt.

"Maybe it wasn't meant to be," Alex replied doubtfully.

"I thought we agreed it is?"

"I'm having second thoughts."

"That's fine. If you won't, then I'm sure one of the others will."

I tiptoed back from the doorway, struggling with a moral dilemma. Should I give these two sorrowful creatures space for their private conversation, or should I eavesdrop for information that might give me an edge in the repartee that was sure to occur over dinner? I chose the former, as, truthfully, I found the situation quite sad. Lee really was acting in a most unbecoming manner. The little snippet of conversation I'd heard had made the situation quite clear: It seemed obvious that Lee had twice tried to seduce Alex, with no apparent success; for Alex's ability to hold out until exactly the right moment was legendary, and one could never be sure, with Alex, that the right moment would indeed arrive. Lee had clearly been throwing the ball back into Alex's court by implying the possibility of an *amour* with J, or Chris, or Law; which, if you know Alex, is a superb strategy, for Alex is known to suddenly want something when that particular something loses interest or suddenly becomes unavailable.

7

The caretakers had arrived while I was resting. They'd managed to sweep up the broken glass from the shattered kitchen window and were clearing the charred Saab debris from the patio. Seeing them with their brooms, I was struck, not for the first time, at how naturally sweeping and other cleaning tasks come to people from certain social classes; more proof, I believe, in support of the Social Darwinist theories that I have long espoused, though not always to universal acclaim.

J and Chris had managed to cobble together a salad, of sorts, from the arugula and bits and pieces of the radicchio. Alex and Law had thrown together the *foie gras* from the noisome livers, and had, of course, made it much too greasy—not that any of my guests, who'd been weaned on frankfurters and tacos, would notice. I commenced the sautéing of the crabcakes while Lee set the table, choosing water-spotted wine glasses and placing them on the table in such a way as to make my housekeeping habits appear as slovenly as those of a single mother of five whose bonbons melt on the floor and whose children defecate in corners as the opening credits of *The Jerry Springer Show* start rolling.

The female caretaker, who is sometimes less confrontational than the male, inquired as to my health and state of mind before she left; I replied with the graciousness for which I am known that the nap had done me good and that I was back to my vivacious self; a lie, of course, since the lingering aftereffects of a migraine are brutal and many. But I have never been one to complain.

"Your friend, Lee...." the female caretaker began; at which point my head began to throb again, as I did not expect the caretakers to be on a first-name basis with my guests any more than with me.

"Yes?" I snapped, attempting to put paid to further conversational liberties.

"I recognize that voice, I think."

"Do you?" I replied, with coldness. This line of conversation could go nowhere; for not only was it unheard of for a caretaker to speak with her employer as if they were on equal terms, it was equally audacious to assume that said employer would be willing to gossip about the houseguests.

"When we got the phone message telling us not to unlock the master bedroom, we thought it was from you, even if you sounded a little different. But I spoke to Mitchell, and we agree—we think it was your friend Lee."

My rage knew no barriers. I'd obviously been mistaken in thinking the female caretaker less ignorant than her husband, a conclusion now cemented in my mind by her blatant attempt to sow the seeds of discord among me and my guests. I wondered what possible motive she could have for attempting to draw Lee into her web of lies and deceit, and asked her as much.

"Never mind. Forget I mentioned it," was the surly response.

A light dawned on the horizon of my mind. The explanation was suddenly as clear as the minds of the twenty-somethings who frequent the downtown hotspots: The filthy-minded female caretaker—a married woman, no less—had developed a case of lust for my friend and ex, and was seeking to separate Lee from the rest of the party so that she could offer her own special brand of "consolation."

Did she really think I was so blind that I could not see through her motives, as clearly as I can see the remains of the receding hairlines of balding men who have shaved their heads in an attempt to camouflage that fact? The question was whether or not to confront her with my epiphany; and this I decided not to do, as I have always made it a practice not to cast my pearls before swine.

After changing into my evening wear, I joined my guests in the dining area. J was wearing the usual baubles, bangles, and beads over an extremely unflattering ensemble. Chris was much less adorned but, as always, had not managed to find any properly fitting attire. Alex looked like an aged drowned ferret, as usual, and Lee's hennaed hair hinted at the considerable and futile effort that had been made to get that burning bush under control. Law had changed into a simple pair of extremely expensive slacks and an even more expensive oversized shirt. Such clothing had to be a gift from an admirer of some means, for the penurious Law could barely afford to keep food on the table, much less purchase a wardrobe masterminded and marketed by overpriced European designers.

"Poor thing, you've had a rough day," Lee began. "Allow us to serve the *foie gras* and salad. You just sit and enjoy." The irony with which Lee said the words was consummate, those three sentences having been expertly crafted to instill as much guilt in me as possible for making my guests feel obligated to help with the cooking duties. Lee has long been second to none in the art of guilt inducement, yet another reason that our relationship has had more ups and downs than the panties of a barmaid in a roadside saloon.

Rather than insisting that I help with the serving—as I'd used up my energy reserves several hours earlier—I sat back as Lee brought in the *pâté*. It was truly reprehensible stuff, tasting even worse than it looked; I needed several glasses of a swill-like shiraz (brought by J and Chris, whose tastes in wine are as developed as the infrastructure of Third World nations) to disengage my gag reflex. The salad, served by Law, was marginally better, though of course laden with too much dressing, which someone (probably the midgetlike J, whose inability in the kitchen, as well as the bedroom, had been much commented upon by some unkind people of our acquaintance, including Lee) had thrown together hastily, unaware that preparing an edible dressing requires more than combining two cups of parsley and one cup of oregano with some olive oil.

Looking around at the seated guests, I couldn't help but think that I could not have assembled a more perfectly balanced crowd if I'd tried. Three men, three women; three gay, three straight—all from different walks of life and different backgrounds, sitting together and enjoying a meal with dear friends. The only things this motley assortment had in common were (1) their utter lack of funds, and (2) their ability to charm unsuspecting homeowners into inviting them for getaway weekends that would provide blissful respite from bill collectors and repo men.

Over salad the conversation turned to current events; a topic that I find extremely dull, as the term is synonymous in my mind with the sexual escapades of heroin-addicted Hollywood starlets and power-hungry politicians with the morals of alleycats and the intelligence of millipedes. Law spoke of this male movie hero's supposed liaison with that female TV star, who, as all the world knew, was living with her same-sex partner; J followed up by discussing the misfortunes of a rock star whose offstage antics would be enough to embarrass such unembarrassables as Britney Spears or Amy Winehouse. Lee then brought up a recent murder in Manhattan, a case in which a prominent psychiatrist ended up having multiple personalities, one of which was a serial killer responsible for the murder of a famous socialite's husband; a fact that surprised none of us, who have all lain on the couch at one time or another and who have concluded that those treating us are often as unqualified for the job as the triple-D breasted candidate who interviews for, and gets, the secretarial position to the CEO. Law, much beleaguered assistant to my very own Dr. Rosenthal, nodded but said not a word for fear of breaching any professional confidences.

"I read somewhere that the husband of the murdered woman is having the devil's own time even staying in his apartment," Alex commented. "Something about the woman owning the apartment, but not having a will."

I experienced a moment of sadness, looking around the grand dining hall of the house that had been in my family for four generations. I have no children, and never will; some of what I own will be given to charity after my death; some will go to friends like Alex, J, and Chris, who deserve nothing but who have been a source of *divertissements* over the years; and much (including the house and my apartment in Manhattan) will go to Lee, with whom I have an unbreakable bond, despite the ability of that individual to behave in ways that would send even the Dalai Lama scrambling for an Uzi. Of course, none of my guests were aware of these provisions in my last will and testament, for I believe that such information is to be shared only with one's investment counselor and attorney, and perhaps one's therapist.

I insisted upon serving the crabcakes myself, partially to ensure that they were properly presented, but also to drink in the oohs and aahs that they receive upon being first viewed and smelled. I brought the plates out, one by one, serving Lee first (secretly hoping, I am not ashamed to say, that the cakes would be cold by the time I'd served all the others) and myself last.

I had said "*Bon apétit*" and raised my fork when Alex said, "Robin, hold just one second. It's time for a surprise." I lowered my fork and feared what might be in store. To my delight, the surprise turned out to be a bottle of _____, truly one of the finest French whites to leave the borders of that haughty and overrated country. Forgive me if I am reluctant to mention this particular bottle by name; but I have found that, in the past, when I have recommended certain vintages, my advice has been heeded so closely that it became impossible to procure those wines for myself afterwards; and, as this bottle is a special favorite of mine, I do not wish to advertise its excellence and therefore diminish its supply.

"Allow me to do the honors," Alex said lightly, disappearing with the bottle into the kitchen in search of a corkscrew.

A moment later, Alex was back, carrying a single glass of the wine on a silver tray. The glass was deposited before me, as before royalty; a feeling which, I am mature enough to admit, was not unpleasant.

I lifted the glass lovingly, sniffed the heavenly bouquet, and brought the glass to my lips. At last, I thought, a moment of sheer pleasure in a day that had been as hellish as certain streets in the West 40s.

Just as I was about to sip, Lee plunged a fork into the crabcakes and began munching. "Hmmm," was the comment. "These crabcakes seem a bit heavy on the saffron."

As bones snap when a prizefighter slaps around the girl-friend who is supporting him; as twigs snap when trodden upon by gluttonous children exiled to summer weight-loss camps; as castanets snap when played by aging Spanish dancers whose pantyhose can no longer hide their varicose veins—so snapped I. To be insulted thus by Lee in my own home, after what I'd gone through! It was all too much. I took the glass of wine from my lips and threw its contents in Lee's face.

"Perhaps some wine will drown out the excessive saffron," sneered I, standing and exiting.

The others looked on, not shocked and, dare I say, supportive of my action.

On my way up the stairs, I heard Alex say sarcastically, "Nice going, Lee. Perfect timing."

J and Chris sighed simultaneously, in that way of theirs. "I guess this means it's our turn," one of them said. I couldn't tell which, as they sound so similar as to be indistinguishable from a distance.

8

It is perhaps best to gloss over the details of the drama that followed; advisable, undoubtedly, not to mention Lee's indignant banging at my door, threatening all manner of horrors instead of tendering the apology that was so clearly called for; wise not to recount the plaintive mewlings of J and Chris, who begged me to return to table and not allow one misplaced *bon mot* to ruin an entire evening, much less a full weekend; prudent not to record the dialogue between me and Law, who was the only personage whom I allowed admittance to my *chambre*. Suffice it to say that Law administered to me in the way that any caring angel would, demonstrating in the process that said angel was firmly on my side, and as vociferous as I regarding Lee's beastly treatment of me.

Sleep does wonders for the souls of the righteous while also showing miscreants the errors of their ways. I awoke at noon the next day feeling refreshed and ready to start anew; for I have never been one to hold a grudge, or to let a minor incident get in the way of a long and sturdy friendship such as that between Lee and myself. Also to be considered was the presence of four others on my estate, in addition to the cretin whose name I just mentioned; and surely the innocents, dullards though they may be, did not deserve to be punished for the misdeeds of one bitter ersatz food critic.

Thus I emerged from my morning ablutions ready to greet the day; and was flabbergasted when, upon opening the bedroom door, I looked down to see a bouquet of miniature blue sunflowers awaiting me. A note from Lee was attached:

My apologies for the uninspired and inaccurate jocular commentary re: the crabcakes. They were sublime. Forgive me. L.

The flowers melted the last floes of ice that had been floating on my heart. For here was the best of Lee, who knows me and my tastes like no other; who'd probably been up early, perhaps running the risk of being seen in Chris and J's entirely unacceptable automobile, darting about the eastern end of Long Island in search of the exquisite flowers that had become favorites of mine since their introduction a few months earlier. Yes, Lee was thoughtless; and yes, Lee had inexpertly chosen the "Habel blue" sunflowers, two of which seemed to have been used as steel wool by the florist's charwoman, as indicated by their smashed petals and honeycombs; but these things I could forgive. For the ability to greet each day afresh, with an optimistic outlook and with matters in their proper perspective, is a gift that I have been given.

On re-emerging into society I was greeted with shy but effusive hugs by all except Lee, to whom I nodded. I certainly would not acknowledge or give thanks for those wilting blossoms; however, Lee understood from long experience that, for me, a nodding of the head is tantamount to a burying of the hatchet.

Chris and J had taken it upon themselves to fix a light repast for lunch. I cringed inwardly, wondering what sorts of atrocities those two codependents had inflicted on my vegetables, breads, or poultry. The meal, as it turned out, was to be capon and Cornish game hens; which birds, as you may be aware, are exceedingly difficult to prepare, requiring the skilled touch of one who respects their limitations; and needless to say, this quality is not extant in the souls of Chris and J, who would have been quite satisfied receiving their nourishment in the form of liquid hamburgers fed intravenously.

The twins, as I sometimes call them in my mind due to their inability to self-actuate, were busily destroying the lovely game hens on the outdoor barbecue whilst Alex and Lee set the patio table. A few of the peacocks wandered about underfoot, perhaps attracted by the smell of mothballs emanating from Alex's clothes; or perhaps drawn by the possibility of being fed table scraps and thus cannibalizing one of their own species.

Alex placed a chipped crystal bowl of salsa in front of me, along with a side plate of blue corn tortilla chips that looked as if they'd come out of a bag rather than being purchased fresh, cut properly, fried lightly, then served warm and slightly salty.

Chris stopped annihilating the Cornish hens long enough to call to me, "Robin, we made your favorite salsa. Just our way of saying 'thank you' for your wonderful hospitality." Though J had gone into the house for reasons unknown, it was unrealistic to expect that Chris would forbear using the first-person plural pronoun, as two symbiotic parasites can never be expected not to speak as one.

I gazed down at the ruinous and murderous attempt at "salsa." The tomatoes looked as though they'd been cubed by a back-alley abortionist, and the onions had been chopped in a crazy-quilt mixture of shapes reminiscent of a child's set of tangrams. Worst of all, the cilantro (the fresh, beautiful cilantro!) had been mangled and thrown into the mixture, stems and all; thus creating a woefully indescribable mixture that looked and smelled not unlike molten lava.

Chris was looking at me expectantly; I was in a horrible bind. Though the child is mindless and banal, one's heart did have to expand just a bit upon considering the natural imbecility that had thought itself capable of preparing a suitable bowl of salsa. The decision at hand was fraught with peril—to taste the salsa and bring joy to Chris's day; or to find a way to avoid doing so, thus ensuring that my innards would not be assaulted by guaranteed gastric violence?

I made my choice. Using my foot, I jarred the table enough to spill the entire bowl of salsa onto the patio; timing the stunt, I might add, in such a way as to completely remove myself from the salsa's trajectory and therefore remain unsoiled by the bloody mixture.

"Oh," I cried, with a faux sense of loss.

Chris and J (who'd just emerged from the house) hesitated a moment, as did Alex, Lee, and Law; then all rushed to my aid simultaneously.

"I thought I felt a bug crawling up my leg," I said. "I do apologize for spilling your lovely salsa before I had a chance to taste it, Chris."

Chris looked angry—a common emotion, as any chef knows, when others do not hold your prize dish in the same esteem that you do—but the anger was replaced almost immediately by a smile and a shrug of the shoulders.

Meanwhile, a gaggle of peacocks had descended upon the patio, greedily lapping up the salsa like a dozen women deep in their cycles who have discovered a pool of liquid chocolate. Better them than I, I thought; and moved away to let the horrid creatures gorge themselves.

"I'll call the caretakers to clean up the mess," I announced on my way indoors. "In the meantime, let's move the *salon* into the house, shall we? I don't think any of us want to eat among buzzing flies and ravenous peacocks."

The guests looked at one another helplessly, something they seemed to be doing quite a bit since arriving in

_____.

Back in the house, I placed a call to the female caretaker and told her that we required her clean-up services promptly. She replied in her usual aggressive monosyllables, as is the wont of the serving classes.

9

The episode with the "salsa" had essentially killed my appetite, so I sat and entertained the masses with sundry stories while they choked down the mutilated hens and drank a product that was labeled "lemonade" but smelled more like a mix of ammonia and bleach. I'd fantasized that I might, just once, experience an afternoon free of intestinal agony, given my abstinence; but this dream was not to be realized, fading faster than the peroxided head of a washed-up actress still desperate for attention. For the smell of the charred hens was enough to send me fleeing up to my lavatory, where I turned to my private supply of Dr. Rosenthal's thoughtfully prescribed 'pineapple pills' in order to regain that tranquil composure that is my trademark.

During my time upstairs, the five had left the soiled plates for the female caretaker to clean (and I could hear the obscenity-laced mutterings of that slattern as she did the job she is so well compensated to do) and gone out to the yard for a game of croquet. Seeing me at the window, Law called out, "Oh, do join us, Robin." Accommodating person that I am, I decided to do so, for I've long been quite expert at the game.

"Croquet—what a lark!" exclaimed Lee, glomming onto Alex as a partner in much the same way that a remora attaches itself to the underbelly of a shark and feeds off its natural juices. It went without saying that Chris and J would comprise the second team; though for several seconds I entertained the thought of asking J to be my partner, which would have led to Law teaming up with Chris, despite the obvious attempts of those two to avoid each other this weekend, as evidenced by their unwillingness to sit near each other or engage in any conversation at all; which would have led to many accusations, later that evening, that J had "abandoned" Chris by partnering with me for the croquet game; which would have led to fireworks of the most histrionic kind. But my energy level had been drained after my gastric bout, and I wished to save the ploy for another time when I'd be able to spectate with more ardor.

This left Law and myself as the third team, an outcome that pleased me perfectly, as Law had been such a dear the previous evening; and I was more inclined than ever to give the sweet thing the money that had been so timorously, so self-effacingly requested several months earlier. I *did* plan to bestow my largesse upon Law at some point, whether sooner or later; but in the meantime, I saw no reason not to string the child along a bit longer. For surely Law's situation could not be as desperate as it seemed; and I did not want to give the impression, to any of my guests, that I was a personal bank from which withdrawals could be made at will. And, truth be told, given the expensive *accoutrements* and costly articles of clothing that Law had worn so well this weekend, I wouldn't have been surprised if Law's need for cash had already been met by another admirer in the same age bracket as myself.

The six of us began playing amicably, but it wasn't long before an unspoken misunderstanding seemed to develop between J and Chris, who seemed to be hitting their balls with an uncalled-for aggressiveness.

My turn came. Lee—in that way that only Lee has of putting me in difficult situations that test my forbearance to its outermost limits—had deliberately set up an impossible shot for me; this being the latest, I was sure, in a long series of passive-aggressive behaviors intended to "punish" me for imagined slights. I carefully scoped out the balls' positions and thought that with just the right angle and force, I should be able to prove to Lee that, as always, I could leap over any obstacle placed in my path by a vindictive ex-lover.

I pulled back my mallet, and then something quite odd opened. I slightly adjusted my weight in order to get the proper angle on the ball, and in so doing, slipped and fell on a patch of mud. As I lay on the ground, a mallet swung at my head, missing it by a mere inch. If I hadn't slipped, my brains would have resembled the chuck steak favored by middle-class housewives who've spent the grocery budget on booze and therefore cannot afford high-quality meat.

The mallet was held by that gangly giant Chris, who looked horrified and shocked—so much so that I actually felt sympathy for the inept buffoon.

"My God, Robin, are you hurt?" Chris asked shakily.

"No, no, I'm fine. But covered with mud, as you can see."

"I'm *so* sorry. I was trying clobber a junebug. It's been getting on my nerves since we started playing. I must have…miscalculated the distance."

As always, I made the effort to understand—for I, too, have been terrorized by bugs of all types, which sometimes invade my homes and therefore deserve the death sentence they receive; and, given Chris's extreme clumsiness, which I suppose I've gotten used to over the years, such a mishap was perhaps inevitable.

"You all finish the game without me," I said, feeling a bit miffed but trying not to show it, as a quick examination had shown that mud had splattered all over my new sweater, which I had recently purchased in a Chelsea shoppe that sells overpriced garments made by Shanty Irish fishwives in their cold-water huts. "I need to bathe and change." Because my friends know that this process takes two hours at a minimum, this was my way of saying that I would not be offended if they were to play through without me.

"Nice going," I heard Lee say ironically to Chris, and my heart warmed; for, as much as Lee drives me to distraction, it was rewarding to hear the nincompoop who'd nearly brained me taken to task via Lee's sublime sarcasm.

I approached the house, giving a wide berth to those filthy peacocks, who seemed to have lain down for an afternoon nap. A closer inspection showed that they'd gone to their final resting place. I silently congratulated myself on having rented the flock before buying my own; for it was certainly preferable to have someone else's birds die than to purchase my own, become attached to them, and then lose them to some sort of avian illness; which, I suppose, is only to be expected when one brings unacclimated birds to the southern fork of Long Island.

10

Needless to say, the reprehensible caretakers were skittish about touching the carcasses of the defunct peacocks. They murmured something about protecting themselves from disease; yet more evidence of their belief that the world revolves around them—for not once during their various whines and jeremiads did they express any concern whatsoever for my health, or that of my guests.

I was sitting in the overstuffed chair that my grandfather had favored, reading an inane piece of trash by a *New Yorker* columnist who suffers from the delusion that she is a novelist, when a wave of panic jolted my entire being. I have always handled stress exceedingly well, and I felt that I'd held my own quite marvelously over the past 36 hellish hours, despite being surrounded by a bunch of feeble-minded dingbats. But as I flipped through the pages of that unbearable tome, a thought intruded on my consciousness: If I had to prepare another meal for my guests, I would not emerge from the evening sane, not even with the help of Dr. Rosenthal's magical concoctions. The mere idea of cooking was simply unthinkable; I would sooner have eaten peacocks tartare than slave over the stove for hours, attempting to transform subpar ingredients into something magical and wonderful, only to then have my efforts ridiculed in the manner that Lee had so callously demonstrated the prior evening.

I abruptly snapped shut the long-winded non-opus, rose to my feet, and descended the stairs. Like the English aristocracy, my guests were playing at various amusements in the first-floor drawing room. Chris and J were attempting to complete a crossword puzzle, an effort as futile as the flirtations of a man with skinny arms at a gay bar. The others were attempting to play Scrabble; which board, you will not be shocked to learn, was covered with two- and three-letter monosyllables with a maximum score of four points.

"All," I declared, "I think a road trip is in order this evening. For a change of pace, let's plan to go to the _____ Inn for drinks and dinner."

Glances were exchanged, in that meaningful way that seemed to be happening quite a lot this particular weekend; but attempting to break the code behind those nods, looks, shrugs, and tics would have required an entire encyclopedia of human semiotics; thus, I let the moment pass uncommented upon, the analysis of human behavior not being something I find particularly stimulating or rewarding.

Shortly thereafter, I returned to my *chambre* to prepare for the evening; if I were going out on the town, extra time would be needed to complete my toilet. I emerged three hours later, looking fresh and fit, with a healthy glow in my cheeks that had been accentuated by a few non-cosmetic tricks I've picked up over the years, and which I share with no one.

My friends insisted upon walking around the once-quaint village of _____; thus was I forced to browse in a series of insipid shoppes full of unremarkable and insanely overpriced merchandise. One or two stores I refused to enter, having had mishaps with either current or previous owners; other shoppes were simply too unbearable in concept, such as the one using androgynous models to sell beachwear—and this I would not enter on principle alone, for I have never been tolerant of women who look and behave like men, and vice versa.

Eventually we made our way to the _____ Inn, where we were served a dark, dingy merlot that had been chosen by Lee, whose taste the sycophantic sommelier had congratulated, perhaps in an effort to sexually titillate my ex, who was, I admit, looking quite alluring that evening, despite buttocks that have grown too ample and skin reminiscent of a pachyderm's. Lee, of course, returned the flirtation, the better to continue the "Torture Robin" game; but I'd taken enough of Dr. Rosenthal's 'blackberry pills' to allow me to maintain my *façade* of *ennui*.

I need not go into the details of the "foods" that were placed before us; "meals" that included pheasant, veal, lamb, tilapia, and swordfish mutilated in ways inconceivable to the human mind. Against my better judgment, I tasted a tiny piece of my Dover sole, which should have been as tender as the posterior of the M in an S&M relationship, but which was, in actuality, as tough as the GED exam for people with the mental capacity of, say, a J, or a Chris, or a Law, or an Alex.

Of all the people at the table, the only one who showed even a modicum of concern for my suffering was the dear Law, who asked why I wasn't eating and offered to switch meals with me. I declined, of course, as Law's meal looked about as appetizing as a grilled inner tube garnished with maximum-viscosity motor oil.

"I suppose I haven't much of an appetite this evening," I sighed. "The last few days have caught up with me, and I am just the least bit tired."

"You poor thing," Law consoled. "Maybe you should take an extra dose of Doctor Rosenthal's 'blueberry pills' when we get back to the house, to ensure a good night's sleep. If you are short on supply, by all means take as many of mine as you need."

And now you see why Law is such a sweet thing—the only person concerned enough for my well-being to care that I would not toss and turn all night. In fact, Law was concerned enough to mention several more times that I should take extra 'blueberry pills' when we returned home; and the pleading was so effective that I agreed to Law's plan, the tendency toward being too indulgent of my friends being one of my weaknesses.

Back at the house, I performed my nightly ritual, applying the various creams and lotions that are essential to my well-being; exfoliating and scrubbing; brushing and combing; until I had washed away the cares of the day. The final step was to help myself to a few of the 'blueberries,' which would allow me to rest with only a minimal intrusion of nighttime demons and golems. Given the stresses of the day, I agreed with Law's suggestion that I should take four pills rather than the usual dosage of two. I had poured a glass of water from the carafe that the caretakers are required to refill regularly (a task that, needless to say, they complete resentfully and inadequately) when the words from the prescription label jumped out at me: UNDER NO CIRCUMSTANCES TAKE MORE THAN 6 PILLS IN A 24-HOUR PERIOD. DO NOT MIX WITH ALCOHOL.

I scanned my memory. I had already taken eight pills that day, for which I can be forgiven, I am sure; as a weaker person stuck in a house with five boors would surely have taken many more than that. Perhaps, though, it would be best if I were to attempt to sleep on my own. I felt I could accomplish this task, being utterly exhausted after 42 hours surrounded by the unpolished and unrefined.

The featherbed welcomed me. I cleared my mind, thinking back to my days as a child in this very house, and soon drifted into a peaceful sleep unmarred by dreams of vengeful ex-lovers, Siamese twins joined at the waist and speaking as one, flaming Saabs, and maladroit cooks obliterating quality ingredients.

I was dozing calmly when, suddenly, I heard a small noise, as if the floorboards were creaking or someone in another part of the house was attempting to stifle an orgasm. I turned my head, opened my eyes, and saw Law hovering over me with a large pillow.

"Law? What are you doing here?" I asked sleepily, a warmth filling my loins at the thought that Law might wish to join me in bed voluntarily.

"Oh, did I wake you?" Law asked. "I'm so sorry, Robin.…I was…concerned about you. Are you comfortable? I thought you might like my feather pillow. I brought it with me from home, and it guarantees a good night's rest."

"Law, how kind of you," I replied, wondering if the fool had lost any remaining sanity; for everyone knows that bedclothes are home to all sorts of personal mites and creepy-crawlies; and though I might not be able to do anything about my own personal parasites, that did not mean I was willing to allow someone else's bacteria into my bed.

"Thank you for the kind offer, dear," I replied, "but I really am sleeping so soundly. It was lovely of you to check on me." Perhaps I should have taken the pillow to save Law's feelings; but, I will admit, it was Law I wanted in my bed, not the pillow, and I was just the slightest bit miffed by what I perceived as Law's sexual teasing.

"Don't mention it," Law said, as semi-sweet as chocolate, though I thought I detected an undernote of anger, which was completely unwarranted, as I had done absolutely nothing wrong. And out Law went, pillow and all, to leave me to my slumbers—slamming the door on the way out in what appeared to be a fit of unjustifiable pique; as if Law had been the injured party, and not I—I, who had been sleeping soundly and been awakened suddenly and rudely by a pillow-wielding simpleton.

11

This latest incident with Law had the potential to disturb my somniloquy, for my body can never fully rest when my mind is agitated. After a few moments' analysis, the explanation hit me with full force: Of course Law had been upset by what could only have been perceived as my abrupt dismissal. Perhaps I'd spoken too soon; perhaps Law had been using the pillow as a sort of decoy in hopes of receiving an invitation to join me for the remainder of the evening; and perhaps the merlot had combined undesirably with the 'blueberry pills,' the result being the diminution of my mental faculties to a point where the subtext of Law's words had been lost on me, in much the same way that any literary or cultural reference is lost on Law.

Having convinced myself that Law's door-slamming was a manifestation of hurt feelings at my unwitting rejection rather than a fit of petulance, I was able to lull myself back to sleep, Morpheus having taken my side in the conflict, as he often does.

Several hours later I was wakened again but what could only be described as a sibilant slithering sound. The room was quiet except for the noise, and I wondered what it could be. The decomposing bodies of the peacocks giving off some sort of noxious, flatulent gas? The hushed noises of copulation emanating from the room of either Lee or Alex? The atrophying of Chris and J's few remaining brain cells, drying up and being released into the west wind?

My senses were further activated by what appeared to be a movement at the foot of the mattress. Was it my overactive imagination, or was there something indeed crawling over the hand-stitched quilt that my great-grandmother had spent months assembling? Going on auto-pilot, which I sometimes do when feeling threatened or overwhelmed, I reached for the lamp that sits on the night-table and flicked on the switch. The creature slithering steadily towards me was a large multicolored snake, quite beautiful in its way, with a skin that would gladly have been purchased by South Americans, in order to fashion boots, belts, and other questionable fashion accessories.

And it was here that my guardian angel, who has a history of being absent when she or he is most needed, finally came through; for I had left the fourth-rate novel by the fifth-rate *New Yorker* novelist on that night-table. What I had considered an appalling waste of paper and ink just a few hours earlier suddenly transformed itself into a weapon expertly crafted by Vulcan himself. I grabbed the intellectually lightweight, but physically heavyweight, volume and in one swoop brought it down on the serpent's head. The impact shattered the wicked creature's skull.

Apparently I'd been screaming while this had been happening, and soon all the houseguests, except for J and Chris, who were most likely recriminating with each other in the guest house, had gathered in my *chambre* to discover what had transpired.

My screams continued, and with effort I retained consciousness; for my victory over the asp had resulted in blood and snakebits all over the aforementioned quilt, which could never be replaced and certainly could never be slept under, ever again; and the thought of losing another priceless family heirloom was such that Law ran to fetch my 'cantaloupe pills,' while Lee held my hand and Alex sipped wine.

After a few hours of alternating rest and consolation, punctuated by my occasional involuntary spasms of grief, my guests began the process of helping me close up the house to prepare for our return to the much calmer and more predictable island of Manhattan.

The caretakers arrived, at their leisure of course, to clean up the mess and to close up the house. The male caretaker examined the remains of the viper and pronounced it a highly venomous "copperhead," expressing surprise that this Southern snake should have found its way to the far reaches of Long Island, as if he were a qualified herpetologist instead of a man who makes his living by unlocking doors and opening windows.

Both caretakers, male and female, were as truculent and churlish as they'd always been; and under great duress I paid them their agreed-upon wages, though the sum was certainly much more than they deserved; all the while looking forward to leaving this place and never seeing their wan, bovine faces again. For, given my easygoing temperament and *laissez-faire* approach to household management, I'd certainly have no difficulty in replacing those soon-to-be-dismissed caretakers with competent, grateful help at a more reasonable price.

12

The final indignity was having to pile myself and my possessions into J and Chris's revolting Chevrolet, a situation that required me to don a hat and dark sunglasses so that I would not be recognized as a willing passenger in such a vehicle. I had wanted to call a car service to bring me back to the City, but J and Chris would not hear of it; it seemed that the two fools wanted to extend the weekend as much as they could by bringing not only me, but also Lee, back to town. Law and Alex, having arrived separately, also went on their merry ways separately, Law to seduce and rob the wealthy, Alex to dazzle the shallow and impressionable.

After sitting in beastly traffic—for which, thankfully, I'd prepared by taking the last of the 'peach pills'—we arrived at the front door of my building around six p.m., exactly the same time that all the *nouveaux riches* return from their weekend getaways and flood the sidewalks of the Upper West Side with their suitcases. I thanked J and Chris, and was able to avoid kissing J because the cramped interior of the car made it impossible. Lee and I exchanged one of our awkward embraces, agreeing that we'd had a marvelous weekend and promising that we'd talk soon. Chris, who'd been driving, began unloading my valises from the trunk.

I was so overjoyed to be back home that I exited the driver's side without paying much attention to my surroundings. All was a blur for a moment as a cab, no doubt driven by a hashish-smoking immigrant, grazed my left side and knocked me down. I shouted a few choice words at the cabbie as he sped away down West 72nd Street, as the others watched in horror.

Lee got out of the car to check on my well-being, surveying me up and down.

"My God, Robin, you're simply indestructible."

Perhaps it was my imagination, but the statement seemed to have been uttered in a tone that could only be described as disappointed.

Part Two

DEATH IN MANHATTAN

13

I have always been a very resilient person. Yes, I have had my share of heartaches and setbacks; does a person exist on earth who has not? Yet my coping mechanism has always been stronger than that of the average human. I understand my needs too well to ever remain fully disengaged with life for *too* long. When the world is getting me down, I simply self-administer the cures that have served me well for lo these many years; cures composed of the physical (long, intense massages designed to release the stresses carried by my corporeal being), the mental (the writing of my memoirs and the composing of Petrarchan sonnets), and the pharmacological (to which Dr. Rosenthal's contributions have at times been essential).

Thus I wasted no time beginning the process of recovering from that highly ungratifying weekend spent in _____. Upon arriving at my Manhattan home, I threw open the apartment door, only too delighted to have left the inanities and inexplicable behaviors of my houseguests behind. My comfortable bed awaited me, as did the various creature comforts of the four walls that had been my home (and, occasionally, Lee's) for more than two decades. And yet for some reason I found myself reluctant to cross the threshold. It was as if some strong masculine force physically held me back from stepping foot into the entryway; and I found myself shaking harder than a college professor accused of sexual harassment.

Nonetheless, the strength of character that has long been my trademark took over, and I was able to force myself onto the parquet floor, where I breathed a bit easier. Picking up the largest of my valises—that which contained the necessary items for my nighttime ablutions—I made my way to the master bedroom suite. My goal had been simply to unpack the items absolutely essential for that evening's ritual, and to then toss my exhausted carcass into a bed free of hissing lizards and pillow-brandishing maniacs.

And yet this proved to be a more daunting task than one could have been predicted. I found myself unable to push open the door of my *chambre,* as I stood, immobilized, at the doorway. I clutched my throat and began gasping for air, dropping the valise on the floor and cracking the parquet tile so lovingly inlaid the previous summer by a rather fetching craftsperson who'd been most willing to provide additional services for a sum considerably below market rate. Once again gathering my reserves and strengthening my resolve, I was able to force open *la porte* and heave my way through.

I sat on the bed and wondered what sort of bizarre nether-world I had entered. My home suddenly seemed like a stranger's hovel, and I felt more ill at ease than an *American Idol* winner whose hair and makeup artists have abandoned her prior to a photo shoot, thus leaving her tooth gaps, bald spot, uneven complexion, and axillary hair visible to the music-purchasing public.

Wondering if perhaps the exhaustion engendered by the hellish weekend had begun to affect my faculties, I truncated my nighttime ritual by more than an hour so that I might wrap myself in slumber, with assistance from the supply of 'blueberry pills' I had borrowed from J, Alex, Chris, Law, and Lee, just in case. And yet I believe I did not sleep one wink. Suddenly the weight of the comforter, given to my father by his maternal grandmother, felt crushing and suffocating; I threw it off the bed in a fit of insomniac pique, where it lay on the floor like the clothes of a high school cheerleader in the motel room rented by her biology teacher. Several times I bolted upright, gasping for air, gagging on the emu-feather pillows I had acquired at great expense from an illegal game farm in Wooloomooloo, Australia, and which had been smuggled into the country by a band of traveling dwarves who occasionally come to the States with their all-pygmy production of *Pygmalion*. Each time I felt blessed somnolence about to triumph, I was awakened by a sibilant sound that disappeared the moment I opened my eyes.

Clearly, this would not do over the long term, I thought as I rose from bed the next morning, dizzy from sleep deprivation. In my quasi-hallucinogenic state I recollected the long-time rumours that my building is haunted by an unfriendly entity. That depressed phantasm had never had the audacity to enter my home in the past, but my exhaustion-induced delusions convinced me that my absence had given the incubus the opening he needed to begin haunting the penthouse. I had pulled out the Yellow Pages and opened to 'EXORCISTS' when it occurred to me that I should perhaps consult Dr. Rosenthal before doing anything drastic.

Dr. Rosenthal's time may be overpriced in the extreme, but those highly in demand are usually too savvy to underprice themselves. And I do pay extra for access to Dr. R's private number, so why should I not avail myself of that privilege? Upon raising the good doctor on the phone, I found my floodgates opening quite wide as I held Dr. R enraptured with my adventures in _____ over the weekend. At several points I paused for effect, holding back those salty drops that threatened to emanate from my ocular orbs as I recalled the loss of the chandelier and the quilt.

Dr. R needed no time to come up with a diagnosis. What I had thought might be a minor attack of the vapors was actually something more substantial: Post Traumatic Stress

Disorder. I balked instantly upon hearing the term, which as everyone knows is merely a euphemism for a weakness of character that causes those "afflicted" with it to whine and carry on about their delicate emotional states. And yet I could not argue with Dr. R's seemingly infallible analysis that my inability to cross the thresholds in my apartment was the result of my PTSD-induced fear that throwing open a door would cause a nearby chandelier to come crashing down on my head; my inability to sleep under my great-*grandmère*'s comforter caused by flashbulb memories of the dead copperhead's blood on the quilt in my modest bedroom at the house on Long Island; those hissing sounds in my unrestful sleep the manifestation of my unconscious memories of that same evil asp that had made its way from the American South, it seemed, solely to attack a slumbering innocent such as myself.

Fortunately, medical science has found a way to lessen the effects of PTSD, and I left Dr. R's later that day with several prescriptions guaranteed to take the edge off. During our visit, Dr. R warned that I must do everything in my power to avoid stress for a minimum of two weeks; so, upon arriving home with a generous supply of the newly acquired 'tangelo' and 'kiwi pills,' I immediately placed a call to Faith Goode, interim director of the charitable foundation that employs my not-inconsiderable talents for finding and developing rising stars in the arts. To these ascendant luminaries the Goode Foundation donates considerable sums for professional development.

Preoccupied with some internecine battles in the Foundation, Faith did not argue with my doctor's assertion that a period of two weeks' bed rest was essential to my continued mental, physical, and spiritual health. In her usual clipped fashion, she snapped, "I don't care what you do, just show up for the vote next month," and hung up. Picturing her hatchet-face as she slammed down the phone on my sensitive ears caused a momentary drop in the effectiveness of not only the 'tangelo' and 'kiwi pills,' but also the 'grape' and 'apricot pills' I'd ingested earlier; but I consoled myself that time away from the Goode Foundation was certainly worth the cost of a conversation with the witchlike Faith Goode, whose moral sense is as developed as the musculature of the Ethiopian populace.

To have time to oneself! Sitting in my comfortable Louis XIV chair in my *chambre de vivre*, I thought with excitement about the many tasks and personal enjoyments I had neglected over the previous months—pleasures that I would now have two weeks to pursue. Certainly there were books to be read, finances to be checked up on, rooms to be redecorated, *accoutrements* to be purchased and soon thereafter returned, elderly great-aunts and -uncles across the Pond to be checked up on. It occurred to me, too, that it had been nearly a week since I'd last seen the dear manicurist whose attentions had been cut short by the call from Lee that had led inexorably toward the events of the prior weekend. Perhaps it was time to get reacquainted with that delightful urchin?

No sooner had I reached for the *teléfono* to reserve my appointment than that selfsame instrument began to shriek. I felt an immediate pounding in my temples and looked at the Caller ID. The call was coming from Lee, whose reason for phoning could only have been to outwardly thank me for a delightful weekend in the country while subtly recriminating with me regarding the substandard food, lodging, guests, and entertainment. You will understand that in my delicate state I wished to avoid this trap and therefore left the urgently ringing phone unanswered.

Over the next two weeks, I received phone calls from J, Chris, Alex, and Law as well, and I consistently ignored the ringing phone as well as the subsequent beeps of the answering machine. My friends know that I sometimes retreat from the world, and they usually can be counted on to respect my need for quiet time, but they all seemed particularly insistent this time. When they could not raise me on the house phone, they tried my cell—so much so that I shut down that noisome device and threw it into a drawer in my *escritoire*, cursing the inventor of that most annoying piece of technology.

Two weeks of 'tangelo' and 'kiwi pill' therapy did work wonders and, as Dr. R had predicted, I awoke a fortnight after beginning my much-needed respite ready to start anew. As I ground coffee beans that I'd had flown in from Xachiolapacatapol, Mexico, to begin my day, the phone began trilling yet again. Resigning myself to the fact that I could not avoid communication with the world indefinitely, I walked to the device to look at the caller ID: The caller was J. Sighing inwardly, I answered.

"Robin, my God. Where have you been?"

"J, how delightful to hear from you. I've just returned from an unexpected mission of mercy.…"

J began sobbing, an unpleasant sound like a horse attempting to whinny while simultaneously trying to dislodge a ball of hay from its throat. This was probably the result of yet another inane argument with Chris, and I waited patiently for the long, drawn-out tale to commence, already missing the gorgeous quiet of my solitude.

"Robin, we've been calling you for days. Lee is dead."

14

Those who have not lost the dearest, as well as the most insufferable, person in their life are incapable of comprehending the battery of emotions that one experiences upon receiving the type of news that had been so unceremoniously dumped upon me. The soporific effects of the 'tangelo' and 'kiwi pills' were immediately negated as the room began to spin and a swoon threatened to overtake me. *Retain consciousness, Robin*, I ordered myself, and with the greatest of effort I was able to follow my own orders.

I listened in disbelief as J outlined the horrific details. Late in the week after our return from _____, J had received a phone call from Lee, who'd invited J (and by parasitic extension, Chris) to the West End Avenue condo, ostensibly for a bit of post-Long Island debriefing. Such behavior was consistent with Lee's insistence upon being privy to the secret goings-on at any gathering, which always required a post-mortem of the event. Certainly, if memory served me, Lee had been too busy cavorting with Alex while on Long Island to pay much attention to the various oddities of Law, Chris, and J. The phone call inviting J and Chris for a late lunch had to have been merely a pretext for Lee's plan to siphon every last bit of blackmail-worthy gossip out of those houseguests to whom insufficient attention had been paid whilst at the house.

Upon arriving on West End that fateful Saturday afternoon, the codependents had been informed by the doorman that Lee was not at home—or, at least, was not responding to the urgent buzzes from the front desk. At this point J whipped out a cell phone to discover Lee's whereabouts, calling not only Lee's home phone but also the cell. Neither phone was answered, and after 15 minutes or so of buzzing, the twins left without giving the situation much further thought, assuming that once again Lee, never the world's most reliable person, had forgotten the invitation.

The rest of that day passed uneventfully, until J and Chris received a curious call from Alex late that evening inquiring as to Lee's whereabouts. Apparently, Lee had also phoned up

Alex the previous day, requesting that a visit be made to the West End condo the following evening. This came as a surprise to J and Chris, who'd been invited for a mid-afternoon get-together. Why wouldn't Lee have invited J, Chris, and Alex at the same time? Unless, of course, Lee had been playing the usual game of divide-and-conquer, which seemed likely to yield the best gossip from multiple uncensored viewpoints.

Alex had arrived at Lee's building at the appointed time and underwent much the same experience that J and Chris had earlier in the day. There followed a series of phone calls among the various friends, including several calls placed to me, which, you may recall, I had left unanswered and unacknowledged in my attempt to recalibrate my emotional barometer.

Of course, speculation began instantaneously that sparks had flown and old passions had been reignited between Lee and myself during that fateful weekend, which led to further salacious suggestions that Lee and I had holed ourselves up together, the better to re-explore the physical side of our relationship while blotting out the intrusions of the world; an idea fatuous in the extreme, and, no doubt, suggested by Alex as a way of throwing the gossip hounds off the trail. However, the inanities of groupthink are difficult to dispel, and once the idea came up, it quickly became the conventional wisdom; and no more was said about Lee's disappearance.

But then the phone calls from outside parties had begun to come in. Dr. Rosenthal has a zero-tolerance policy for no-shows, and when Lee failed to make an appointment early the following week, Dr. R had furiously ordered Law to determine Lee's whereabouts to reschedule the appointment and to remind Lee that the missed appointment would be charged as per usual. Law had tried to raise Lee, as had Lee's employer, the City of New York Parks Commission, which retained Lee as a *feng shui* consultant and was very much in need of advice regarding the proper celestial orientation for a new pavilion being built in Central Park. None of these attempts were successful, and a sort of groundswell of concern arose that *Lee might not be well*.

Thus began an intervention spearheaded by J, an inept creature usually incapable of walking and chewing gum simultaneously. Yet in this instance J was, apparently, masterful, and by Wednesday the crowd of friends gathered at Lee's dwelling to insist that the doorman give them access to Lee's apartment. I had been invited, via voice mail, to *rendezvous* with that motley crew; but as I had been ignoring all messages, I had not received the invitation.

The doorman had resisted all imprecations to grant the party unauthorized access, but had quickly been prevailed upon. For, despite their mindlessness and self-absorption, my *amici* can be quite resourceful when faced with a challenge. So Alex drew the doorman aside and mentioned a rumor circulating on West End Avenue that said doorman had been seen scurrying ratlike down the street with packages from Barneys New York and other pretentious retailers—packages that had been intended for building residents, yet had somehow never made it to their rightful owners; a horrible rumor which, Alex implied, could be downright damning should the building's management get wind of it. With eyes thus opened to the urgency of the situation, the doorman grabbed a set of keys from a lockbox, led the merry band of concerned thugs to Lee's doorway, unlocked the door, and stepped aside to let them in.

The place had been preternaturally quiet, a sure sign that Lee could not be at home; for if Lee had been there, surely those insufferable popera CDs by the likes of "Andrea Boccelli" and "Josh Groban" would have been playing in the background; a noise that had induced many a migraine in my delicate cranium during the Lee cohabitation years.

The group fanned out to search for Lee, with Chris checking the coat closet in the entryway first, an action that may strike you as odd, but which becomes decidedly more understandable when you know that Lee was once robbed, then blindfolded, tied up, and stowed in that selfsame closet by a street urchin whom Lee had taken in as an act of "kindness," though it would not be cynical to assume that there had been an expectation that such kindness was to be reciprocated quite intensely at a physical level.

It was J who entered the bedroom to see the huddled mass of musty and unkempt blankets curled up in the bed. Lee had always been a notoriously restless sleeper, though that situation had begun to improve with the help of those effective little 'blueberry pills' that have become a pharmacological staple among those of my acquaintance. The immediate assumption was that Lee was deeply in the Land of Nod courtesy of the 'blueberries,' though for everyone's peace of mind a consensus emerged that, irate though Lee might be, they should awaken that recumbent form just to make sure everything was indeed fine.

Law thought that a few light slaps on the cheek would awaken the slumbering rhinoceros. But the first slap was enough to prove that Lee would never awaken again. For Law's hand lightly smacked a cheekbone that was not slack as a result of too much sun over the years, but rather one that was as cold as ice and as stiff as a Viagra-induced erection. On the cluttered bedstand next to the bed was the bottle of 'blueberries,' almost empty.

Not knowing what else to do, Law, one of the more level-headed and calculating of our group, called Dr. Rosenthal for advice. Horrified at the thought of losing the income stream from a patient who required as much attention as Lee, Dr. R had rushed over and declared what everyone already knew—that Lee had indeed gone to that place of final rest, or eternal torment, depending on the type of life one has led; in Lee's case, most likely the latter.

The following day, the medical examiner/autopsist had filed the paperwork outlining the cause of death: a heart attack, no doubt brought on by Lee's fat-laden diet and equally fat-laden thighs, buttocks, and mid-section.

And throughout the whole process, I had been holed up, listening to Mozart, reading several demanding philosophical treatises, and dallying with the manicurist, who had gone from delightful to increasingly tiresome over that two-week period. My upset at losing my closest companion was only slightly offset by my relief at not having been a member of the party that had found the corpse; for everyone knows that the dead have a very distinct and unpleasant odor about them, a scent that, given my heightened olfactory sensitivities, would have stayed with me until my dying day.

15

Several years ago, a huge-bosomed and tiny-brained celebrity died unexpectedly on one of those islands somewhere off the coast of nowhere, and a time-consuming brouhaha ensued over the disposition of the body, which had begun to deteriorate so rapidly that pundits began predicting that the starlet's silicon implants would be the only remaining parts of her intact at the time of her burial, or cremation, or assumption into heaven, or whatever fate awaited her mortal remains.

At the time, I had steadfastly refused to pay any heed whatsoever to the media frenzy regarding this most minor of

American bimbos; but, this being the twenty-first century, I was unable to filter the ubiquitous details completely from my consciousness. But these wretched memories came back to me forcefully when a similar controversy erupted over the rights to Lee's body.

It had long been my assumption that I would be Lee's executor, and that I, as the person who had been most loved, and most tortured, by Lee over the years would have the final say on the proper treatment of the remains. Yet this proved to be anything but the case, for reasons so buried in legal mumbo-jumbo that my frail but resilient constitution was nearly overwhelmed on several occasions. Had it not been for Lee's lawyer rather obviously making a play for me, while simultaneously informing me with a malicious and overtly sexual wink that Lee's *corpus* would need to remain in a deep freeze at the City morgue until the reading of the will, I might have slipped into a fugue; however, the *frisson* of sexual interest on the part of the noisome but not-unattractive barrister did manage to keep my senses engaged, for what is the purpose of flirtation, really, other than to make one feel completely alive, even in the face of mayhem and death?

All of this is to say that my dear friends and I had to wait several days for the reading of the will, and during that period I felt it best to remain active. For it has always been my experience that idle hands allow the hobgoblins of the mind to take over; and remaining alone in my *maison*, or being driven to the brink of insanity at the homes of weepy friends such as J, Chris, and Alex, would certainly not have allowed the various neural pathways of emotion in my brain (and perhaps even those of *mon coeur*) to begin processing Lee's permanent absence in a way that would permit me to move forward with the many small tasks that are collectively called *la vie*.

So, after many a salty drop had been shed, and after many garments had been rent in a manner that would have done the most overwrought of Italian matriarchs proud, I took charge of my emotions and decided to visit Lee's apartment. Such closure, I felt, was essential to my well-being; and it seemed only fitting that the intimacy of our long-standing relationship be brought full circle in a private place where my surfeit of emotion would not be viewed by prying and gossipy eyes. Of course I still had a key to Lee's apartment, just as Lee has always had keys to mine, though I rarely had cause to visit Lee's abode, as I had never felt particularly comfortable in Lee's surroundings, filled as they were from floor to ceiling with uninteresting bric-a-brac and the works of street artists to whom The Goode Foundation would not have donated a breath if they were suffocating.

I managed to slip past the doorman of Lee's building unnoticed. I did not want to attract any attention, nor lay myself open to accusations of untoward, acquisitive behavior regarding Lee's personal effects; but more than that I wished to avoid the doorman, with whom I'd had an altogether unsatisfactory "incident" several years earlier.

Upon entering Lee's darkened, dusty, musty apartment, I felt a momentary hesitation undoubtedly fueled by my recently diagnosed PTSD; however, the effects of the 'tangelo pills' kicked in more or less instantly, aided by some newer colleagues that Dr. R had recently prescribed: the 'strawberry pill' for anxiety and the 'avocado pill' for attention deficit, to which I seem to have become susceptible in recent months.

Drawing in a breath, I made my way into the small pre-war bathroom where Lee kept many of the grooming *accoutrements* necessary to tame that wild mane of flaming red hair that had long been Lee's trademark and least appealing feature. On a trip to Madagascar many moons ago, Lee and I had found a native shop selling beautiful handmade grooming implements at impossibly low prices, and we'd purchased several that had become favorites, which had almost made up for the fact that we'd gotten caught smuggling them through Customs; for, it turned out, our interfering nation has an issue with products made from endangered or protected species, and as a result the Customs officers (if not quite so easily bribed) would have made me relinquish the ivory hand mirror I had purchased from a Negro craftsman; and they very likely would have done the same with the tortoise shell hairbrush Lee had purchased which, in a delightful play on words, had actually been crafted from a tortoise's shell.

It was this tortoise shell hairbrush I sought, as it had long been the one item of Lee's I coveted. And yet more than half an hour of turning the bathroom inside out yielded not a single tortoise shell implement. Various acne medications, yes; expensive concoctions hand prepared by Chinatown herbalists to melt away cellulite, yes; but no tortoise shell hairbrush. Nor was the hairbrush in Lee's bedroom, on Lee's bedstand, or anywhere else in the apartment. I wondered if perhaps the tortoise had somehow been revivified and walked away, back to Madagascar, only to be caught by the same craftsman and turned into another hairbrush. Certainly it deserved a better fate than spending its life attempting to unsnarl the unsightly snarl of orangey spaghetti that was frequently Lee's head. "*Bon chance, mon ami*," I whispered quietly to the tortoise, wherever he might be.

During the time of our official "romantic" relationship, Lee had kept a journal to which I had never been privy. It had been kept under lock and key, and my various efforts to steal glances at it had been met with the fiercest of resistance by Lee, who insisted that the leather volume was the "private space" so necessary when one is cohabiting with another. Lee likened the journal to the room of one's own that Virginia Woolf had so wished for, a simile that quite pleased Lee but could not have been more pretentious, for Lee's ability to write prose was easily outstripped by any fifth grader in New York City, making the comparison to Mrs. Woolf the greatest of overstatements. Nonetheless, I had let the matter drop and only occasionally tried to gain access to Lee's scribblings and ravings; but I had never succeeded.

However, that was then, and this was now. Lee and I had never been overly demonstrative with each other, perhaps as a result of the myriad small feuds and monetary thefts that had plagued our relationship almost from day one; but it was obvious to all that Lee adored me, and I felt sure that the diary would be the one place where all those unuttered kind words might finally be found.

Unfortunately, the diary proved as elusive as the tortoise shell hairbrush.

My attempt to delve more deeply into Lee's impenetrable psyche thus thwarted, I went in search of other physical objects that would allow me to experience memories of Lee more intensely. Sitting on the uncomfortable sofa, I spied the princess telephone that had long been a campy favorite of Lee's. Attached to it was the answering machine that Lee had long used as a weapon against me, screening out my calls and pretending not to be home when I was most in need of a willing ear and a kind word. Perhaps the voice mail messages would provide some insight into Lee's final hours or days; or, failing that, at least offer a few salacious bits that I might use to my advantage at some point in the future?

I rewound the tape, pushed the PLAY button, and sat back expectantly, waiting to hear the voices of various old and new friends dramatically entreating Lee to return their calls. But the tape was empty, which was odd in the extreme. Lee had always made the number of messages waiting on voice mail a contest between us, a competition for popularity that Lee had been hell bent on winning, even at the cost of my mental tranquility. Lee *never* erased messages until the machine was full; this was Lee's method of feeling popular and very much *in social demand* when affected by the doldrums, which plagued Lee as frequently as STD's plague the promiscuous.

But surely Lee's cell phone, one of those expensive models that allowed Lee to take photos of unsuspecting shirtless men at construction sites, would have some messages on it? I walked quickly to Lee's bedroom and began searching the nightstand where Lee's cell phone should have been. For Lee was obsessive-compulsive in many ways, some of which were the perpetual insistence that keys *always* be placed in exactly the same slots on the key holder, that the vodka always be added to the martini *after* the vermouth—and that the cell phone *forever* be placed on the nightstand when not in use, so that it might be easily retrieved when wanted, or easily answered in the wee hours when one's friends call with various and sundry inflated crises.

But the nightstand yielded nothing, except for some rather prurient magazines and Lee's passport, which I absent-mindedly stuck in my jacket pocket. I had searched for that brain-cancer-causing device for ten minutes when it occurred to me that I might be able to locate it by simply using my own to call it. I did so, listening for the insufferable electronic tones of Beethoven's Fifth to alert me to its whereabouts, but I heard no ringing anywhere in the apartment. Lee's cell phone had disappeared, along with the tortoise shell hairbrush, the diary, and the answering machine messages.

As I stood there puzzling, the explanation dawned on me: Lee had spent the remaining hours of a futile existence destroying the very items that would mean the most to me.

Sensing an impending death, Lee had decided to torture me to the end. Knowing that I would want the hairbrush, Lee had tossed it down the trash chute; knowing that I would seek to read the journal, Lee had torched it; knowing I would want to eavesdrop on private voice mails, my former partner had deprived me of that joy by deleting all messages and tossing the cell phone out the window. For what other explanation could there be?

I sat on the edge of Lee's deathbed, on the verge of hyperventilating but working hard to reclaim the tranquility of my mind, when a thought struck me. Lee had long held a safety deposit box at the local branch of an old-world New York City bank; perhaps it held the various treasures I sought, and more. It was certainly worth a look.

16

I have never been one to allow sartorial matters to prevent me from showing up promptly for all appointments; that is to say, within an hour of the agreed-upon time. For Manhattan traffic and transit are the most convenient of scapegoats, allowing lateness to be somewhat fashionable and perhaps even useful in those social games played by New Yorkers of all ages, races, and genders. Such psychological warfare, while regrettable, is simply essential to retaining an alpha position in any type of relationship, whether personal or business; and though I am loath to play oneupspersonship, such strategies are sometimes necessary.

That said, on the day following my visit to Lee's apartment, I did find myself faced with a bit of a dilemma as I stood in front of my *armoire*, selecting clothing for the meeting with that lascivious attorney who clearly had the destruction of my virtue uppermost in his mind; and I was torn. In such situations one must be careful not to show too much skin or too much of the body's elegant form; for the art of eroticism lies in what is *not* shown, rather than what is. To better drive one's admirers wild with desire, one must hint at what lies beneath the surface rather than call direct attention to it through various tight garments and such. On top of this challenge I was faced with the obligation to wear something discreet and tasteful, out of respect to Lee's memory, as various friends and hangers-on would be at the reading as well, and one did not want lips wagging about the inappropriateness of one's dress.

In the end, I settled for a pair of black linen slacks, simple leather shoes, and a somewhat daring *mauve* jacket that declared proudly that life must go on in the face of tragedy. Certainly the jacket accented my shoulders and trim waist, which could only pique the attorney's curiosity as to what lay beneath; and the slacks had just the right amount of cling to suggest rather than define.

I encountered a dankly somber atmosphere when the attorney's somewhat truculent amanuensis showed me into a tackily decorated conference room of some sort, where J, Chris, Alex, and Law were already gathered. The lawyer sat at the front of the room, wearing a look not only of impatience but also, to the trained eye, one of extreme desire. I took a chair directly across from my admirer, murmuring unpleasantries about the density of Broadway (the avenue, not the theatre experience; though that too has been weighted down, by one flop after another, in recent years) and the impassable streets of the West 50s. Which, of course, no experienced New Yorker could argue with.

"Now that R. Anders has arrived," the *roué* began, with a lascivious sneer, "I would like to thank all of you for coming.

I know this has been a difficult time for everyone. Lee was a good friend to all of us."

Nods of assent, murmurs, and the choking back of tears followed this banal pronouncement, and I waited for the proceedings to become more interesting, while simultaneously avoiding eye contact with the barrister. For everyone knows that attorneys live for, and thrive on, attention, and they become exceedingly frustrated when others do not willingly provide the adoration they believe is their due. In choosing to pursue me sexually, the attorney had not realized what a formidable competitor I am in this regard; and while I had not yet decided whether to give in to his obscene needs, for now the attorney needed to know that Robin Anders is a force of nature to be reckoned with, but, more than that, to be respected.

"Now, if everyone is ready, I'll read the will," the attorney began, pretending not to notice the way I was studiously avoiding his gaze.

"I, Lee Harris, being of sound mind and body, do hereby bequeath the following of my worldly possessions to my friends and loved ones.

"To Chris Blackheart and J Croux, I leave my copies of the following books: *Facing Codependence: What It Is, Where It Comes From, How It Sabotages Our Lives*, by Pia Mellody and Andrea Wells Miller; *Codependents' Guide to the Twelve Steps*, by Melody Beattie; and *Awakening in Time: The Journey from Codependence to Co-Creation*, by Jacquelyn Small. May this treasure trove of modern wisdom bring you much happiness, my dear friends!

"To Law Lessness, a wild, untamed child, I leave the name and phone number of my financial advisor, Zachary Allison, so that you may learn, at your tender and impressionable age, the value of a dollar, as well as various techniques to better manage your income, so that you are no longer in thrall to your more well-heeled elders.

"To Robin Anders, I leave my friendship and the tortoise shell hairbrush of which you are inordinately fond, and envious. May it serve as reminder of your younger days, when your hair was thick enough to warrant such a magnificent grooming device.

"Finally, to Alex Mann, I leave my entire estate: my condominium on West End Avenue, all the possessions therein, and the revelation that you are not only my heir, but also my progeny. Though aware of your existence, I had never expected to see you again after that fateful day I took you, a tiny infant, to an Upstate orphanage. Yes, Alex; we met purely by happenstance at a party in Greenwich Village a decade ago, and our friendship developed from there, despite our age difference. We always have had an inexplicably close bond, and now I know why: You are indeed the fruit of my loins, the baby we'd named Jody. Yet I think Alex suits you more—it is a strong name, a name full of character and life, much like the person who bears it. Your parents want you to have everything that was once ours, so that you may have the life now of which you were earlier deprived by our selfish actions.

"By the time I die, I hope to have told you this in person, but I made a promise that I would ensure you are provided for, and I want you to know the truth in case anything happens to me before I can find the courage to speak with you. Thanks to wise investments, you will now find yourself the possessor of a small fortune that should grant you a life of leisure for the rest of your days. The money will be kept in trust for you until such time as you turn 30, at which time it becomes yours. You will turn 30 approximately two years from the date I sign this will, and until then the money will earn a lovely amount of interest and set you up even better for the future. Farewell, my dear Alex, and know that your selfish parents loved you—and that at least one of them was proud to have known you as an adult. More details are provided in a letter I have written to you, which I have left with my attorney."

You could have heard the proverbial pin drop. Then, if possible, the room got even quieter when the lawyer concluded the reading by saying, "Signed by my own hand, Lee Harris," and the date the will had been signed—less than a week after our return from the holiday weekend on Long Island.

Not wanting the attorney to witness the temporary loss of my *sang froid* at these exceedingly disturbing turns of event, I glanced to the other side of the room, where Alex sat, arms folded. Was it my imagination, or was that latest member of the *nouveau riche* wearing a rather smug grin?

17

Many questions remained to be answered, of course; but the shock of the revelation combined with the disappointment of being all but disinherited kept our small party silent. The attorney, raping me with his eyes, closed our meeting by saying he needed to have a private conversation with Alex—no doubt to provide the promised letter and to discuss Lee's funeral arrangements—and the rest of us were free to go.

Perhaps the attorney did us a favor, as prolonged exposure to one another would likely have ignited the tinderbox that had been stuffed full of wood shavings during the reading of the will. J and Chris, clearly hoping to have been more substantive benefactors of Lee's nonexistent largesse, left the attorney's office with nary a word to anyone. Law, perhaps plucked by having a set of unflattering character traits immortalized in a last will and testament, departed silently as well, no doubt to begin searching for new sources of potential upkeep and/or revenue, since Lee, always reluctant to provide such succour in life, had proven equally stubborn in that regard after death.

Whilst the members of my dwindling social set went their separate ways, I felt it incumbent upon me to have a word with Lee's newly revealed heir.

"Alex…," I began, cautiously.

"Did you know, Robin?"

I thought for a moment. In similar circumstances I have been known to occasionally pretend to possess bits of knowledge to which in reality I am not truly privy. In this case, however, I felt that being anything other than completely straightforward would only backfire on me later. For I have always had a sort of sixth sense about these matters, and it has rarely steered me wrong.

"No, Alex. I did not. I am as shocked as you are. You *are* shocked, yes?"

I flashed back—as one with a nearly eidetic memory sometimes does—to our weekend on Long Island, when it seemed that Lee and Alex had spent an inordinate amount of time together. Upon arriving at the house, Lee had seemed exceedingly anxious to have a room adjoining Alex's. I had assumed a motivation powered by carnal urges, but perhaps Lee'd had a nobler purpose? Had Lee told Alex—a *protégé* nearly three decades Lee's junior—that their relationship was one of blood, not of friendship? And if so, what had the ramifications been? The implications were positively Oedpial and/or Electran, given the speculation that had been swirling around the exact definition of Lee and Alex's relationship over the last several years. For the time being, however, it was best not to spend one's time considering the Freudian aspects of the situation; for everyone knows that eneuretic Austrian never did get it quite right.

"Yes, Robin. Completely shocked. When I turned 21, I looked for my biological parents, just to know where I had come from. But everywhere I looked was a dead end, and after a while I figured that if they'd wanted to be found, they wouldn't have covered their tracks so carefully. It didn't really matter, in a way…I love the people who adopted me. *They* are my parents. But now, to think that I'd actually been friends with one of my biological parents for years, and never knew about it.…it's a little overwhelming.…"

"There, there," I clucked, giving Alex's shoulder a pat, which is always preferable to hugging. "How could you have possibly known? It wasn't as if the two of you looked alike or shared the same mannerisms, all those little things that speak to a familial bond." And it was absolutely true: Lee was an overweight redhead with a thick build and big bones—a slobbering green-eyed Irish setter, freckly and clumsy and ungainly, yet not unintelligent. In contrast, Alex was a prematurely gray, brown-eyed combination of ferret and Siamese cat, all long delicate limbs and sibilant S's, with a matching set of nearly crossed eyes that had to be a gift from Alex's other parent.

I took my leave and began a slow, steady stroll back to my apartment. I needed some time to breathe, and while the mix of oxygen and other elements smothering Manhattan cannot actually be considered *air*, it was a relief to finally be free from the attorney's cruel sexual stare. I wondered how long it would be before my answering machine yielded a message from the attorney's secretary stating that he needed to "see me" in his office urgently.

I'd deal with that scenario when it arose, but at the moment the more pressing need was to get home to the 'plum pills.' How like Lee to dramatically announce the existence of a long-lost child in a will, when the assembled masses would gasp in shock at the revelation. But why had I not been told? Surely I, as the keeper of Lee's deepest and darkest secrets, deserved better treatment? Was this the reason Lee had placed several calls to me upon returning from Long Island—calls that I had gleefully ignored while tending to my own mental health? Or was this the situation to which Lee had been referring with that oblique comment about the past rearing its ugly head, or returning in a "haunting" way?

And while it went without saying that I had no actual need for any of Lee's worldly possessions, nor the desire for same, it certainly would have been delightful if Lee's will had given me anything beyond a contraband hairbrush and a slap in the face. After all the years we'd spent together! Certainly Lee had always been vindictive; and certainly Lee had never quite grown accustomed to my ability to come out on the winning side of any argument; but this disinheritance felt extreme even for that vengeful individual. Could Lee have been temporarily insane? Such things have been known to happen when one is in sexual thrall to another being, and Lee's hints to me on Long Island had indicated a nascent relationship with Pat that had the potential to become obsessively physical.

And—speaking of—had anyone bothered to call poor Pat with the news of Lee's demise? Certainly Pat, whom I'd not yet had the displeasure of meeting, would wonder where Lee had disappeared to. I would need to make some discreet inquiries about town to find Pat's whereabouts so that the news could be broken and an invitation to Lee's memorial service tendered. I supposed all this was Alex's responsibility now; but could such a selfish individual really be counted on to do the right thing?

No—it would fall upon me to contact Pat, as indeed the bulk of all demanding projects lands squarely on my shoulders. I suppose this is the price of being competent. However, I decided to look on the bright side, for a conversation with Pat might offer some interesting insights into Lee's final days.

But before calling on Pat, I had another visit to make: to the bank that held Lee's safety deposit box, where I hoped to find that ridiculous tortoise shell hairbrush that was now, by rights, officially mine.

18

This will come as no surprise, but I have always had a flair for the poetic. This might explain why, as I walked to First Gotham Bank the following morning, I couldn't help but think in literary terms about the relationship Lee and I had shared. Sometimes a simple object becomes an incredibly potent symbol, and this was the role that *keys*, both physical and metaphorical, had played in the Robin/Lee *amour*/friendship/relationship/rivalry. We both knew the *keys* to the other's personality; and we had each played a *key* role in the other's life for decades. Given our strong individual needs for privacy and solitude, we had both always been exceedingly reluctant to let others into our physical space, so the fact that Lee held *keys* to my homes, and I held a set of *keys* to Lee's various locks, might be seen as a physical manifestation, if you will, of the ties that bound us inextricably.

That said, something I'd always wondered about was the size and heft of Lee's keychain, which contained more keys than one really could need at any given time. Certainly one needed the keys to the apartment of oneself and one's lover, as well as the keys to one's office. But Lee's keychain held a minimum of 15 keys of assorted sizes and shapes. Whenever I commented upon that extraordinary number, I was given a very distinct brush-off. This of course had the exact opposite of the intended effect; rather than quenching my curiosity, it only made me all the more determined to discover the locks into which those various keys fit.

Thus, one evening toward the end of the first year of our relationship, I'd cooked a romantic dinner for two, carefully mixing several of Dr. R's less bitter-tasting powders into Lee's portion of the delicate whipped potatoes I'd prepared to accompany the *chateaubriand*. These had the intended effect of knocking Lee unconscious for more than twelve hours, which had afforded me the opportunity I needed to run to the hardware store and have copies of all those keys made. These I put for safekeeping in my apothecary cabinet, where they had remained untouched—until now.

The original keys had various marking and numbers on them, and I'd been sure to transcribe those markings onto small pieces of masking tape which I'd affixed to the copied keys. Such careful replication was necessary, as I'd felt certain at one point that Lee had been carrying on behind my back with someone who shall remain nameless—because I never did succeed in learning that person's name. I *had* learned, however, through various inquiries and occasionally by following Lee at a discreet distance, that the likely *paramour* lived in Apartment 208 of a sordid little high-rise on the Park; and indeed, one of the keys was marked "208." This fact I had kept in the back of my consciousness to use in an argument against Lee, which I'd done with great aplomb a year or so after the keys had been copied. The look on Lee's face when I hurled my accusation told me I'd hit the mark; and while the emotional devastation wreaked upon me was indeed extreme, the sheer shock that Lee's *faccia brutta* had registered was almost enough to compensate for the trauma.

Flipping through the keys, I found one marked "6905." This, I felt, had to be the key to Lee's safety deposit box. It had that sort of banklike look to it, and I knew that Lee's salacious side would not have been able to resist a box number that begins with those two digits. To confirm my suspicions, I called First Gotham Bank, told them my name was Lee Harris, and said I needed to get into my safety deposit box. Then I laughed with *faux* embarrassment and said I couldn't remember which of my many keys was for the box: Was it the one with 6905 etched into it? The fatuous young woman assured me that indeed it was. I requested her name, as such an exceedingly dimwitted person could prove useful in the future.

My next step was to pull out the passport I'd retrieved from Lee's nightstand. (The poor dear, spending literally hundreds of dollars in an attempt to have a decent passport photo taken, only to end up with *that*.) I did blink back a tear or two as the two shriveled green peas that were Lee's eyes looked back at me dimly from that daguerreotype, but fond memories did not stop me from pasting my own much better picture on top of Lee's. Such defacement of government property was regrettable, but necessary if I were to retrieve my tortoise shell hairbrush before Alex absconded with it.

At the bank, I asked for Selma Rayuathapan, who, it turned out, was quite a lovely young thing. Any casual observer would have noticed her immediate sexual interest when I introduced myself as Lee Harris, with whom she'd spoken earlier on the phone. After asking to see my I.D. and glancing cursorily at the doctored passport, the silly young thing actually put a wiggle in her hips as she led me to the safety deposit area, the better to convey her interest in a *liaison* of some sort. Needless to say, I returned the flirtation, as it is good to remain in practice in the art of seduction.

The key marked 6905 worked like a charm. As Ms. Rayuathapan batted her eyelashes coquettishly in my direction, I began unloading the box's contents. Here was a gold

pocket watch that had been in Lee's family for several generations, a timepiece neither valuable nor particularly pleasing
in design, but one that for some reason held sentimental value for my ex. An Altoids tin held a few insignificant baubles
I didn't recall seeing before, an unremarkable ring and pendant made with inferior gems, I believe onyx and peridot
respectively. A few small certificates of deposit hinted at Lee's
dwindling monetary situation; anyone who expected to find
shares of Microsoft or Apple in that box would have been
sorely disappointed.

The last item was an envelope marked "Sent via
Messenger." Lee's name and address were also written on the
envelope in a spiky hand, most likely with a cheap fountain
pen with a substandard nib. Curious, I pulled out the sheet of
low-quality foolscap within, unfolded it, and read thus:

My dear Lee:

As I do not have much time left—a result of
my own decision—I feel that the time has come
for the sort of direct honesty we shared nearly
three decades ago, and that we have revisited,
with only limited success, from time to time.

I have tried and tried to reach you, via your
home phone and your cell phone, but various
mutual friends tell me that you have escaped to
Long Island to the weekend home of that insufferable Robin Anders, about whom I have heard
much that I can only hope is not true. This is not
the type of information to be left casually on a
voice mail, so I commit it to writing here, so that
you will have a direct record of the information
by my own hand.

I always felt that I couldn't leave until I had found the baby, someway, somehow. And the detective I hired has finally succeeded. He has found our child living *right here in New York City*. Of course, the adoptive parents did not retain the name we'd hastily given the child. The fruit of our loins now goes by the name of Alex, adopted from that Upstate orphanage by Manfred and Emily Mann more than 28 years go.

If/when you look up our dear Jody, please apologize from the bottom of my heart that I could not be there with you. I really can stand the torture of this illness no longer, but I want to do what I can to compensate our love child for our abandonment. The terms of my will leave everything to Jody/Alex. Please, in memory of all that we have shared, I ask two things of you: First, find Alex and share our tragic story so that I may make posthumous amends, and second, be sure that my estate gets to the child no matter what happens. Should you decide that Alex is not mature enough to handle a significant sum of money at this time, I believe it will be fair for you to set up a trust account to be dispersed at a proper time. It will be a source of comfort to me that I shall go to my grave knowing that you will immediately take steps to ensure that dear Alex is amply provided for.

I have enjoyed our reacquaintance, and only wish it could have listed a bit longer.

With something akin to fondness,
Pat

Well, this maudlin piece of dreck certainly did shed some light on various situations, didn't it? I congratulated myself on discovering single-handedly how Lee had become aware of the existence of a love child born a quarter century earlier, and why the terms of the will had been changed so precipitously. In addition, I had discovered an intriguing new piece of information—the identity of the child's other parent: Pat.

Finally, though I will not say surprisingly, the envelope confirmed the suspicions that had plagued me for the entire tenure of my relationship with Lee. For the return address on Pat's envelope contained that mysterious, contentious number also found on one of Lee's many keys: 677 West **th Street, Apt. 208.

19

Never let it be said that the job of a sleuth is easy. One spends an inordinate amount of time simply bustling about, going here, going there, in search of information that will lead to the inevitable shocking revelation that one could never have expected. In the meantime a great deal of money and energy are expended, often in inverse proportion to the amount of useful data gathered. Occasionally along the way one does meet, and take to bed, an intriguing and mysterious stranger, and while some more exhibitionistic narrators may feel comfortable in revealing such details, I have always believed that a person of good breeding does not kiss and tell.

Pat's letter had hinted rather strongly at imminent self-destruction. But one must not take these things on faith, based as they were on the scribblings of a person driven mad with guilt and emotional pain. Whether Pat was alive or dead would not be difficult to ascertain, were it not for a rather essential piece of missing information: Pat's last name. I vaguely recollected Lee having mentioned it once or twice, but in this era of information overload I tend to gloss over data that I perceive as irrelevant, or not of lasting value.

While my desire to speak to any of my friends about the situation was positively nonexistent, it did seem likely that at least one of them would know the mystery surname. Thus, continuing in my newfound role of information-gathering sleuth, I picked up the phone. J answered my call on the first ring, as is the habit of those many young, desperate Manhattanites for whom a ringing cell phone is social validation and a heightened sense of self-esteem all rolled up into one glorious ball of neurosis.

"Say, J, do you remember Lee's chatting about an ongoing relationship of some sort with a Pat Someone-Or-Other? You do? You know, it occurs to me that one of us should at least phone poor Pat up, just in case news of Lee hasn't reached…Yes, yes, I know; Lee did indicate as much…But J, listen to me for a moment instead of prattling on, will you, dear? As I was beginning to say, I'd like to give Pat a ring, and I realize that I simply have no idea how to get in touch…did Lee ever mention Pat's last name to you? Oh, yes, Armstrong. I do believe that's it. Would you hold a moment, please? I have another call coming in."

Of course nothing of the sort was happening, but inventing an excuse is so much more polite than hanging up abruptly. I hit the # button on the keypad, waited a moment, then hit it again, which I'm sure made some sort of beeping noise, as of me clicking back into the current conversation. "J, dear, I must take this. Thank you so much for the information. I'll be in touch." And I rang off, congratulating myself for getting J off the phone in record time.

As luck would have it, directory assistance did list a P. Armstrong at 677 West **th Street. I dialed the number, of course not expecting anyone to answer, as everyone knows that Manhattanites simply do not answer their phones while at home for fear of being perceived as somehow socially undesirable, the idea being that if one has friends and/or sex appeal, one is certainly out and about, doing things and being seen/done, rather than sitting home by one's lonesome, desperate for some equally undesirable individual to ring one up and ask one out.

And sure enough, a voice mail greeting did pick up and play on the fifth ring. I listened as a husky voice said matter of factly, "Hi. This is Pat. I'm not here right now, so please leave a message. I'll call you back when I can."

I hung up the phone, as I have never had much interest in speaking to electronic gadgetry. I'd try Pat again later, but in the meantime I had another idea.

My fingers trembled as I pushed the digits that would connect me via cellwave to my dear Law. The time we'd spent together in _____ was still fresh in my mind, and memories of those days, and nights, were just a bit titillating. A young person of uncommon resourcefulness, Law might have an easy method of uncovering more information about Pat. Working in my favor, perhaps, was the fact that Law was employed on a part-time basis as Dr. Rosenthal's general office assistant. Maybe Pat's name had come up in Lee's conversations with Dr. R, and maybe Law had overhead and made a mental note of the dialogue? Or perhaps Law and Lee had discussed the topic directly? Stranger things have happened, for Law—despite seeming apathetic and diffident—does have a knack for catching details and using them for personal benefit.

Like everyone else in New York City, Law makes a priority of answering the cell and chatting, even while at work. As I expected, my call was answered instantly with a delighted, "Hello!"

A few personal and private pleasantries, uttered with the usual undertones of sexual urgency, were exchanged. I then fed Law the same line of nonsense I'd fed J about wanting to phone up Pat with information regarding Lee's passing.

Law drew in a breath and came close to gasping.

"But Robin, don't you know? Pat died while we were on Long Island. Lee found out when we all got back to the City. I assumed Lee had told you...."

Law trailed off, and another piece of the jigsaw puzzle clicked into place. Lee had indeed called me shortly after our return, leaving a few cryptic messages on my voice mail—messages, you may recall, that I hadn't had the fortitude to listen to as I attempted to deal with the fallout of my Long-Island-induced PTSD. Besides, even if I'd listened to them at the time, I'm sure I would not have paid them much heed, as Lee's messages always had a way of seeming much more urgent than they really were, and over the years I'd learned not to enable that behavior by responding to it.

I listened as Law provided the details. Pat, also a patient of Dr. Rosenthal's, had lost a valiant fight with a particularly stubborn illness. Unable to bear the pain any longer, Pat had decided to end it all in the privacy of that Central Park high-rise, but not before writing that final note to Lee, as well as a kind letter to Dr. R, hand delivered by messenger one day after the fact, asking Dr. R to kindly make the necessary arrangements so as to spare Lee the worry and upset. All of this was a matter of public record; the *Times* had reported on it, as had various other local tabloids; and thus was Law able to recount the details without compromising any ethical or professional standards of conduct.

So it seemed a double tragedy had taken place not far from the nucleus of my cell: the suicide of one of Alex's parents, followed by the tragic death of the other a week later. The intensity of it was almost too much bear, but a couple of the 'asparagus pills' that Dr. R had prescribed for use *solely in the case of emergency* proved moderately effective in increasing my coping skills.

Law filled in the remaining details as I listened intently. Dr. Rosenthal had of course canceled sessions immediately upon receiving Pat's note and had rushed over to the apartment, but not before calling the police and asking them to have an ambulance meet the entire party at the high-rise. And, of course, when Dr. R speaks, the police listen, due to Dr. R's discreet but well-known status as therapist to the New York elite, including the commissioner of police, various FDNY personnel, and of course the mayor. Though you did not hear that from me.

The superintendent of Pat's building had produced a set of keys to apartment 208, and the troop had barged in to find poor Pat lying peacefully in bed, a bottle of pills not unlike my very own 'blueberry pills' empty on the bedstand. Pat's glassy eyes and rigid posture told the party everything they needed to know. A day or two later, most likely just as Lee was receiving Pat's letter, the Medical Examiner declared Pat a suicide. The details of the estate were still being sorted out, but this Law did know for a fact: Pat had appointed Lee executor.

Apparently, Lee took Pat's death quite hard and had asked Law to help sort through Pat's possessions, and the two were to have met at apartment 208 a couple of mornings after Pat's death—the same day on which J/Chris and Alex had been scheduled to arrive at Lee's abode in the afternoon and evening, respectively. When Lee didn't show, Law placed a phone call or two, of course not knowing that Lee lay permanently inert back at home. The rest, of course, is history, as Law connected with our various other friends over the next several days, and the realization grew that *something was wrong*.

And this is where a detective's work is never done. How easy it would have been to simply take the rest of the afternoon off, to have a manicure and/or a pedicure; for uncovering information in this fashion is tiring in the extreme, both mentally and physically. But as always my curiosity rose to the forefront. While I'd had the key to apartment 208 in my possession for years, I'd never actually used it—in fact, had not even known until this very day to whom it belonged. Would I ever again have such an unfettered opportunity to explore that den of sexual iniquity? In using that key, not only might I gain answers to many of the questions I'd had in the years of my relationship with Lee; I might also find that elusive tortoise shell hairbrush that still seemed to elude me. For, surely, Lee must have spent many an evening at Pat's, which meant that my hairbrush might still be there, filled with clumps of Lee's coarse but thinning hair.

Now was as good a time as any; so I returned to my home, retrieved the key from my apothecary cabinet, took an hour or so to fix my hair and refresh myself, changed clothes, and returned to the streets where I hailed a cab, but not before stopping at a local boutique to treat myself to something small, for the only thing in the world that could even begin to mitigate the distressing events of the past several days was a new pair of shoes.

20

One of the benefits of being a lithe and elegant person is my ability to walk about unnoticed, to slip into and out of the various cracks and crevasses of *La Città di Nova York* without attracting undue attention. My movements have in the past been described as catlike and graceful, even balletic, and my extremely light step is well nigh undetectable when I am attempting to keep a low profile.

My lightness of foot served me well as I slipped into Pat's building, that overblown pre-war monstrosity that had gone atrociously upscale in the 80s. Taking advantage of the door-man's divided attention as he signed for some dry cleaning, I simply floated under his radar and into the elevator, where I pushed the button for the second floor.

The hallway was one of those prototypical Manhattan hall-ways, painted an atrocious celery color with a carpet to match. This particular hue has always particularly offended my sensi-bilities, and normally I would have fled the scene, but a deeper motivation caused me to soldier on. Fortunately, apartment 208 was not far from the elevator at all, so I was not forced to endure the greenish assault on my senses for too long and thus did not even need one of the 'eggplant pills' that are some-times required when my refined sensibilities are brutalized.

As this key was a copy of the key on Lee's chain, it had that new-key feel to it, slipping into the slot only through my various wrigglings and coaxings, not unlike various intimate situations in which I have found myself during my adult life. And I had to force open not one but three identical locks in such manner, as Pat's apartment was tripled-armed to pre-vent any manner of break-in.

My developed sixth sense began tingling as soon as I'd entered the *foyer* and quickly shut the door behind me. The air was stale; clearly Pat had been fond of those unisex colognes that smell good on neither men nor women, and the lingering scent of this noxious concoction hung in the motionless air of apartment 208. But I had that curious presentiment that one feels when one enters a hotel room and senses that *one is not alone*. Perhaps the spirit was corporeal, perhaps otherworldly; but I had come this far, and I was certainly not about to let any person or phantom stop me from regaining the hairbrush that was rightfully mine. Grabbing a bumbershoot from the umbrella stand, I brandished it like a saber, flipped on the light switch, and entered the main living area.

Before my astonished eyes lay a scene of sheer chaos. The cushions of an avocado-colored couch were strewn about the room, and various bric-a-brac of questionable taste lay in pieces on the synthetic carpets. It seemed as if a volcano of paper had exploded in the center of the room, raining its ash on every planar surface of the apartment. In the kitchen, cabinet doors were agape, their contents spilled onto the *faux* marble flooring. If anything, the two bedrooms were in even worse condition. Beds had been upended, pillows slashed and unstuffed, dresser drawers pulled out and rifled through.

Sifting through the mess on the floor, I pulled out some tarnished silver frames featuring photographs of the same individual: with friends, laughing it up at one of those pretentious Madison Avenue eateries; staring wistfully into space in a candid shot snapped by some looker-on or admirer; arms draped around this friend or that one; lying on a couch in close proximity to Lee, both wearing expressions of lust and/or postcoital bliss.

So this was the infamous Pat, all wispy yellow hair, long limbs, and big green Siamese cat eyes like UFOs from some emerald planet. About the lips and mouth I could detect the character flaws that had determined that self-destruction was preferable to battling an aggressive illness; for Pat, despite what some would call a conventional attractiveness, had the receding chin and beaten-down look of an extraordinarily weak-willed individual.

What could the home invaders have been looking for? I suppose money and jewels were the obvious candidates. It seemed quite likely that the street friends of the building staff had been given access to Pat's apartment to search for those objects that could be sold easily at pawn shops; though, not having seen Pat's home prior to its being "tossed," as the English bobbies say, I had no idea whether such valuables were indeed kept in the place, or whether Pat stored them elsewhere. Or, in fact, whether Pat had owned anything of value at all.

Stepping over the mess into the master bathroom, I was greeted by a surprising sight. The room had been thoroughly cleaned out. Nothing was left in the vanity or wall cabinet—not a toothbrush, not a comb for Pat's fine, lifeless hair, not even a canister of dental floss for Pat's horselike teeth. The same was true of the smaller powder room in the further reaches of the apartment—it too had been stripped of all its ointments and unguents, and lay as bare as the head of Mr. Clean.

I suppose I could have gotten on my hands and knees to have searched through the millions of sheets of paper that lay about the floor, but my gut instinct told me that my hairbrush would not be found among the ruins; nor would all the searching in the world generate any leads as to its whereabouts.

As I closed and locked the apartment door behind me, I had a sudden thought. Could Alex have done this? As executor, that newly wealthy creature would have access to Lee's papers and keychain, as well as, perhaps, additional information about Pat's worldly possessions. But such an explanation made no sense on several levels. Why would Alex destroy the contents of a place that was part of the recently inherited estate?

Well, none of this was any of my business. My interest began and ended at a hairbrush that, it seemed, I was unlikely to ever recover. The thought caused me great distress as I took the elevator to the lobby floor, so much so that I had to take one of the chewable 'tomato pills' that Dr. R has prescribed for emergency use when potable water is not readily available. In my distress, and my fumbling to get the 'tomato pill' into my oral orifice as quickly as possible, I hit the wrong button on the elevator panel, "B" instead of "L," and thus found myself on the building's basement level.

As the elevator doors began to close, a wash of inspiration flooded over me. I stuck my foot into the closing doors and wedged myself out. The usual scent of phosphates and fabric softener from the laundry room hit me rather violently, and I nearly swooned, but the 'tomato pills' do have the benefit of being fast-acting, which saved me from being found in a dead faint in the basement of a building I had no right to be in.

Still trusting my hunch, I wound my way around various corners until I came upon that mainstay of supposedly upscale Manhattan apartment buildings: the storage cages. A left turn and then a right led me to the cage marked "208," a floor-to-ceiling mesh enclosure about 10 feet high and 10 feet wide. Pulling out my key, I tried the lock and *voilà*—with a bit of fiddling, the door swung open.

Obviously the lowlifes who'd ripped Pat's apartment to shreds hadn't thought to visit the promised land of the basement, for the contents of the storage cage remained undisturbed, covered with a fine layer of oily dust, no doubt the remains of the undergarments being laundered only a few feet away. Pat seemed to have quite a taste for rather bizarre African artifacts, as well as other types of native *objets d'art* from around the world. Possibly some of these pieces might have value at thrift shops in the vicinity of St. Mark's Place, but Alex need not worry that Sotheby's or Christie's would be fighting for the auction rights.

From the corner of my eye I spied a much smaller object that might prove to be of interest, however. It was a jade-green metallic box, a little smaller than a shoe box, sealed shut with a combination lock. It also had a handle, which made it quite easy to grab the box and carry it out of the building subtly, which is exactly what I did upon relocking the cage and taking the elevator back to the lobby. For the box did seem just the perfect size in which to hide a Madagascarian tortoise shell hairbrush. As I left the building, I thought I noticed an ominous shadow looming behind me; but because minor hallucinations are sometimes an unfortunate side effect of the 'tomatoes,' I paid it no heed and went on my merry way.

21

I have found in my long residence on the island of Manhattan that most residents have two distinct sides to their characters: the outward, upstanding citizen who desires nothing more than to dine on the finest oysters at the best restaurants with the longest waiting lists, and the larcenous money-grubber who understands that a certain amount of filthy lucre is required to maintain even the most basic standard of living in *La Grande Pomme*.

Thus one sees those struggling young artists frequently posing for photos that they desperately hope will never come to the attention of their parents; those dedicated and serious young actors taking parts, under various false names, in films with little dialogue but a great deal of action of the flesh; those singer/songwriters whose part-time jobs at upscale eateries afford them ample opportunity to earn a little extra cash by selling goods purloined from the walk-in freezer or liquor store room. Even Law, as I have perhaps hinted at, has been known to provide certain physical succour to the wealthy in times of need; though what that young fleshpot of Egypt does with the money, other than waste it, is something I have never been able to ascertain.

All of this is to say that I did not need to make very many calls to find someone to help me deal with that rather stubborn lock on the mystery box I'd found in Pat's storage cage. Upon arriving home, I'd attempted to unlock the combination with various combinations of 2, 0, and 8—a rather brilliant idea on my part, I thought. However, I was unsuccessful, and all that turning of the dial proved exceedingly rough on my always-sensitive skin. In addition, the efforts took a completely unacceptable toll on the manicure I always try so carefully to keep from damage.

In a masterstroke that allowed me to solve two problems at once, I placed an emergency phone call to my manicurist, explaining my need for an immediate appointment as well as my equally pressing need for someone able to deal with a pesky lock. With the promise of an ample tip, the manicurist showed up at my door late the following morning, brandishing not only the usual manicure kit but also a set of large, bulky tools, including one rather ominous looking device that managed to snap the lock off Pat's box faster than a trailer park denizen loses her virginity on the evening of her 13th birthday. Why or how the manicurist had access to such tools was none of my business, of course; nor did that sensual but simpleminded individual ask for any details of the box or its contents, knowing full well that services provided in New York City are rendered on a no-questions-asked basis, and that silence is built into any rate that is quoted and agreed upon.

The previous days had been stressful in the extreme, and I did need an outlet for the various emotions that had threatened to overwhelm my delicate equilibrium since receiving news of Lee's untimely passing. *Mystery box be damned*, I thought, and proceeded to entertain myself with the manicurist in various ways that compensated that expert lock snapper quite handsomely.

Of course I needed a bit of refreshment following the afternoon's activities, so after a long bath and a nap greatly aided by one or two of those wonderful 'peach pills,' my energy level had been restored enough to begin the strenuous mental acrobatics required to continue piecing the jigsaw puzzle together. Fortunately, I felt very much up to the task, as the ability to see connections among the unconnected, links among the unlinked, and ties among the untied, is a talent I have been blessed with.

Bracing myself for what I might find, I flipped open the metallic box. The contents were disappointing, to put it mildly. Apparently Pat had been quite the sentimentalist and had never forgotten that child conceived in sin and given up for adoption so many years earlier. Several black-and-white photographs showed a much younger Pat and an infinitely thinner Lee gazing lazily at the camera. One or two shots showed an overwhelmed-looking Pat holding a tiny infant wrapped in swaddling clothes, and one shot that seemed particularly tear-stained showed mother, father, and child together, none of them seeming blissfully happy. Really, I told myself, I was quite lucky never to have had to meet this Pat Armstrong in person, for I have never been able to abide maudlin, self-centered people who keep photographs of themselves and cry over them in moments of weepy nostalgia.

A small leather (more likely plastic) sack held a couple of pieces of costume jewelry: a ring of onyx, a pendant of peridot. Holding these up to the light, I inspected each more closely. Where had I seen such trifles before? The answer struck me forcefully: They were very similar to those I'd found in Lee's safety deposit box. Turning the items over, I found an inscription on the back of each: the onyx ring inscribed with a cursive L, the peridot pendant inscribed with a P.

So these were the thanks I received for making Lee the center of my existence for so many years! And all the time that I'd spent suffering at Lee's hands, receiving only abuse in return for the loving care I'd given, Lee had maintained a spiritual and (it was now clear) physical bond with an ex from the long-ago past! Is this what having children does to people—tying them together in an inextricable knot that can never be loosened? In the midst of my despair, having had my worst suspicions confirmed, I maintained enough self-possession to thank God that I'd had the foresight never to become a parent; for the ability to rid oneself of an undesirable mate is essential to one's self-preservation, and to have that ability limited in any way, shape, or form, even by the fruit of one's loins, is not a situation to be tolerated.

Blinking back a tear—for no, I would not shed even a single drop for that two-timer, that backstabber—I continued rifling through the box's meager contents. Stuck at the bottom of the box was a yellowing envelope with a preprinted return address: Upstate Home for the Unwanted and Despised, Glens Falls, NY.

Setting my jaw, I opened the envelope and unfolded the pages within—a photocopy of the adoption papers, in which "Mr. and Mrs. Smythe" consented to leaving their six-week-old child, "Jody," to the care and feeding of the Sisters of Perpetual and Infinite Justice until such time as "appropriate" parents might be found. At the bottom of the certificate, on the line reserved for the signature of L. Smythe, I recognized the penmanship of the late Lee Harris. The "y" in Smythe could belong to none other than Lee—I would recognize that overlong loop anywhere. The "t" was also unmistakably Lee's, with its long crossbar slanting upward from bottom left to upper right, with a slight devil's-tail spike on both ends. The capital "L" could belong only to Lee, as well—as oversized, grandiose, and bloated as the person who scribbled it.

P. Smythe's signature was much more mousy and tentative, the trembling hand of an unsophisticated soul who had never strayed from the cursive method taught in school, who crafts each letter according to the style set by the second grade teacher rather than placing a distinctive flourish upon key letters such as the capital "S" and the lower case "y." Each letter was round and almost exactly the same size as all the others, with the capitals not soaring much higher than the final "e." A more pedestrian signature could not possibly be imagined; making me wonder yet again what Lee's yin could possibly have seen in Pat's yang.

Hold the phone, Robin, said an urgent voice in my head—and so attention-demanding was the voice that I looked up to see if someone had perhaps sneaked into my apartment while I examined the contents of the box. I had spent a not insignificant amount of time reading Pat's suicide/mash note to Lee just a day earlier, and I'd taken in every last word of that epistle while noting its spikiness, its up-and-down orientation, its tightness. But that hand bore zero resemblance to Pat's signature on these adoption papers. And the capital "P" with which Pat had signed the suicide letter could not be more different than the small, nondescript "P" I saw here.

Which could mean only one thing—that the person who'd given up baby Jody for adoption with Lee could not be the same person who'd written the suicide letter.

I sighed deeply. Even in death, Lee was presenting me with the same types of problems, enigmas, and puzzles that had been the trademark of our relationship.

22

Ihave always had a strong work ethic, sometimes to the detriment of my own mental and physical health. Working tirelessly for The Goode Foundation has been a major part of my existence for more than two decades now, and though the process of giving a foundation's money to deserving young, attractive artists is enervating in the extreme, I have always felt it is my way of giving back for the many privileges of my existence.

Sadly, my untiring efforts on behalf of The Goode Foundation have not always received the recognition they deserve, as the three Wyrd sisters who run the place (inefficiently) are usually too busy fighting their own battles. This has become worse since the death of their father, who failed to put in place a proper succession plan, which has in turn led to much political jockeying. In a delightful turnabout, however, this battle was working in my favor as I investigated the tenuous links among Pat, Lee, and Alex. Obsessed with their own Machiavellian schemes, no one at the Foundation noticed or cared about my absence from the office. Faith Goode, the interim director, reiterated rather shortly that she didn't care what I did, as long as I showed up for the vote, and hung up on me once again. Meanwhile, her sisters Hope and Charity were leaving me coddling and sycophantic voice messages, in a rather transparent attempt to get my support. These I ignored, as there were more pressing problems to be solved.

Perhaps a place to start would be the Upstate Home for the Unwanted and Despised. This might be a good place to begin unraveling the mystery of Alex's birth—and Pat's signature. Perhaps Pat, clearly the more oversentimental and mawkish of the two parents, had simply been unable to bring the child to the Home, sending Lee and some unknown third party to do the dirty work. This could explain why Lee's signature matched that of Parent #1, but Pat's signature did not match that of Parent #2.

Directory assistance held no listing for such a place in Glens Falls. I asked the flirtatious operator if he might look up "Orphanages" in the vicinity via the business listings, and I was informed that no homes for unwed mothers or anything even remotely similar existed within that area.

I have never considered myself a Luddite, though I do feel that my approach to electronic gadgetry is somewhat old-fashioned. Yet despite my intense loathing of the Internet and all its perversity—its welcoming haven for splinter groups like the transgendered, for whom I have absolutely no patience—I had bowed to the twenty-first century and gotten a connection so that I might receive those "emails" that seem to fly with regularity among friends, as a sorry substitute for the lost art of conversation.

So it was with reluctance that I booted up the machine, went to one of those so-called "search engines," and typed in UPSTATE HOME FOR THE UNWANTED AND DESPISED. I found the information I was looking for almost immediately. The home in which Jody/Alex had been so unceremoniously abandoned 28 years ago had long since closed its doors; most likely as a result of out-of-wedlock births becoming acceptable and even desirable, especially among those of the social classes who used to be rightfully embarrassed by such situations.

My eyes widened, my stomach tightened, and my heart began to race ever so slightly when I realized the next source of information I would need to consult. Pat's letter to Lee had indicated that a private detective of some sort had been engaged to find their child, and that said detective had succeeded in learning the child's name and whereabouts. A call or visit to the detective would certainly yield quality information; however, I was ignorant as to the detective's identity. I pictured an obese, balding, flatulent man smoking a cigar and tossing out salacious comments to his secretary.

Who might know the detective's identity? I could think of only one person who might possibly be privy to that information: Pat's attorney, the person who'd drafted the will leaving Pat's fortune in trust with Lee for the recently found heir. For we all know that New York attorneys are privy to more gossip than Liz Smith and Cindy Adams, our own doyennes of dirt.

And who would know the identity of Pat's attorney? To my speculation, only one person: Lee's lustful lawyer. This would mean that I would have to advance our cat-and-mouse game to the next level. Rather than playing the waiting game as the attorney stewed in the juices of lust, I was going to have to make the highly unorthodox move of placing a call—or, worse, making a visit—in order to request the information.

As you may have realized, I have never been one to back down from a challenge. Thus, with a renewed sense of energy, I picked up the phone and dialed Lee's attorney's office, requesting an appointment for the following morning. I was kept on hold a completely unacceptable length of time; and, indeed, in any other situation I would have written serious letters of complaint, while beginning a smear campaign against the office staff; but in this case, I knew that the waiting time was part of the attorney's ongoing war of attrition against my virginity; and armed with this knowledge, I was able to keep myself calm and almost polite when the secretary returned to the phone and announced officiously that I could be seen at 9 the following morning.

Placing the phone back in its cradle, it occurred to me that I should retrieve Pat's letter from Lee's safety deposit box, so that I had it in evidence when necessary. Perhaps that young woman with the unpronounceable name at the bank could be bullied or charmed into making a copy for me on the bank's photocopier; but if she were unmovable, I could always take the letter, make a copy elsewhere, and return it to the box.

So I applied my sunscreen and various moisturizers, retrieved the key to Lee's box and the altered passport, and took myself down to First Gotham Bank, where I was brought into the safety deposit box area by a young man whose sexual attentions would very much have been welcomed at another time, but were an unwanted distraction when my mind was cluttered with so many details.

Turning the key in the box, I studiously avoided the clerk's intense stare, knowing that eye contact could only send the wrong signal. Rather, I kept my eyes focused on the box, but eyes cannot focus on emptiness. Yes: Much to my chagrin, while I sleuthed around Manhattan, attempting to serve the cause of justice, someone had come and emptied the safety deposit box of all its contents.

23

As a person who has never sought the spotlight, I have likewise always been reluctant to make a mountain out of the proverbial molehill. While weaker folk might have run out of the bank, tearing out their hair and screaming about conspiracies and secret societies, I felt absolutely no urge to indulge in such histrionics. Perhaps the 'tangelo pills' had helped somewhat in this regard, but I believe the larger part of the explanation lay in the layer of icy intellect that I am known to bring to any given situation. The safety deposit box's missing contents could no doubt be recovered, as long as I were willing to exert my considerable brain power in that direction, without distraction, for an extended time period.

Thus I strolled back deliberately to my home from the bank, using the constitutional to bring order to the chaos of the situation. Was the removal of the box's contents related to my visit a few days earlier? Or was this merely a coincidence, as insubstantial as the bulges in the trousers of the Brooklyn Italians who invade Manhattan on weekends looking for ladies to bed?

The answer could no doubt be found quite satisfactorily with a single phone call. Upon arriving home, and after a much-needed hour's footbath, I placed a call to Alex, ruminating as the phone rang on how much of one's social life is now conducted without actually seeing anyone. For, unlike those of my generation, for whom social contact was the very manna of existence, today's young urbanites are socially fed by the curious phenomena of the *cell phone* and *text message*, which allow one to claim multitudes of "friends" while going about one's business and not really spending any time with them at all.

"Alex, dear, it's Robin. How are you holding up? I've been so concerned."

There was long, heavy sigh. "Dealing, Robin. Dealing. So many details to be attended to. And of course, at any other time, I simply would have phoned up Lee and asked for a helping hand....And it would have been given, graciously and without reserve. Could it be, Robin, that our friendship was founded on a sort of *psychic knowing* of our bonds of kinship? It makes one..."

I have been acquainted with Alex long enough to know that this sort of conversation could go on indefinitely if not nipped in the bud.

"It makes one feel very, very lucky to have experienced that bond with another," I put in hastily. "I, too, shared an eternal bond with our departed friend, and in moments when I begin to feel overwhelmed, I focus on the many fond memories, the shared confidences, the sense that Destiny had decreed we would forever be in each other's lives. That said, Alex, I did want to bring something to your attention. In looking over some mementos, it occurred to me that Lee had held a safety deposit box at First Gotham Bank for many years. I didn't know if you were aware of it, of if Lee's—attorney—even knew of its existence. It may contain valuables of some sort, so I thought I would mention it to you."

Alex sighed, a quasi-whinny different in tone and tenor than the previous sigh, which had been more protracted and self-pitying. "You're talking about the First Gotham on **th Street, yes? I just got access to the box this morning, and I went to retrieve the contents. They're now here with me."

In other circumstances I would have made subtle inquiries into the treasures the box may have held, but since I already had that piece of information, I thought I could cement my reputation for being a subtle and nonintrusive friend by not asking any further questions. Nor did Alex volunteer any such information, which should not have been a surprise, for Alex has always been rather paranoid and secretive.

Pretending that my buzzer had just been buzzed to announce guests, I rang off and began preparing for an evening of relaxation at home. Having showered and changed into my evening clothes, I began applying those various unguents that have always been an important part of my youth-maintenance routine. Out of the corner of my eye, on my dressing table, I noticed the list of invitees I'd made for the Long Island weekend trip. I looked over the names with a sigh, noting how elegant my penmanship is, even when I am rushed or in brainstorming mode, as I'd been the day that Lee had rung up to suggest that fateful gathering. For penmanship is very much a part of oneself, and in one's script, as in one's clothing and grooming, one makes a statement regarding *who one is* and *what one believes*. My letters betrayed the studied hand of a master scribe, with their soaring heights and daring lows, their forays into adventurous letter formation, and the impeccably placed dots on the i's and j's. Really, such handwriting could not have been more different from Lee's, which betrayed an underlying sense of insecurity; and it just as easily outclassed Pat's, with that intense spikiness as of an erratic EKG readout.

And then it hit me.

Scientists sometimes describe insights so blinding that their vision is temporarily dimmed, as if the brilliance of the thoughts shine a supernova of light upon their consciousness. This was almost exactly what I experienced when I realized that my hypotheses of the previous day could have been completely misguided. I had been thinking that perhaps Lee and some mysterious person from the past—other than Pat—had gone to that Upstate orphanage to dump chubby, unattractive baby Jody into the ample laps of the Sisters of Perpetual and Infinite Justice. But what if Pat's signature on the adoption papers had indeed belonged to the late Pat Armstrong—and that Pat's supposed deathbed letter to Lee had been written by someone *other than Pat*?

Might a weakened Pat have dictated the letter to a third party? I supposed that was possible, but the more likely explanation was much more disturbing. Someone other than Pat had written that letter to Lee, attempting to pass it off as Pat's hand. And who would benefit most from such a letter? *Look for the money and you find your answer*, as we gumshoes are fond of saying—and one did not have to look far for the solution. The one and only person who benefited from Lee's death was Alex.

But surely Lee would have recognized Alex's handwriting, and not have been taken in by so transparent a ruse? Then again, maybe not. A person as self-focused as Lee rarely pays attention to anything not perceived as relevant to one's self, and certainly Lee would have seen no benefit in time spent noticing and/or analyzing the penmanship of others.

I remembered with great clarity the effort Lee had put into ensuring that I had placed Alex in a *chambre* adjoining Lee's at the house on Long Island. Perhaps during those moonlight games the two had played, Lee had confessed the possibility that a child from the past was threatening to re-emerge? Could Alex have used that situation, and Pat's illness and impending death, to personal advantage?

I gasped as another possibility occurred to me. Alex, always in desperate need of cash, might not have trusted Lee to keep Pat's money safely in trust—for as most of our friends know or suspect, Lee had demonstrated a very marked proficiency for embezzlement during the tenure of our relationship. Which, in the final analysis, might have given Alex a motive to help Lee along to the great beyond.

But Lee had died of a heart attack. This could not be—the *m-word*, could it? That most horrific of all crimes, next to the wearing of white after Labor Day—the taking of someone's life?

No. It was simply impossible. But suddenly I felt I absolutely had to see a sample of Alex's handwriting.

But how could I achieve that goal? *Think, Robin, think*, I told myself. The 'blueberry pills' I'd taken after my nightly ablutions had begun to kick in, and I was not thinking as clearly as I might have wished, but once again Athena, Goddess of Wisdom, shone her light on me. I recalled that a month or so prior to the Long Island weekend, I'd been invited to an absolutely unbearable *boîte* at Chris and J's apartment. The food had been execrable, and the libations even worse, yet I had suffered through the evening with that great good humor for which I am so well known.

Yes, this is relevant, for the following reason: My circle has, over the years, gotten in the habit of writing small personal thank-you notes to the party's host or hostess on overpriced cards purchased at Platypus. I, of course, usually discard such cards upon reading them, as I am morally opposed to clutter. In contrast, J is known as a packrat of epic proportions, and the pigsty that is Chris and J's apartment is testament to the fact that nothing ever gets thrown out. Thus J might still have a thank-you note from Alex, which would give me a good sense of that wretched creature's handwriting and how it might, or might not, resemble that of Pat's deathbed letter.

By this point the 'blueberries' had achieved almost maximum effectiveness, but I do somewhat recall calling J and asking if such a thank-you note from Alex might be retrieved. I was characteristically enigmatic about my reasons for wanting said item, but asked J if we might meet for lunch the following day—my treat, of course, provided the requested thank-you note be delivered as requested.

These vague memories were confirmed the next morning when, upon arising, I checked my answering machine to find a message from J confirming our lunch plans and indicating that the requested document had indeed been found. Before meeting J, however, I had one important social call to make.

24

Recent years have seen the development of a disturbing trend in Manhattan. Once a place where residents took the utmost pride in their appearance, we have become an island of dirty, unkempt slobs. Women leave their apartments without cosmetics properly applied, and with their hair looking no better crafted than a bird's nest. Men have taken to walking about in a type of footwear commonly referred to as the "flip-flop," thus treating strangers across the City to views of their misshapen, smelly feet in stores, restaurants, theatres, and other social gathering places where, in the past, the well-reared gentleman would sooner have appeared naked than gone barefoot. However, I suppose the joke is on these unfortunates when it rains, and the feces and urine of a million dogs flow like the waters of the Hudson River onto their exposed digits.

All of this is to say that I have always believed that certain sartorial standards must be upheld at all costs, which is why I arose several hours early to prepare for my morning meeting with the attorney. As everyone knows, lawyers are forever looking for the upper hand in any situation, whether legal or interpersonal. Given all at stake in this meeting, I simply could not allow myself to be bested. Every hair had to be properly brushed into place, creams needed to be applied, and the proper *ensemble* had to be chosen. Together, all these preparations would signal to the attorney that I was a good and proper match, not only intellectually but also, perhaps, physically—and then if, and only if, I were to consent to a corporeal dalliance.

New York City is filled with people who believe their time is more valuable than yours, and I had little doubt that the attorney fit very snugly into that category. Thus I chose to arrive twenty minutes late for my appointment. Upon announcing myself, I sat down and wondered what the attorney's first volley would be. Would I be made to sit in the waiting area for a longish amount of time, as a way for the attorney to demonstrate the upper hand? Or would I be received immediately, in an effort to make me feel small and rude for showing up late?

The latter proved to be the case. The sour-faced receptionist escorted me into the attorney's office only a minute or two after my arrival, asking if I'd like a cup of coffee or tea. I declined on the grounds that I prefer my teeth to remain pearly white rather than become stained by caffeine-laden hot beverages. Only God knows if this was a subtle and unintentional "dig" at the receptionist, whose own teeth were dingier than the underwear of a navyman six months at sea.

I was looking about the office distractedly, my gaze lingering momentarily on several handsome leather-bound volumes with legalistic titles, when the door opened and the attorney walked in. It was obvious to even the most casual observer that many hours had been spent in preparation for my arrival. Clearly, scent had been freshly applied, and a set of rosy cheeks hinted that perhaps a bit of "pinching" had been done just seconds earlier. The stride was purposeful and resolute, that of a commanding officer taking charge of a situation and all the people in it—including myself.

When sexual tension is crackling in the air, it is best to speak sooner rather than later. This keeps the situation under control and disperses libidinous energy.

"Thank you for taking the time to see me," I began. "As you might imagine, this has been a difficult week."

"Yes, I'm sure. To be honest, however, I'm not quite sure why you're here. The terms of Lee's will are quite clear. You're not planning to contest them, are you?"

So this was to be the game! To cast me in the role of antagonist! But best not to show any emotion that might give the attorney an advantage.

"You may be sure that I have no such motivation. As I believe you know, Lee and I were longtime friends. We had been together, as a couple, in the past, but for the last several years were on a purely platonic basis. I confess that the revelations of Lee's will were surprising to me, but not shocking, as I had always suspected that Lee had quite a sordid past. Still, I am troubled about a few things regarding Lee's death, and I am hoping you can help me achieve some closure."

The attorney said nothing but stared at me, an unnerving, frankly lascivious stare that nearly caused me to lose my *sang froid*. Fortunately, I had taken a larger than average dose of the 'mango pills' before leaving the apartment, and I was able to continue speaking as though we were having a workaday conversation rather than an intensely sexual *tête-à-tête* filled with *double entendres*.

"Specifically," I continued, "I am hoping to talk with Pat Armstrong's attorney about a few questions I have regarding Lee and Pat's child."

"Do you mean Alex Mann?"

"I mean Lee and Pat's child." Such double talk was necessary; for, as you know, my recent ruminations had begun to suggest to me that Alex may not have been the result of a long-ago coupling between the aforementioned lovers.

"If you don't mind my saying so, I can't really see where this is any of your business."

My blood boiled, my nostrils flared, my eyes shone with repressed urges. "Excuse me, but I believe it is. I shared a deep and special bond with Lee, and I want some questions answered about the person with whom my ex-lover had a child. I am not asking you for anything other than the name of Pat's attorney. I'll have this conversation with him, or her, and you won't need to have a thing more to do with it."

There was a moment of silence as the attorney's rigid, combative posture became ever so slightly more relaxed. "Is that it? You could have asked me that on the phone. You didn't need to come here in person."

Ah, thrust! Parry! Feint! Acting as though I had manufactured a nonsensical, unrealistic reason to visit the office, to make the next move in our cat-and-mouse game!

"Perhaps I am old-fashioned in this regard, but I am unaccustomed to working via telephone, especially when the person who answers that instrument is—your receptionist, I believe? You must know that she is a rather rude individual and that her telephone persona, as well as her in-person demeanor, leaves much to be desired. So I suppose I cannot be blamed for wanting to talk with you about this directly, rather than jumping through a series of ridiculous hoops erected by some adoring but incompetent underling."

"Veronica? What on earth are you talking about? Everyone loves her. Most of my clients come to me only because they want to see *her*."

"Be that as it may, I must tell you that she is a cancer. I know you are an attorney, not an oncologist, but conventional wisdom tells us that tumors must be chopped out and destroyed quickly, before they infect the surrounding area and do systemic damage. But I'll say no more on this topic. As the adage goes, a word to the wise is sufficient."

Advantage Anders. For the first time, the attorney seemed lost for words. However, this delightful victory did not last long. The attorney grabbed a pad and began scribbling something onto it.

"Pat Armstrong's attorney is Kevin Jenkins. Here's his contact information."

I took the proffered slip of paper without a word, turned heel, and walked out of the office slowly, the better to remind the attorney that I'd won this volley, and that Robin Anders never leaves a room without accomplishing certain goals first.

* * *

I had a bit of time to kill before meeting J at a pretentious little café on Ninth Avenue for lunch, so I did a bit of window shopping, marveling at the inverse relationship between gentrification and public urination. For, in the old days, one could not walk the sordid streets of Hell's Kitchen without skipping over many a yellow stream emanating from every alleyway; now, in contrast, as the rents have risen and the socially ambitious have moved in, those with urgent bladder needs are more likely to use the facilities of a local bar or restaurant. Leave it to a social climber like J to suggest a restaurant in such a neighborhood.

I arrived at the café a bit early and treated myself to a few cocktails as I awaited J's arrival. The server did seem to develop an inordinate affection for/attraction to me almost immediately, which is why I suppose my drinks were served so strong (as if Robin Anders's sexual favors can be guaranteed with the application of alcohol!) and why I felt a tiny bit tipsy when J arrived garishly clad, as usual, with all manner of rings, bracelets, and pins, and sporting yet another new hair color. I dispensed with the small talk and ordered J to produce Alex's thank-you note immediately, ignoring the simultaneous look of confusion and adoration in J's sludgy hazel eyes.

I fairly ripped the note from J's hands, sure that I would

find a handwriting that exactly matched that in the letter from Lee's safety deposit box. But I was wrong. Alex's penmanship did not resemble "Pat's" in the slightest.

I felt a curious hollowness in my stomach, an odd emptiness. *So this was what being wrong felt like.* I suppose I can be forgiven for not recognizing the sensation immediately, for I have experienced it so rarely.

25

I awoke the following morning in my silken bedclothes feeling quite refreshed. Always a very energetic person, I do admit that conflict sometimes depletes me, and that unpleasant yet highly titillating experience with the attorney had exhausted me. I didn't quite recall how I'd gotten home, as the 'mango pills' seem to have hit me more strongly than usual during my lunch with J, and those rather strong cosmopolitans had certainly not helped.

Still, one cannot fret over such matters, and all was explained when I went into the master living area and found a note from J, asking me to call when I'd arisen, to quell any fears for my safety. J really could be such a dear when set loose from the shackles of that intense and problematic relationship with Chris; and I vaguely recalled J's attempts at lunch to discuss some "issues" that the two of them had been having of late. However, as I mentioned, the effects of the mangos/cosmos had caused a momentary lapse in my ability to concentrate; and, having heard far too much of the ups and downs of the J/Chris relationship over the years, I suppose I would have tuned out anyway.

A lunch spent with J more than fulfilled my weekly time quota with that uninteresting individual, and I really was not in the mood to have an extended phone conversation. Thus, making use of my ample knowledge of the ways of Manhattan life, I simply dialed the phone number of J and Chris's apartment. This would certainly not be answered on a weekday, which allowed me to leave a brief and chipper message regarding my continued well-being, as well as my heartfelt thanks to J for seeing me home the previous day.

Looking at my calendar, I realized that three days had passed since the reading of Lee's will, and, despite numerous good-faith efforts on my part, I was no closer to being in possession of that tortoise shell hairbrush that was rightfully mine. However, one of my better qualities has always been my ability to channel unexpected negative energies into productive uses. Thus I strode with great purpose into my *chambre* and began rifling through the garments I'd worn the previous day in search of the contact information for Pat's attorney. I located the piece of foolscap and examined it closely, half expecting it to contain some sort of mash note from the attorney, who did not seem above putting amorous advances in writing. However, the paper was free of any such innuendoes; and I reminded myself that the attorney had already proven to be quite a master chess player in this game of sexual pursuit, and that I must not expect such an expert to make any amateurish missteps this early in the game.

I placed a call to The Law Offices of Kevin Jenkins, J.D., LL.M., introducing myself as Robin Anders of The Goode Foundation. This may not have been strictly kosher, in that I was phoning for personal reasons rather than on Foundation business. But any attorney worth his salt on this island knows of the Foundation and its many, many connections, as well as its ability to make things happen for those whom it considers "friends." Not surprisingly, I was put through to Mr. Jenkins almost immediately.

"Hello, this is Kevin Jenkins."

"Mr. Jenkins, good day. This is Robin Anders calling. I wonder if I might take a few minutes of your time."

"Yes, yes, of course. But no need for formality. Please call me Kevin."

I hesitated for a moment. As you know, I prefer to be addressed by my proper title, especially by strangers, or those who work in the service-oriented professions. I have been known to correct people who take ungranted liberties in this regard somewhat ferociously, as I have always felt that a too-quickly-established familiarity breeds nothing but contempt. However, in this case, I did not expect an ongoing relationship with this "Kevin Jenkins"; and I certainly did not have a lot of time to waste. Lawyers, as you know, can be highly obstructionist when they are in the mood to erect barriers to the gaining of knowledge, and this was not something with which I wished to deal—not when I had so many other things on my plate. This seemed to be one of those situations where I could get by on my not inconsiderable charm, chatting with "Kevin Jenkins" as a social equal and exchanging confidences as only two good friends feel comfortable doing.

"Well, that is lovely, Kevin. And please call me Robin. I won't keep you long, as I know you must be a busy man. A dear friend of mine, Lee Harris, recently passed away. Lee was a good friend to Pat Armstrong, who I believe was a client of yours."

"Kevin" sighed. "Yes, that's true. I hadn't known Pat very long, but we had developed a fondness for each other. I'd known about...the illness...but I had no idea that it would drive Pat to suicide. Very tragic."

"Yes, Kevin, I'm afraid there is tragedy all around us. But there is a ray of hope in the darkness. Were you aware that Pat and Lee had a child together nearly 30 years ago? They put the child up for adoption, but Pat had recently gone searching for the long-lost baby and, apparently, had succeeded with the help of a private detective."

The air was silent for a moment as "Kevin" took in my words.

"Hmmm. Well, that does explain a few things I'd wondered about."

"Are you able to share, without violating any confidences?" I put just the right amount of flirtatiousness into my voice.

"I don't see why not, Robin. Pat had originally come to me to have a will drawn up. I believe Pat had been mostly alone in the world, so the original terms of the will had divided the estate up among various charities and distant cousins. But a month or so after we drafted the original will, Pat called to ask if I could recommend a private investigator. I've worked with a good one, Junior Makeba, so I recommended him. Pat didn't mention what Junior's services were needed for—and I don't usually pry into such matters. You know, the Manhattan code of silence."

I murmured my assent, having taken advantage of that very code with the manicurist/lockpicker quite recently.

"Anyway, I did see Junior a couple of weeks after that, and he thanked me for the referral. I guess I didn't think much about it at the time, but a couple of months later Pat came in and changed the terms of the will, basically leaving everything in trust for some young person, with Lee Harris as the executor of the estate. It seemed to be an emotional matter, so I didn't ask a lot of questions. And then, of course, I got the news a few weeks later regarding Pat's suicide. My office contacted Lee Harris, who put us in touch with [here "Kevin" mentioned the name of Lee's attorney, whose foul name I have vowed will not besmirch my manuscript], and the will was probated quite quickly. What a shock to hear a little while later about Lee's death, as well."

"I wonder, Kevin, would you be able to give me the phone number of this 'Junior Makeba'? I would love to ask him a question or two. Do you think he'd have any ethical concerns with talking with me about the investigative work he did for Pat?"

"Kevin" laughed. "Robin, as long as you're willing to pay, he's willing to talk." I heard the shuffling of a Rolodex. "Here's his number."

I took down the number and exchanged a few further mindless pleasantries with "Kevin Jenkins," who, if I had to guess, must have graduated from a second- or third-tier law school and had set up his own practice when none of the larger firms in Manhattan would have him. And it was not hard to see why—while a pleasant enough individual, he lacked that *savoir faire* that downtown firms seek in their newly hired associates. The fact that he was actively consorting with an individual named "Junior Makeba" only strengthened my belief in the likelihood of my conclusions.

As I was about to ring off—after making the usual promises of difficult-to-obtain tickets to performances by artists supported by The Goode Foundation—I recalled something "Kevin" had said earlier in the conversation. During the course of my investigation, there had been numerous references to Pat's condition, which I'd assumed was some sort of aggressive cancer. But not a soul had ever confirmed my assumption with any hard facts.

"One last thing, Kevin? You mentioned Pat's 'illness.' I am wondering—what condition could have been so bad as to cause one to commit the ultimate act of self-destruction? Was it a particularly violent cancer?"

"Kevin" inhaled—clearly this was a man of some feeling, a man with whom I might have considered a dalliance at one point in my life, during those rebellious days as a teenager when I took pleasure in driving my parents to distraction by bringing home all manner of suitors far below us in social ranking and distinction.

"Actually, no. I believe it was Parkinson's. I never asked directly, of course, as I don't like to pry. But I did see it progress. The last time I saw Pat, it looked like the disease was really beginning to get the upper hand. The poor thing could barely hold the pen to sign the will."

My disappointment was profound. For I'd just received a slice of information that could explain the discrepancy between Pat's signature on the adoption papers from thirty years ago and the recent suicide note. Of course it made sense that Parkinson's Disease would degrade a normally steady penmanship into the type of intense spikiness I'd seen in Pat's note to Lee.

Which meant that, perhaps, there was no mystery to be solved at all—except, of course, for the location of my missing tortoise shell hairbrush.

26

As much a person of reflection as a person of action, I pondered the Mysterious Affairs of Lee and Pat as I made my way to the Greenwich Village headquarters of The Goode Foundation. Though a somewhat lengthy absence from one's place of employment does provide just the right amount of cachet—after all, only those of the highest rank and regard are permitted to be away from the office for three or four weeks at a time—one must be careful not to let others become too accustomed to one's absence. Assistants must be reminded that one's sabbatical is not to be taken advantage of, and fellow staffers must be reminded of the essential role one plays in the day-to-day workings of the place, even if one is not physically present.

As I suspected, my assistant, a child of privilege, had used my medical leave, and the subsequent time I'd spent investigating the case, to allow papers to pile up and folders to remain unfiled. This creature and I had long maintained a bit of a dangerous dance that more or less constantly threatened to spin out of control. As a gatekeeper, she was second to none, protecting me from all manner of unwanted phone calls and visitors, not because she cared about my nerves or schedule but because it gave her great nasty satisfaction to turn supplicants away and hang up on them. This is a priceless gift and one that must be managed properly, though I did rather often find myself wondering if being saved from the importunities of aspiring artists was worth the cost of an assistant who made it clear that she did not need the job and did not care whether or not I liked her.

While idly looking through some applications for various fellowships and stipends, it occurred to me that I might ask my new friend "Kevin" to fax me the signature page from Pat's will. I was curious to see Pat's signature and whether or not it matched the handwriting that I remembered from Lee's suicide note. So I placed another call to my new admirer, who assured me that faxing the requested materials would be no problem at all. In return for this small favor he asked if I'd be able to secure tickets for a soon-to-be-held invitation-only recital by a Ukrainian pianist sponsored by the Foundation. As this practice of one hand washing the other is the way business is done in this City, I promised to have my assistant personally deliver the tickets as soon as I received his fax. Five minutes later I held that fax in my hand, and my surly assistant was headed out the door with the tickets, mumbling and grumbling about being treated like a common messenger, and promising to have a talk with Faith Goode about my inappropriate use of tickets, my assistant's time, and the like.

Despite my nearly photographic memory, it was difficult for me to determine whether the spiky hand from Pat's suicide note was the same as that on Pat's will, which had been signed a little more than a month earlier. Certainly both pieces of penmanship were spiky and jittery, but more than that I could not tell. Besides, the will contained only Pat's signature, nothing more, while the letter to Lee had been more of a heartfelt missive in which Pat's last name hadn't even been included. I folded up the fax and placed it in my jacket pocket, planning to compare its signature against the adoption papers in Pat's metallic box when I arrived home.

In the meantime, a call to Junior Makeba might shed some light on the murky waters in which I'd unknowingly immersed myself. Of course it was foolish of me to expect one as shady as Junior to answer the call, which I'd had the greatest trouble punching into the keypad, as I have never quite accepted that decidedly unfashionable "646" area code and had vowed long ago never to call anyone with such a prefix.

Voice mail clicked in almost immediately and I was greeted by the rudest of recordings, delivered in a lilt that I would have guessed belonged to someone from either Botswana or Swaziland, or perhaps Jamaica: "This is Junior. Leave a message." I reluctantly did as directed, mentioning "Kevin's" name and requesting a return call.

I had no sooner left the message and hung up the office phone when it began ringing. Of course! This was only to be expected when one sends one's assistant to dispatch concert tickets, thus allowing all manner of undesirable calls to get through. Or could it be that Junior Makeba had been screening calls but had already listened to my message and was calling me back? I'd left both my office number and my cell number.

I tentatively picked up the phone. An unexpected voice greeted me.

"Robin? Thank God I found you."

"J, is that you?"

"No, it's Chris."

"It's unusual to hear from you during the day, Chris. Is everything all right?"

"Well, to be honest, Robin, it isn't. We've just had the most unsettling experience."

What could such an experience have been? An abstract thought? A momentary lapse into good taste regarding clothing or furnishing? The satisfactory completion of the *TV Guide* crossword puzzle?

"Whatever happened, Chris?"

"Our apartment's been robbed. J is simply inconsolable. Fortunately, I have been able to keep a more reasonable head on my shoulders."

I sat patiently, two unspoken questions uppermost in my mind. Why on earth was I being informed of this singularly uninteresting occurrence? And, more importantly, who on earth thought that J and Chris would own anything worth stealing? Any thief with a practiced eye would know that a close inspection of their designer clothes and "expensive" jewelry would reveal their Chinatown origins; and the location of their apartment, situated as it is on a most unappealing street of the East Village, would have hinted at the extreme unlikelihood of any possessions that could be expected to move quickly on the black market.

Chris blathered on. "Oh, it's so awful, Robin. We feel so…so…*invaded*. Things would be so much easier if Lee were still with us! We feel so *alone*! The police were here and have taken pictures and the like, but they want me to go down to the station to sign some paperwork, and I really don't want to leave J alone right now."

This last line was delivered with a heavy hint. Under other circumstances I would have done my utmost to ignore the subtext, but I suppose I was feeling just the slightest bit competitive with the dead Lee, whom everyone seemed to be invoking as a paragon of virtue who could always be counted on in a time of crisis. If only they knew of Lee's many shortcomings, if only they had suffered at Lee's hands as I had! They might not be so sanguine.

"Chris, would you like me to come over? I could stay with J for a while."

"Oh, Robin, *would* you? I'd be so grateful. You know we try not to bother you, but this is really an extreme case, and when I couldn't raise you at home or on your cell…"

I pulled my cell phone out of my jacket pocket and looked at it. Sure enough, there were several missed calls from J and Chris's apartment that had somehow not gotten through—an all-too-common occurrence in these tall buildings where cell service is as poor and unreliable as the services of a low-paid prostitute who's received a better offer.

"…and, Robin, I know this may be a bit too much to ask, but is there any chance you might bring over some of those 'pineapple pills' that you have spoken so glowingly about? J really is most overwrought, and could probably use a bit of 'help' with relaxing.…"

"Yes, yes, Chris. Of course. I'll need to go home to get them, but I can be at your apartment in about an hour."

I hung up amidst Chris's effusion of thanks. While having to go home first was inconvenient in the extreme, this little detour was very much in my best interests. For, to cope with

J's weepy anxieties, I certainly was going to need the help of those rarely taken 'tangerine pills' that I keep in my private lavatory for cases of emergencies.

Hailing a cab outside the Foundation, I sighed. For, as always, the altruism that is central to my character had won out once again. Certainly I'd not expected to spend the remainder of my day this way, but this was not the first time I have dropped everything to aid a friend in need, and—knowing my friends' willingness to exploit my genuine love of humanity—it would most assuredly not be the last.

27

I have never been one to indulge in the sort of overwrought dramatics that have become, it seems, a staple of life in this overcrowded and far-too-small borough. I suppose this is only to be expected in a city of aspiration such as New York, where actors of all ages, colors, and ethnicities flock, desperate to be noticed, discovered, and desired by the increasingly few luminaries who control the purse strings of Hollywood and Broadway. Gathering a large number of people with such personality traits into a fairly condensed area is bound to bring about all manner of competition for attention: who has the biggest biceps (he or she with the most steroid usage), the bluest eyes (he or she with the most costly contact lenses), the most money (he or she with the greatest paucity of morals), and so forth. There is also, I have found, a sort of rivalry among Manhattanites regarding *who has suffered the most*, or *experienced the greatest privation*, which has allowed Dr. Rosenthal to develop quite a successful practice. The good doctor simply sits back and lets the vain and self-centered talk about themselves for an hour, then collects a $300 check from an individual who lives in an apartment no larger than a shoebox.

In short, I fully expected J and Chris to behave as though they were the first human beings in the history of the universe to have had their apartment burgled and their worthless possessions stolen. And, indeed, when I arrived at the recently invaded domicile, Chris appeared rather worked up while J sat in a faux naugahyde chair, staring idly into space, hair tinted a most unnatural eggplant color as the latest in the unending series of unbecoming dye jobs. Perhaps this was the beginning of a fugue state into which J was about to lapse, and to Chris I suggested as much. Chris hurriedly reassured me, however. While awaiting the arrival of the much-needed 'pineapple pills,' J had made do with six Benadryl tablets, which Chris had found somewhere deep in their medicine chest; and this explained J's turgid somnolence.

Like an angel of mercy, I quickly administered the 'pineapples' to a pliant J, who seemed to be engaging in a sort of mumbling stream-of-consciousness monologue that would have done Molly Bloom proud. Various phrases as hackneyed as any Hallmark card dropped from J's lips, as I extricated my hand from the vise-like grip in which J held it—"priceless treasures," "memories of a lifetime," "an indescribable feeling of loss," "things will never be the same," and so forth. I patted J's head sympathetically, hoping that the 'pineapples' would work quickly with the Benadryl to drop J into the state of mute somnolence that was so clearly the solution to the day's problems. And sure enough, almost immediately J's words became slurred and, if possible, more incoherent; which cued me that it was time to have a more serious chat with Chris, to investigate the details.

"It's odd, Robin, very odd. I'd had an audition that had gone very well with a director who made it clear that I'm one of the top choices for the role." Which was code, of course, for the fact that Chris had most likely performed an extremely acrobatic session of oral gratification upon said director, and was likely to be rewarded. "I was thrilled at being seen so early, and there's that new place on Great Jones whose soft-shell crab sandwich I've been wanting to try for lunch....You know how J gets when I try new restaurants on my own or with others. So I called up J, who has actually been home quite a lot lately, due to the lack of work, and we *rendezvous*ed at the restaurant.

"Anyway, we ran into two friends of ours—Michael and Michael, I think you know them—and before we knew it, we were all laughing and having a good time, and spirits were ingested, and so forth. So, what should have been a two-hour lunch turned into a four-hour marathon."

"Yes, Chris, yes…but the details of the break-in?"

"Well, my point is that the thief, or thieves, must have been watching our place, because it had to happen in the four hours that J and I were both gone. Whoever it was could have seen me go out in the morning, and then waited for J to do the same. By the time we got back, almost everything was gone. My watch. All of J's jewelry—they took two entire boxes! All the cash we had in the place." Which I knew couldn't have been much. "And our iPods and iMacs, which we'd personalized to the hilt. That's what hurts the most."

"How did they get in?"

"It had to be the fire escape. That's what the"—here Chris's voice became *sotto voce*—"police officer said. The window was open when we got back, and it looked like some thin-wristed thief was able to open the lock on the bars."

I crossed the unkempt, overcrowded, filled-with-junk, tiny living room to the fire escape, which was only three stories from the ground. Sticking my head out *la fenêtre*, I considered that it might have been possible for some professional cat burglar to jump onto the ladder from the ground, sprint up a few flights of the narrow metallic stairway, lift open the sash, and then reach in through the bars, most likely with some made-for-burglary tool, to skillfully unlock the lock and gain access to those exceedingly undesirable living quarters.

I attempted some words of solace in the form of a rhetorical question. "Doesn't it make one wish that these vermin who prey on the honest and hard working would work as hard at a chosen profession as they do at 'casing' joints and then robbing them?" I was not surprised at the alacrity, and ease, with which I found myself slipping into the argot of the private investigator.

Chris nodded forlornly, then hastened out the door to sign the paperwork and, perhaps, exchange phone numbers or bodily fluids with the aforementioned police officer. I wondered briefly if my "help" with J had been recruited solely for this purpose, to provide a credible cover story while Chris stalked an officer of the law, attempting to sweet-talk that individual into a physical dalliance. No matter; this was not my concern, unless of course J should find out and attempt to hold me accountable; but we would cross that bridge if we came to it, and given the very high effectiveness level of the 'pineapple pills,' I very much doubted that J would have any recollection of the day whatsoever, anyway.

Without recourse to any quality reading material, I idly turned on the television. To my surprise, a DVD was already playing one of J's more recent films, and I was treated to the sight of that well-toned but slightly-out-of-it individual lying on a bed, legs high in the air, receiving the rather urgent thrustings of a somewhat hirsute gentleman. J did not appear to be having fun in the least, though the hirsute gentleman seemed considerably more engaged, even if his movements seemed more epileptic than sensual. One wondered why, exactly, J would keep such a DVD out in the open, unless watching one's soul mate being so roughed up was titillating to Chris; but again, this was none of my concern, and besides, I had seen J's work in the past, under circumstances I need not go into at this time, and I can assure you that in a contest between the manicurist and J for my affections and arousal, the manicurist would win hands down, every time.

I turned off the DVD and flipped through the channels of network TV, not finding anything remotely interesting. The stresses of the day had been extreme thus far, so I can be forgiven for allowing my eyes to close as I sat in a rather overstuffed chair while J snored loudly in the corner. But no sooner had I entered a dreamland populated by my dear Law and the manicurist, working in concert to provide me with a garden of earthly delights, than I was awakened by the shrill tones of my cell phone.

I fumbled for the phone and flipped it open.

"Ya, this Junior. I have call from Robin. I call back."

For a moment I wondered who this "Junior" person might be, but then I remembered with a start.

"Yes, Mr. Makeba, this is Robin Anders. I was given your phone number by Kevin Jenkins. I wonder if I might ask you a few questions."

"You have questions? I have answers. For money."

Say what you will about immigrants, at least they are honest. All they want is money, and they aren't afraid to say so. Such truthfulness, while rude, can be refreshing, and the lilt in Junior Makeba's voice made the words sound more mellifluous than they would have sounded coming out of the month of, say, some Brooklyn P.I. whose lips had never once formed the letter *r*.

"There's no need to worry, Mr. Makeba. I can pay for your services. To make a long story short, I am a friend of the late Pat Armstrong. I understand that you were of service in helping Pat locate a long-lost child.…"

"Ya."

"I was wondering if you could tell me that child's name and where he or she lives."

"Pat Armstrong and baby. Very popular this week."

"Popular? How so?"

"No money, no info."

"I said I will pay you."

"You say you pay, but Junior sees no money in his hand right now."

"I can assure you I will send you a personal cheque as soon as we have rung off."

Junior laughed heartily. "No cheque. Cash only. First."

"I must say, Mr. Makeba, you don't make this very easy."

"Life not easy. But Junior here to help."

I supposed I could have attempted to use on Mr. Makeba the intimidation techniques I have perfected, but a little voice inside me told me they would not work on this alien, who could not be manipulated in the way that starving artists and cash-poor friends can. Never one to fight the inevitable, I sighed and gave in.

"Very well, Mr. Makeba. I will pay you in advance."

"Ya. Good. I meet you tomorrow."

"Can you give me copies of the paperwork, or any other documents you may have found, related to Pat's child?"

"Ya. Junior will have. Meet tomorrow at noon. Five hundred dollars. My home."—and here he mentioned an address that filled me with horror. For it seemed that Junior Makeba lived in a far-off land known as "Washington Heights," in an upper part of Manhattan populated by an exceedingly unsavory group of people, whose many faults need not be gone into here. I have long made it a practice to never go north of

Lincoln Center, as civilization does drop off precipitously after the mid 60s, and even more so after that last vestige of Culture, Columbia University, in the one-teens; and certainly, if 116th Street was against my wishes, 179th Street was geometrically more so.

I sputtered and was about to protest, but the phone was already dead. Perhaps Mr. Makeba had gone into an area with bad cellular service, but more likely he'd been done with the conversation and had simply hung up.

28

Though I have always been quite adventurous—some might even say *intrepid*—I will admit to being somewhat cowed at the prospect of going so far North on the island, into that no-man's land of crack houses, brothels, and middle-class housing. For a person of my obvious breeding and means would likely stand out like a sore thumb amidst the pregnant teenagers and nascent terrorists from Middle Eastern nations, which would make me a likely target of aggression based on sheer envy and malice.

I had not yet replaced my burned-up Saab, as there'd been absolutely no time to do so; and certainly taking the subway was out of the question, as I know nothing about the NYC public transit system, feeling as I do that mass transportation is really intended for those of limited means, who do not mind sitting elbow to elbow with fellow members of the Great Unwashed.

I had originally thought that a simple cab would do, but my refined sleuthing sensibilities kicked into gear. Was it not my goal to "blend" with the area's residents? If I were truly to be perceived as a "resident" of the "hood," must I not do everything in my power to get around as the locals do? This meant that I should of course engage the services of a private livery car, with blacked-out windows and one of those boomerang-like antennae on the trunk. This, as all savvy urbanites know, is the preferred means of transportation for drug dealers, and I could imagine that Washington Heights, home to many a supplier of illegal substances, would be fairly swimming with these dark-hued Lincoln Towncars, which would allow me to come and go unnoticed, unthreatened, and unmolested.

On the bright side, even a casual watching of the news teaches us that narcotics dealers have very expensive taste in clothing, which meant that I would be able to wear my usual garments. The one thing I lacked was a pair of those sunglasses that are so common in the ghetto-like regions, and which I felt were necessary to be perceived as a part of "street life." Thus, while waiting for the car to come pick me up, I dashed down to one of those overpriced shoppes on the park, where I purchased a set of sunglasses that the sales clerk assured me were the model of choice of various "hip-hop"-type people who apparently are a staple of today's musical airwaves.

The driver arrived as promptly as can be expected in a city choked incessantly with cars and trucks, and I settled myself into the back seat to enjoy the ride. The driver was, not surprisingly, one of those swarthy-skinned men with geographically unplaceable accents who seem to have become a staple of the driving business in recent decades.

Peering through the window, I gazed idly at the streets I know so well, that have been a part of my life for longer than I care to admit. I have never believed that one should fight too much against that which one cannot control, so I stopped myself from inveighing internally against the arrival, and conquest, of storefronts like "Starbucks" and "Duane Reade," which seem to have taken over every block of this city at a rate faster than the spread of lice among dirty schoolchildren of the Deep South. As always, people walked along the sidewalks laconically yet aggressively, refusing to yield to oncoming pedestrians while expecting the oncomers to do exactly that. While observers from other parts of the country, or world, may find this practice somewhat rude and overbearing, it is sadly necessary if one is to make any progress whatsoever; and all good New Yorkers know this, and cope accordingly, with right of way given according to a series of urban rules that I have very clearly formulated but do not quite have the energy to set forth here.

The surroundings became considerably less familiar as we traveled north of Cathedral Parkway, also known as 110th Street, via Broadway, that diagonal road that is a vestige of the early days of New Amsterdam and that I have long thought should be corrected to work with the grid more properly. I felt myself becoming considerably more anxiety-ridden as our journey continued, for once one is past the environs of Columbia University, one might as well be in the Bronx— and I am sure I need not burden you with my thoughts regarding that less-than-bucolic borough and its peoples, who have long been a source of ill repute to the larger City.

As we entered northern Harlem and then "Washington Heights," the storefronts took on a distinctly more "local" flavor, with, it seemed, the majority of the retail establishments promising all manner of products for 99 cents or specialties such as Sonny's Jamaican jerk chicken, Pablo's Cuban beef patties, or the Colonel's Kentucky fried chicken. At various stoplights I watched as the elderly, crazy, and non-English-speaking came and went, oblivious to one another and to me; causing me to reflect yet again on the monumental self-centeredness of New Yorkers, and to give thanks that I had escaped such a character flaw.

Junior Makeba, it turned out, lived directly in view of that grandiose edifice known as the "George Washington Bridge," an overrated engineering feat that has the dubious distinction of connecting Washington Heights to New Jersey, whose many problems need not be gone into here. Suffice it to say that in all my years of living in Manhattan, I have managed to never once cross the Hudson River and sully myself with the soil of the so-called "Garden State," and I admit that I am somewhat proud of that fact; for in a day and age in which standards are compromised on a daily basis for reasons of convenience or expedience, one must more than ever hold on to one's most deeply held beliefs.

Though urban literature is filled with the stories of colorful characters who sit at windows and on front staircases—I believe these are known as "stoops"—I admit I had no expectation of seeing fiction bloom into life in the shadow of that austere bridge named after the Great Founder of our country, to whom I am somewhat related on my father's side. And yet, there they were, all manner of babbling women and men, chatting amiably in a number of languages not heard since the Tower of Babel, wearing their colorful clothes and eating foods not commonly ingested stateside. Children skipped rope and played some manner of ball, almost as if they had seen Norman Rockwell paintings and decided to emulate them in the concrete jungles of the streets and alleyways.

The driver double-parked the car—the only type of parking available on these mean streets—and promised he'd wait. I didn't expect my appointment with Junior to take very long; the exchange of five hundred dollars for a few pieces of paper could surely take no longer than a few minutes. I climbed the "stoop" and was smiled at by some dark-skinned ladies who sat there, bouncing chubby infants on their knees and discussing in their native language how they would be spending their large welfare checks. I rang the buzzer for apartment 4, expecting to hear Junior's money-grubbing voice bark at me from the loudspeaker; but no such response was forthcoming. I tried buzzing several more times, but still received no response.

One of the ladies took pity on me. "You lookin' for Junior? Go upstairs. Buzzer doesn't work half the time."

I nodded my thanks—not wanting to engage in any actual verbal conversation with the ladies, who might have had switchblades hidden in the folds of their sundresses—and made my way up a filthy staircase cluttered with rusty toys and a carpet that would have made the eyes of Columbia University's microbiology department light up with joy. On the second floor, the outline of a number 4 that had once graced the apartment door indicated that I'd found Junior's place. I knocked tentatively at the door, which was slightly ajar.

"Mr. Makeba? Mr. Makeba, hello? It is I, Robin Anders. I'm here for our appointment." I dropped my voice slightly. "I have the money."

Still no response.

This was most odd. Would Junior have left the apartment door open like this, for anyone to simply waltz in and steal whatever he or she wished?

I knocked again, and the door swung open a bit farther.

I stuck my head into the apartment tentatively.

"Mr. Makeba? Mr. Makeba?"

Something definitely was not right here. Throwing caution to the wind, I walked into the squalor of Junior's apartment, with its empty bottles of mango soda and its "girlie" magazines featuring large-breasted Nubian women, all thrown casually on the floor amidst a piece of shag carpeting that smelled distinctly of that heady weed known to some as *ganja*.

In a small galley kitchen, melamine dishware encrusted with something brown and sticky was piled high in the sink, over which was pinned an attractive three-quarters profile shot of Jesus. A small table held a stack of African newspapers that appeared to have been read chaotically and then tossed aside. Photos made it appear as if coverage were devoted mostly to this coup or that, such-and-such a junta, and so on; and while the bloody pictures hardly made for pleasant viewing, they were preferable to the magazines in the living room, to which I objected morally due to their objectification of women. For, as a person who has been sexually objectified on more than one occasion in my life, I always do find the reduction of human beings to their various genitals to be highly distasteful.

There wasn't much more to the apartment. I walked slowly into the small hallway and stuck my head into the bathroom, which featured chipped pink tile, a cracked oval mirror, and a large vat of green hair gel balanced precariously on the sink. The only other door in the hallway had to be the bedroom, or perhaps a closet if this were a studio apartment.

Pulling my sleeve around my hand so as to avoid contact with all manner of unpleasant germs, I jiggled the doorknob. "Mr. Makeba? Hello? Am I disturbing you?"

The door pushed in rather than pulled out, which meant I had probably stumbled upon the bedroom. Using my elbow, I found the light switch and flicked it upwards. A single bulb hanging from the ceiling came on and illuminated a man I could only assume was Mr. Junior Makeba, lying shirtless on his bed, his lifeless eyes staring at the ceiling and a thin trickle of blood at each side of his mouth. Around his throat was some sort of white silk scarf, which—unless I missed my guess—had been rather quickly tightened around Mr. Makeba's throat while he smoked his daily ration of *buta tye*, a "joint" of which lay in ash near his cold dead right hand.

Could life be any more inconvenient? Here I had gone to a huge amount of trouble and inconvenience, braving the wilds of a lawless part of the City, to meet Junior on his own ground, simply to get the smallest bit of information; and now I was going to return home, much the worse for wear but without any of the documents I needed to figure out what exactly had gone on between Lee and Pat. But someone—a two-timing husband whom Junior had exposed? a rival drug dealer? a scorned mistress?—had gotten to Junior before I had.

I have always been one to take life's many disappointments in stride, and to not allow myself to become overly emotional regarding situations that are beyond my control. Yet the noxious smells of Junior's apartment combined with the disturbing proximity to New Jersey and the eye-scarring view of Junior's corpse conspired to send me scrambling for two of the 'persimmon pills' that I carry with me in case of urgent need. These I took without benefit of water, for I was afraid to touch anything in the apartment lest my fingerprints be left behind as evidence of my presence.

I wanted to flee as fast as my legs would carry me, but the 'persimmons' had the desired effect of helping me control the raging river of my thoughts and consider my options. I could simply leave the apartment and let someone else report Junior's murder/death to the authorities. This would be the easiest and best way out of an unpleasant situation. But if and when the police came knocking, those two welfare mothers on the "stoop" would certainly be found, and would they mention the attractive white stranger who'd come looking for Junior? Of course, it was more likely that they would say nothing, as everyone knows that the code of the streets, particularly in neighborhoods such as Junior's, require people to have seen nothing and to say nothing cooperative to members of law enforcement; but it was possible that those ladies were relatively new to the country, having sneaked in at one of our many porous borders, and might have seen "snitching" as a path to assured citizenship and the uninterrupted flow of government support.

Besides, was it really *right* to leave cold, stiff Junior Makeba as I'd found him? I have always considered myself a person of the highest moral sense, and, try as I might to bow to pragmatism, I could not quite convince myself that finding a corpse and *not* reporting it was the correct course of action from a humanistic standpoint.

But how to do the right thing while not becoming overly involved in a situation that could only monopolize my time and force me to spend untold hours filling out paperwork and fielding questions to which I had no answers? If I were to call the police on my own cell phone, they'd certainly have a record of the incoming call and be able to trace my number, location, and identity almost instantaneously.

No, the better idea was to call from a place that could not be traced to me. I hurriedly searched the apartment, hoping to find a phone line of some sort; but the search was a futile one. However, I did spy Junior's cellular phone—or, at least, a phone that I assumed to be Junior's—sitting amidst the detritus of the living room floor. Once again wrapping my hand in my sleeve, I picked up the phone and dialed 911 with the corner of a matchbox that had been sitting on Junior's bedroom floor.

"Hello," I said matter of factly to the operator. "I have just come to a business associate's home for a meeting, and I found him dead. Perhaps murdered, I'm not sure. His name is Junior Makeba and his address is...." Without waiting for further questions, I hung up, beat a hasty retreat from the apartment, and climbed into the waiting livery cab.

Half an hour later, as I walked into my building, the doorman began gesticulating and waving something wildly. I held out my hand in a "Stop! in the name of love"-type gesture to indicate that I was in no condition for idle chatter, then took the lift to my home, where blissful respite from the rigors of detective work awaited me.

29

The morning after my highly unsatisfactory meeting with Junior Makeba's corpse, I was awakened by an urgent rapping at my apartment door. This was an occurrence not be tolerated, for even when my neighbors call on me they are required to have the doorman announce them before they appear on my threshold. I was tempted to ignore the persistent rat-a-tat-tat, but I knew the continued din would quite likely make a migraine appear; and that, as you can imagine, was the last thing I wanted. So I threw on my dressing gown and walked unhurriedly to the door, my pique growing with each step. The caller was about to experience the full and uncensored wrath of Robin Anders. Few of those who have encountered this fury have emerged unscathed, but I felt not one whit of sympathy for this unwanted and unwelcome guest, whoever he or she might be.

I flung open the door with great force, only to find my doorman standing there quivering. And I felt my anger slipping away. Despite his often-unwelcome loquacity, I have always held a certain fondness for him, as he is a bit of a sad soul who has always looked to me for support and the occasional kind word, a sop which I have bestowed when the mood has struck me. Certainly I'd trained him well; and I knew that he would not have disturbed me without very good reason.

"Ex-excuse me," he stammered; and my heart continued to melt, for he did look most fetching in his tailored door-man's outfit, which clung to all the right places.

"Whatever can it be at this early hour?" I asked, neglecting to call him by name, as I have never quite been able to remember it.

"I'm – I'm sorry. I waited for you to come back down-stairs yesterday so I could give this to you, but you never came back, and I thought it might be important."

He held out an envelope on which someone had written in a nondescript hand:

Robin Anders
Apartment 1215
Urgent

I recalled the doorman's wild gesticulations as I'd flown into the building the previous day; and I vaguely recalled his waving something at me as well. It must have been this very envelope.

"Where did this come from?" I asked; for it is indeed rare to receive hand-written, hand-delivered notes these days, when thank-you notes are routinely sent via Internet and hand-lettering seems to have gone the way of the passenger pigeon.

"I don't know. I had to leave the desk for a few minutes to help Mrs. Bennett with her packages. I asked José to give it to you if he saw you last night, but it was still on the desk when I got here a couple of hours ago, and I thought I should bring it up to you, just in case."

Of course it was impossible to stay angry; the situation was akin to training a dog particularly well to serve your needs. Could one then fault the dog for doing precisely what you had trained him to do, even if it contradicted another important guideline?

I assured the doorman that I appreciated his efforts, took the envelope, and closed the door. I wondered if the "urgent" nature of the envelope had something to do with the internal warfare down at the Foundation, which I had been studiously avoiding for weeks. Several of the Goode sisters had begun redoubling their efforts to secure my vote, and I really did not wish to be sucked into their vortex.

I supposed that if I didn't like the contents of the envelope, I could always claim not to have received it; thus there could be no harm in opening it. I did so and read as follows:

> Robin,
>
> I didn't expect to find you at home, and have been unable to raise you by phone. I have an urgent matter I need to discuss with you. I don't mean to sound desperate or dramatic; but a few things have come up on which I very much need your counsel.
>
> I know it's short notice, but I am hoping you'll join me for lunch tomorrow. I've made reservations for two at Oaxaca! in the Empire State Building at 1 p.m. Can you possibly meet me on the 86th floor Observation Deck at 12:30? That seems as good a place as any to go over these matters, away from the prying eyes of the nosy. Let's head down to the restaurant after we've had a chance to chat. And who knows? You may find yourself in possession of a certain hairbrush that I may have found among Lee's personal effects....
>
> My cell phone isn't working properly—I dropped it in hot oil as I was frying up some plan-

tains last night—so you won't be able to reach me that way. I'm just hoping I'll see you tomorrow. If that doesn't work, I'll enjoy a solitary lunch and hope to talk with you later in the week.

My best,
Alex

Included in the envelope was a ticket for the Observation Deck. Naïve Alex, thinking that a member of the Goode Foundation's Board of Directors would need to pay for access to the deck! Still, it was a thoughtful gesture—much more thoughtful, in fact, than could usually be expected of Alex, whose focus on all matters Alexian has always been monomaniacal.

I was, of course, slightly irritated at the assumption that I could be summarily summoned to a place as tourist-heavy as The Empire State Building, that rococo steel edifice whose place in the heart of popular culture is entirely unwarranted. But I could not become truly angry with Alex, for I so often ignore my cell phone and the messages waiting thereon that I suppose I force my friends and admirers to track me down in creative ways, such as notes left with my doorman. And the note *did* seem quite heartfelt, and it was difficult to pass up a lunch at Oaxaca!, which serves quite an intoxicating oxtail soup. If I were lucky, Chef Pedro Martinez Villarosa Garcia y Vega de la Vargas—a personal friend of mine, whose daughter has been aided by the Foundation on occasion—might even be prevailed upon to whip up that delightful sturgeon and starfish ceviche that has long been a favorite of mine. Along the way, I might also collect my long-overdue hairbrush and put this rather time-consuming and annoying sleuthing behind me. Yes, it was time to move on to bigger and better things, and what better way to celebrate the successful completion of a "case" than with fresh oxtail soup and/or ceviche?

The grandfather clock in my sitting room indicated a time close to 11 a.m. If I were to cut my morning routine short by half an hour, I should be able to meet Alex on the Deck at close to the requested time. Of course, I would need to be at least fifteen or twenty minutes late, to send the signal that I cannot be ordered about quite so peremptorily.

I threw together a suitably stunning *ensemble* sure to give the tourists on the observation deck something memorable to talk about with their overweight relatives back home in the Midwest, then called down to the desk to have the doorman order a cab.

The taxi driver delivered me to the Empire State with a minimum of honking, cursing, and insane monologue, which is the best anyone can expect from a cab ride in this City. Subtly flashing my Goode Foundation ID at various queues, I was moved to the head of the line for the elevator that would bring me and ten or so large farm-type personages up to see the view. Normally I do not like being in such close quarters with strangers, suffering as I do from just a touch of claustrophobia; but, having anticipated this very situation, I had helped myself to two of the 'strawberry pills' before leaving home.

The deck was somewhat lousy with people, which made jostling for position at the edge a bit of a challenge. Fortunately, many years of living in Manhattan have sharpened my elbows a great deal, and these I made use of quite liberally, occasionally using a well-placed kick to aid in my efforts.

As I hacked my way through the crowd, I spied a prematurely grey head to my right; this could only have been Alex, whose slender back was unmistakable. Of course, Alex was completely oblivious to my presence, standing still and drinking in the sights of Manhattan below us. Eventually I cut through enough of the human kudzu to find myself standing next to Lee's heir.

"Alex?" I asked tentatively. Others would of course have touched their friend to announce their presence, but the Observation Deck of the Empire State Building is no place to give someone an unexpected surprise.

And it was here that my sixth sense—that oracular ability that has sometimes descended upon me when I least expect it—kicked into overdrive. The air got thick and time froze as I sensed imminent danger. My adrenaline surged as I watched a tall masked personage pushing through the crowd toward me and Alex. Nothing about the scenario felt right; my very pores were tingling with dread. And as I caught my breath, the masked marauder pulled out what appeared to be a small knife, which was then plunged into the back of the unsuspecting Alex as I used every bit of my catlike physical prowess to twist out of the way.

But the surprises did not end there. The victim hunched over in shock, turning partially toward the crowd in the process—and my horrified eyes saw that the mangy gray head did not belong to Alex, but to some other wizened creature.

"Stop! Stop!" I cried, hoping that someone in the crowd would do something to intervene and stop the assailant, who'd dropped the knife and fled. But no one in this post-Kitty Genovese world was willing to stop the attacker, who disappeared from sight as the victim—a witchlike woman of indeterminate age—lay bleeding and flailing on the floor of the deck. While I wanted nothing more than to help, the sight of the blood had quite a deleterious effect on my stomach, and I had to turn away and let the crowd tend to the unfortunate victim.

The chaos was unlessened when I felt a tugging at my sleeve.

"Robin? Are you all right?"

I turned to find Alex staring at me, looking more than a bit confused.

"Robin, what happened? What's going on?"

Never one to suffer fools gladly, and still suffering from the shock of the aforedescribed act of violence, I responded with force, "What do you mean, 'what's going on?' You fool! A woman has just been stabbed by some ruffian, who escaped through the door. Didn't you see anything?"

"No, I just got here. Someone was running in the other direction with a mask on as I got off the elevator, but I had no idea a crime had been committed. Are you all right?"

"Am I *all right*? I most certainly am not. I was standing directly next to the victim when she was stabbed. It could have been me." And this was not a comforting thought in the least, as it brought up unpleasant memories of a near miss or two I'd had during my weekend on Long Island with my friends several weeks earlier.

"Well, thank God it wasn't. What incredible bad luck!"

"Bad luck indeed. Why, Alex? Why of all days to suggest meeting in such a ridiculous place would you choose today, when madmen are roaming the streets of Manhattan looking for people to stab?"

"Choose today? What are you talking about? I'm only here because you asked me to meet you. And it is more than a bit inconvenient, I must say."

"Alex, have you lost your mind? *You* are the one who invited *me* here."

"I did no such thing. I got your note, and it seemed important, so I dropped everything."

"My note?"

"The one you left with my doorman."

"But I'm here because of the note *you* left with *my* doorman."

The realization hit us simultaneously; and I must say the experience was quite unique, as I have never seen Alex's uncomprehending eyes grasp a concept quite so quickly before.

By this point, the police and paramedics had arrived and were loading the bleeding lady onto a stretcher. Since she was screaming rather dramatically, I took that to mean she was still alive, which was probably a good thing, though a crone with a voice like that might best be put out of her misery rather quickly. The police were going to want to start asking questions, and I wanted none of that, especially having been at another murder scene 145 blocks north just the previous day. Taking Alex by the elbow, I led the two of us out the door while chaos still reigned, thus escaping the burning questions and lustful eyes of New York's Finest.

In the elevator, Alex turned to me. "Robin, do you think that assault was intended for you?"

"Alex, based on that woman's shape and hair color, I'd say the more likely intended victim was *you*."

30

I have always been able to recover quickly from life's vicissitudes. For the bitch goddess Fortuna has long proven my ally; and thus my ability to survive misplaced croquet mallet blows to the head, poisoning by mysterious Southern asps, exploding cars, and salsa tainted with botulism stood me in good stead on that observation deck. I wondered what would have happened if Alex had arrived on time for once. Might that highly unpunctual individual now be lying in a hospital somewhere, the victim of one of New York's many psycho/sociopaths? The irony was not lost on me; the very same lack of respect that Alex showed for friends and associates in arriving late for every social event had proven not only *not* to be an undoing, but a life saver instead. Which only lends credence to a theory I have long espoused: that the laws of nature, which apply everywhere else on earth, do not hold any sway in New York City.

Since we were already at the Empire State Building, and I'd so had my heart set on that delightful ceviche, I saw no reason not to stay and enjoy lunch at Oaxaca!, as food always tastes better when one has had a brush with death. Sadly, Alex seemed to have no appetite after the incident and left in a bit of a huff, implying none too subtly that I seemed more focused on a good meal than on the continued well being of a friend. I allowed that implication to hang in the air, uncommented upon, for such accusations should not be dignified with a response.

Fortunately, Chef Pedro MVGyVdlV was indeed presiding over the kitchen, so not only was I able to order the ceviche, I was also treated to various other tapas that the good chef whipped up upon being told of my arrival. The other diners looked on enviously as Pedro joined me for a few minutes, so that we might chat about various and sundry gustatory matters. I commented on the waitstaff's high level of visual appeal, at which comment Pedro merely nodded; for, as is well known in gourmet circles, Pedro is as much of a *roué* as any master chef in Manhattan; and perhaps more so, given his fiery Latin blood.

Thus it was with a very delighted palate and a slightly intoxicated brain—for who, really, could resist those luscious pomegranate margaritas that are Oaxaca!'s trademark—that I made my way back to my home base. Good food, I have always maintained, makes the cares of the day melt away, and I was feeling very much close to my usual animated, happy-go-lucky self as I approached my building. So happy was I, in fact, that I did not allow thoughts of the still-missing tortoise shell hairbrush to enter my mind.

Unfortunately, my happy mood was not destined to continue. And this is why:

I have always been a highly organized person. Some might use the term *fastidious*, but with only the best of connotations. For I was raised to believe that there is a place for everything, and that a well-organized life is essential to psychic fluidity. To this end I have an innate sense of the proper placement of physical items.

This explains why a chill went up my spine as I entered the parlor and realized instantly that *something was amiss*. The books on my various bookshelves appeared to have been moved ever so slightly. The drawers of my apothecary chest had clearly been opened and searched through; I always close every drawer completely, so as to maintain as planar a surface as possible on the drawer fronts, and yet this plane was downright bumpy, due to the drawers being incompletely closed. I rushed into my bedroom and noticed various *objets d'art* awry. Every other room in the apartment had been fondled in like fashion.

The very real sense that I might begin hyperventilating forced me to down three of the 'apple pills' that I keep in the medicine chest—the contents of which, I noted, had clearly been sifted through as well.

What was I to do? Clearly, calling the police was out of the question; that would have made my third brush with the law in two days, and while those men and women in blue do hold a certain rough-hewn allure, I did not wish to subject my already fragile mental state to their questioning and, most likely, their lustful stares. Besides, it did not appear that anything had actually been *stolen*. Various priceless works by well-known painters and sculptors had been left untouched, and every last piece of my parents' heirloom jewelry remained ensconced in the velvet case which my maternal grandfather had purchased more than a century earlier on a real estate junket to India. The money that I keep on hand to pay, and tip, various servicepeople was left undisturbed in my end-table. Even my clothing, which some pervert could have stolen for purposes of *frottage* or other dark sexual practices, remained hanging in my various closets, clearly having been manhandled but not bearing any new stains.

But how did the person or persons unknown get into my apartment? The door had not been forced; and it did not look as if the windows had been jimmied open. An enterprising sneak thief might have gained access from the roof—this is the penthouse apartment, after all—but I could not understand how.

And then it struck me: I was not supposed to have known that anyone had been in my home while I dined on ceviche and tapas and as tourists got stabbed in my vicinity. I was to have gone to my slumbers that night, blissfully unaware that my home had been invaded and searched. It was only my intense powers of observation, and my hawklike eyes, that had exposed the goings-on in *Chez* Anders during the afternoon. Clearly, I was dealing with a master burglar, one who could get past the doorman and into my apartment unnoticed.

A technique I learned while very young is to distract my thoughts when they are heading in an undesirable direction. The 'apples,' which calmed me somewhat, helped me along this road; and I remembered that I needed to check on a few matters while they were still fresh in my mind. First and foremost, I wanted to re-read the note that had been left for me at the front desk of my building, the one supposedly written by Alex. This might prove to be a valuable piece of evidence in the ongoing investigation, which—on the basis of the day's events—seemed that it might continue longer than I had hoped. For surely that note had been written to lure me out of my home so that the cat burglar could enter it. I also wanted to compare the handwriting to that of the thank-you letter Alex had sent to J and Chris after that awful party of several months back, which I still had in my possession. I'd placed it in Pat's green metallic box, along with the copy of the adoption papers, the photos, and those cheap baubles that Pat could only have been holding onto for sentimental reasons. I supposed I should have compared the handwritings prior to leaving for my luncheon appointment, but at the time I'd been too fixated on the ceviche to think of much else.

I distinctly remembered leaving "Alex's" delivered-by-doorman letter on my dining room table, and I went thence to retrieve it. But it was nowhere to be found; not on the table, not on any of the chairs, and not on the floor in the immediate vicinity. And, with that crystal clarity that is a hallmark of my thought processes, I began to understand what the burglar had been seeking. I rushed into my study to retrieve the green metallic box, but the effort was futile. It, too, was gone—vanished into thin air. Or, much more likely, carried off by someone who knew my brilliant mind was slowly and craftily unraveling the threads of his or her plot, and who wanted to destroy any and all evidence.

I picked up the phone and dialed Alex's cell number. The call was answered promptly. After the necessary queries regarding state of mind, et cetera, I asked Alex if I might take a look at the note "I" had supposedly written requesting the meeting on the Observation Desk.

"I still have it, Robin, but I don't think it'll tell you much."

"Well, for now I am wondering if the penmanship looks at all like mine."

"Oh, but it's not written by hand. It looks like a computer printout."

And here is where Alex's doltlike qualities had nearly led to premature death. For anyone who knows me, knows that I am unyielding in my dedication to handwritten correspondence; in this era of impersonal electronic communication, I insist on writing all notes by hand, to give that personal touch that is so lacking in the Modern Era.

Anyone less self-absorbed than Alex would certainly have been suspicious upon receiving a typewritten note from me, and despite the nearly-murdered Alex's delicate frame of mind, I pointed out this fact.

"Actually, I *had* considered that, Robin, but the note indicated that your carpal tunnel syndrome has been acting up, and that you were finding it difficult to hold your usual fountain pen, and write with your usual flourish. Here, let me read it to you."

Some papers were shuffled loudly in my ear, and then Alex continued.

"Dearest Alex, I know it is short notice, but I have recently come upon some information regarding your dear parents that I feel is imperative to impart to you immediately, if not sooner. This information is best conveyed in person, I believe; and the sooner we are able to meet, the better, as there is an urgency about some of these matters. Would you kindly meet me on the 86th Floor Observation Deck at the Empire State Building at 12:30 today? This will be a good place for us to chat, and we can then have lunch at Oaxaca! immediately following. I enclose a ticket for the deck, courtesy of the Foundation. I fear my cell is out of commission right now, so I will not be able to receive any calls from you to confirm; but I know you will show up as requested. I apologize if this is peremptory of me, but the matter really is quite critical. I also must apologize for this drab computer printout, as my Carpal Tunnel has been rather bothering me lately, and it brings me great pain to attempt to hold my favorite fountain pen; while, with wrist guards and the like, I am able to at least type. Until 12:30, Robin."

And here was more proof of Alex's lack of intellectual and perceptive abilities; for how could such a letter possibly have been written by me? The overlong sentences; the contorted syntax; the false sense of drama—none of these are hallmarks of me or my written communications.

However, I would comment on none of this; as I could see no benefit in doing so. Instead, I continued on another track.

"But how did you come upon that note, Alex?"

"The doorman said that a messenger brought it. He signed for it and then brought it up to me. As I mentioned earlier, the timing was highly inconvenient, but as a courtesy I thought I should at least hear what you had to say. Now I see that it was a rather transparent ploy."

Indeed. Armed thus with some highly useless information, I proffered my good wishes for Alex's continued existence and rang off, but not before requesting Alex to hold on to that letter, as it might prove useful as "evidence" at some later date. For it seems that modern detection is filled with all sorts of techniques regarding fingerprinting, DNA, and the like, and one could only assume that the letter contained traces of these, and perhaps more.

Sometimes when the world becomes too stressful, I will retreat into my world of one and indulge in a glass of wine, or two, to recalibrate my equilibrium. Thus I retrieved a bottle of my favorite vintage—the same, actually, that had been served as a delightful surprise to me on Long Island several weeks earlier—uncorked it, poured it, sniffed the fragrant bouquet, and began the simultaneous process of thinking and sipping.

Certainly the previous week had been a highly eventful one; and it occurred to me that I had been so busy, chasing various "leads" around town in my search for answers and the tortoise shell hairbrush, that I hadn't taken time to look at the big picture. Individually, many of the details seemed to be odd little occurrences that could be easily dismissed in a world of sensory overload. But, taken together, a larger and more ominous picture emerged.

Pat was dead; and Lee had followed shortly thereafter. Various items were inexplicably missing from Lee's apartment, and Pat's apartment had been ransacked much more vigorously. Items had been stolen from Pat's storage locker (by me); Chris and J's apartment had been burgled; phony invitations had been sent to me and Alex; a tourist who had the great misfortune to resemble Alex from behind had been stabbed as I watched in horror; and my home—my castle—had been expertly broken into, and certain contents stolen, while I feasted on Mexican delights.

There had to be more than coincidence at work here. Every single person who'd spent the weekend on Long Island with me had been drawn somehow into a mysterious web of death, theft, and deception. Everyone, that is, except Law, who seemed rather absent in all this. Which made one wonder if Law was truly an innocent and unaffected party, or if, as always, that sultry individual was the repository of a mother lode of information that was being kept close to the vest. For Law has always been in the subtle position of being confessor to all, confider in none; a situation that has worked greatly to Law's advantage in the past and could, quite possibly, be working that way at this very moment.

31

I have long believed that speaking is not always the most revealing method of communication. For subtleties of the nonverbal variety are often more telling than words; a truism I fear I have demonstrated in many a social encounter with those into whose company I have been thrust unwillingly. To the outward world, I am gracious Robin, kind Robin, socially expansive Robin; but I am playing the role demanded by my executive position at the Foundation, which requires witty conversation with dolts and light repartee with moneyed philistines. But a practiced observer would notice a certain physical distance, a moderate shrinking away from those undesirables whose favor I am currying with my velvet tongue; and the fraudulence of my words is exposed by the language of my body, whose near undetectable cringing is an outward manifestation of the mental and spiritual distaste to which I dare not give voice.

All of this is to say that focusing on the area below the neck is often a very effective way of sensing what lies beneath the surface. If I'd paid more attention to such nonverbal hints on Long Island, I might at this very moment be in possession of that much-sought-after tortoise shell hairbrush, and I might already have solved the mysteries of the various break-ins and the attempted murder of Alex. But I'd been so concerned with playing the gracious host that I'd perhaps not paid as much attention to the undercurrents of intrigue, jealousy, sexual innuendo, and gossip as I normally would have. Now I was faced with this increasingly tiresome puzzle that was trying the limits of my well-known tenacity; and it was all my fault.

Upon this realization, I resolved to renew my focus, to begin a more stringent line of questioning and observation. And there was no time better time to follow through on this resolution than the afternoon after the break-in at *La Maison Anders*, during my biweekly scheduled appointment with Dr. R. Perhaps that occasionally perspicacious individual might have some insight into the various enigmas of recent weeks; but the person who might provide even better answers and even more striking insight would also be at Dr. R's office, thus allowing me to kill the two proverbial birds with the one proverbial stone.

While my sessions with Dr. R last only an hour, I do schedule (and pay for) ninety minutes' time, which allows me fifteen minutes on either end of the session to arrive at my leisure and collect myself emotionally afterwards. For Dr. R has no qualms about putting me through my paces therapeutically, forcing me to engage with those issues I have long struggled with: my intense intelligence, which sometimes isolates me from the Common Person; my all-too-soft heart, which is easily trampled upon and broken; my generous nature, which can be exploited by the unscrupulous; my saintlike patience, which allows all manner of unacceptable behavior to continue far too long; and a host of other personality quirks that need not be gone into here. In short, as Dr. R is a bit of a bear about paying for all time spent in the office, I long ago worked out the aforementioned ninety-minute deal.

But today my pre-appointment fifteen-minute hedge could prove entirely useful from another vantage point. This would allow me the uninterrupted time I needed to engage with Law. For I really had spent very little time with that sensuous individual since that odd evening in my *chambre* on Long Island, when I'd rejected the offered pillow-cum-sexual-advance. Yes, a conversation or two had been had since the return from Long Island, but Law had been more than usually unavailable in recent weeks; and this had to mean something.

To ensure that I would engage Law's undivided attention, I dressed myself in a manner somewhat more provocative than usual; as Law has always been a bit of a fetishist about certain body parts, and outfitting oneself in a manner that calls attention to those parts is almost a guaranteed method of piquing Law's interest. To be reduced thus is something I usually resist; however, these are quite simply the rules of the game, and it is far less time consuming to work within these constraints than to attempt the psychological warfare that would be required to alter them.

Dr. Rosenthal's office is located in one of those curious buildings built within the last two decades but, though various *trompe l'oeils*, has been made to resemble the pre-war buildings so heavily in demand throughout this City. On the outside, the edifice is stolid, serious, heavy, colonnaded and marbled, with the requisite number of artificially antiqued stained glass windows on the entry floor; the inside is all cheap modernity, with industrial carpeting, inexpensively framed "prints" purchased from MoMA, and the paper-thin walls that are the bane of many a New York apartment dweller. When Dr. Rosenthal moved here, the aesthetics and acoustics of the place almost caused me to search for another therapist in more hospitable surroundings; but after much cajoling I'd decided to remain in the good doctor's care, as we had developed an understanding and working relationship over the years that would be exceedingly difficult to replicate.

I arrived at Dr R's unexcitingly furnished offices almost exactly at the beginning of my allotted ninety-minute session.

As I entered through the opaque glass doors, I spied Law engaged on the telephone, attempting to schedule an appointment for some difficult patient, who seemed entirely inflexible regarding the available dates and times.

Law looked up from behind the window of the small hallway-cum-receptionist's-office that connects the waiting room to Dr. R's treatment quarters, flashing me the brightest of smiles and waving a smooth wrist adorned with a rather pricey timepiece. My practiced eye assured me immediately that this wristwatch, of a brand currently favored by various Hollywood Whores and Wall Street Wannabes, was authentic; and not only authentic, but of a style exceedingly hard to get one's hands (or wrist) on, unless one has friends in the Right Places. I was momentarily shocked, for while Law has always been resourceful, one cannot truthfully say that Dr. R's receptionist is truly Well Connected. I was momentarily taken aback that Law would have asked some other friend to obtain that bauble, when I could easily have done so with just a phone call or two; but perhaps I had brought this on myself by not acceding to Law's requests for various monetary favors, even though I'd had every intention of giving in at some unspecified point in the future.

So this was to be Law's game—actively showing off an expensive gift purchased by some other admirer. Well then, so be it. Robin Anders has never been one to be intimidated by those who throw money around in an effort to win favors from the young and impressionable. For, as I have always maintained, character and personality will always win in the end.

Law hung up the phone with a huff.

"Aargh, she is simply impossible. Robin, how good to see you. You're looking well, as always."

"As do you, Law. Your top is quite *chic*. Is it a _____?" Here I mentioned the name of a currently fashionable design-er who is making the rounds of the downtown orgy-and-drug circuit, and who'd once had the audacity to apply for a Goode Foundation Design Grant. During the interviewing process, I'd met and taken an intense dislike to that individual, for all the usual reasons: She was overconfident and undertalented, confident but neurotic, blasé but grasping. One of these unfortunate combinations alone would have been enough for me to vote against her application; and the combination of the three was quite deadly.

"Why, yes. I felt quite lucky to get it. I'd seen it on the runway, and mentioned that I liked it to my friend Kelly, who made an unexpected gift of it to me. But—and I can admit this only to you, Robin—I actually don't completely *love* it. What I *do* love are the stares of envy as I walk down the street. Isn't that awful?"

And therein lay all the maddening but alluring qualities of Law, in a few simple sentences. For Law's words could be translated thus: "Well, Robin, this is my way of showing you that I have other admirers, too, who are willing to help me in ways that you seem reluctant to. And if I grant those other people favors as a token of my gratitude, you have no right to complain. But I'm charming, aren't I? In the same breath, I can admit to being a completely shallow, vain, money-ori-ented person, while also showing you that I'm delightfully *aware* of my own shortcomings, which makes them much more acceptable, even fun."

Such unwarranted self-assurance requires a specific type of response. "You are young, dear Law. As you mature, you will realize that such stares of envy are fleeting and not worth the price of the plastic surgery that removed the lines from around those envious eyes."

Law looked down, perhaps somewhat abashed; and having scored my point and re-established the upper hand, I continued.

"But, on a side note"—here I smiled conspiratorially—"have you heard what has been transpiring? About J and Chris's apartment being broken into? And about the attempt on Alex's life?"

Law sighed. "As a matter of fact, I just spoke with Alex this morning, who told me all about the drama at the Empire State, as well as what happened to J and Chris. What is this City coming to? Are *any* of us safe from having our homes burgled or being assaulted in public?"

"Did Alex tell you that the assaulted person was of similar build and similar hair color? I find that intriguing, to say the least. Alex is wealthy now, you know. I wonder if someone could have been plotting something foul, but mistakenly attacked the wrong person."

"Oh, but haven't you heard? The police found the man who attacked that poor woman. He was a jilted former lover, I believe, who'd stalked her around the City waiting for the proper time to strike. It seems that she'd left him at the altar decades ago, and he'd been wanting to humiliate her in public, just as she'd done to him. All the details are in today's *Times*. Here, I was just reading the article.…"

I waved my hand dismissively as Law began to shuffle through the papers. For, as Law should have known from our long acquaintance, I long ago gave up reading any sort of newspaper, especially one as elitist and snobbish as *The New York Times*, whose writers very much love the sound of their own words and who manage to make every story, every scenario, and every headline about themselves. I have never had much patience for this kind of self-centeredness, and I find that I have even less with each passing day.

32

It seemed that my *tête-à-tête* with Law had no sooner begun than it was interrupted by Dr. R, that head shrinker extraordinaire who'd been taking my money for decades but had never provided quite the number of psychological insights that one unrealistically expects from mental health professionals. However, I suppose I cannot hold the good doctor completely responsible in this regard, for I am significantly more complex than the average New Yorker, and one cannot expect therapeutic methods used on the masses to work equally well on me.

"Ah, Robin. Come in. You're looking very natty today."

I nodded my assent—for it certainly was true—and walked through the door into Dr. R's counseling room, that rather inelegant and austere place where my heart is laid bare biweekly.

"Give me just a moment, would you, Robin?" As I helped myself to a bottle of water from the many on Dr. R's desk and situated myself in the "patient's" chair, I heard that good Freudian asking Law a few questions.

"Law, have you called Alma Moravian about her missed appointments? I really want…"

"How many times do I have to tell you—Yes, I've called her and left several messages. She hasn't called back yet, despite my numerous requests. You know, I wish you wouldn't act as though I have control over your patients' behaviors. It's not my fault that she hasn't called back yet."

"Very well. Please inform me if and when she does."

Though I have never been one to stick my nose where it

does not belong, I felt compelled to comment on this exchange as the good doctor took the seat facing me.

"Doctor, forgive my bluntness, but I am shocked that you would allow yourself to be spoken to in that tone by an office worker." For, as you know, I am quite fond of Law; but such entirely unacceptable snippiness must never be tolerated from one's underlings.

"I know, Robin, and normally I am more strict, but I have the distinct impression that Law is experiencing some stresses that may be causing these bouts of ill temperament. I know better than to ask for details, of course—one must keep that certain professional distance with one's employees—but all the signs are there. Since I am in the business of healing, I think it prudent to weather the storm rather than to provoke a confrontation. Besides, it is very difficult to find reliable help these days; and my clients are all quite fond of Law; *et cetera*."

"Well, Doctor, you know the saying: Spare the rod and spoil the child. However, let me not overly concern myself in your affairs."

"How have things been?" This was Dr. R's cue for me to begin the usual free association of thoughts that has become the hallmark of our sessions, and I began in earnest. As always, the doctor nodded and scribbled on a pad, occasionally interjecting a question or two that would set me off on another five-minute spiel of psychologically rich narration.

"I hear your anger, Robin," suggested Dr. R, after I'd confided my recent discovery that Lee had kept a key to Pat's apartment for lo these many years. "But you do know that anger is only to be expected upon the death of a loved one. And you have many justifiable reasons to be angry. I am glad you are expressing your anger here rather than bottling it up; for holding on to emotion, as we have discussed, is rarely healthy."

"Yes, I am angry; I own that emotion completely. And, strangely enough, I feel that it has given me quite a bit of strength to get through the last few trying weeks. I feel that I have indeed processed much of the recently discovered information in a healthy way, but I keep getting stuck on one thing: this mystery personage, 'Pat Armstrong.' It is exceedingly difficult to know whether to direct my anger at Lee, who, after all, was an adult completely capable of making decisions; or whether this 'Pat' was an active player in seducing Lee's attentions over the years. It would be so much easier on me if I knew for certain. If Pat was nothing more than a partner-stealing, craven beast, then perhaps Lee can be forgiven. For, as you know, Lee was obstinate in many areas but incredibly weak-willed in others."

"Perhaps, but as we have discussed many times, in this life we are often forced to deal with situations on the basis of limited knowledge; and we must make the best of those situations and not let them get the better of us. In these cases, it is useful to believe what it is helpful to believe. So if your healing process is speeded by considering Pat a demon, then craft your emotional scenario with this script, let it play out, and then put it behind you."

"Doctor, how can you be so inhuman? Pat was a patient of yours. And by all accounts, someone who relied on you greatly. To be notified of a patient's suicide via messenger! To be the one to find the body, and to have the responsibility for making the arrangements! Surely this indicates that you had a strong bond with Pat. It seems fair to assume that you know more about my ex-lover's lover than any other living creature. So what can you tell me, Doctor? You need not handle me with kid gloves. I am served better by the truth than by some cockamamie story I have made up in my mind to fool myself into thinking my ex-lover was lured into a trap set by a particularly devious imp."

Dr. R leaned back, eyeing me over folded arms. "Robin, as I have mentioned in the past, it is entirely inappropriate for me to discuss other patients with you. You wouldn't want me talking about *our* sessions with anyone else, would you?"

"But that argument does not hold water, Doctor. Pat is no longer alive; how can doctor-patient privilege adhere? I am not asking you to give me any details of treatment, but rather a sense of the individual whose arms Lee preferred to mine."

Dr. R sighed, for as always I had made a very valid point.

"Very well. In many ways, Pat was your polar opposite. Rather unassuming, nondescript even. I had always felt a tremendous loneliness at the core, there; and, during our sessions, I came to understand why. Simply giving an infant away is never a good way to assure one's long-term mental health, and this fact had weighed on Pat increasingly as the years went by. I think that holding on to Lee, in that special bond that only two adults who've had a child together can understand, was a way of making up for the loneliness, the sense of isolation that is all too common here in New York City, one of the most densely populated places in the country but also certainly one of the loneliest.

"Since the details were all made clear by the terms of Pat's will, as well as Lee's, and are a matter of public record, I can tell you that hiring that detective and tracking down the child was a path I completely supported. While I hadn't known quite how seriously Pat's disease had progressed, I suspected the terminal nature of the illness; and I have always believed that amends must be made and closure must be had. Pat was unsure of Lee's support in this regard, which is why Lee wasn't informed until, sadly, it was too late. In a nutshell, Robin, I tell you this not so that you can have closure yourself, but rather because I think it will prevent you from demonizing Pat, who was probably no better or no worse a person than anyone else on this earth, or even in this room."

And right there you have the reason why I have stayed with Dr. Rosenthal through thick and through thin. For no one else knows me quite as well, or understands that my deeply philosophical nature responds so strongly to such Truths.

"Thank you, Doctor. As always, you have given me cause for reflection. It must have been difficult for you to sit there and watch Pat shaking and twitching, getting worse as the months progressed."

"Yes, but Pat was never one to dwell on the physical. As you might imagine, our discussions were mostly about emotional matters. Of course, as a medical doctor, I had put together a diagnosis in my own mind based on what I'd observed, but it wasn't until I saw the medical examiner's report that the Parkinson's diagnosis was confirmed."

"Do you always get reports on the cadavers of your patients?" I hated to think that, upon my ultimate demise, my innards would be as exposed to Dr. R as my brain cells had been.

"Not at all. But the medical examiner is a friend of mine, and frankly, given the way Pat chose to involve me so closely in post-suicide matters, I felt I had a right to know."

This did mollify me, somewhat, while leading me to raise another question that had been bothering me.

"And had you any idea of Lee's heart troubles? I confess, I always thought that Lee would be much more likely to *cause* heart attacks than to suffer one. Not once, in all the years we cohabited, did Lee ever mention any sort of palpitation, murmur, or irregularity. But I suppose I should not be shocked; as it has become crystal clear that Lee hid many, many things from me."

Dr. R was silent for a moment, then responded cautiously. "Yes, come to think of it, I do remember Lee mentioning a diagnosis of some sort as well as a new medication. But I did not press the matter. As you know, Lee preferred to lead all discussions and not be questioned. I assumed Dr. Larribee had it all under control and thus made no further inquiries. But I will admit that I was shocked, and saddened, by the death, as were so many others. Lee really was an extraordinary individual. And, as you are well aware, Robin, extraordinary people can be extraordinarily demanding; but the work is often worth it."

In this regard I had to agree with the doctor; as I have occasionally been accused of being somewhat opaque, and yet those who choose to orbit Planet Robin usually find that the results are well worth the effort.

That annoying bell—the one that signals the five-minute interval prior to the end of the session—dinged, and I remembered one final question I'd wanted to ask the doctor.

"Before I go, Doctor, I did want to ask you for a prescription for that new medication, Dezonerol. I have read several articles about it, and I think it may be quite effective in aiding me at those times when my attention span is divided among too many competing duties."

Dr. Rosenthal looked uncomfortable. "Are you *sure* you need this medication? I do get phone calls from your pharmacies on a somewhat too regular basis, asking for my approval to refill prescriptions early. Several of the pharmacists have seemed rather…concerned."

I waved my hand dismissively. "Leave them to their worries, Doctor. You and I know how essential these small treatments are for my occasional lapses into mental distress; and I can assure you that, while I do stockpile them for cases of emergency, they certainly are not a facet of my daily existence. The prescription, please."

Dr. R grabbed a pad from the desk and scribbled something on it, then pulled off the prescription and extended it to me. "Here you go, Robin; as you certainly know what is best for you. But please do me the favor of bringing this to a pharmacy other than the ones you currently use. This will minimize database cross-searches and ensure you get what you need."

This seemed like an entirely reasonable request, so I acceded, took the scrip, and folded it into my pocket, gathering my things and bidding the doctor a fond *adieu*.

I blew a kiss at Law, who was once again on the phone, as I exited the office. But Law made it clear through various handwaves that I was not to leave yet. I stood my ground while Law scribbled something on a slip of paper, then handed it to me. I took the paper and read:

TOWN AND COUNTRY PHARMACY
WEST 73RD @ BROADWAY

I smiled, and Law smiled back. Once again the dear child had done me a huge favor, giving me the name and location of a pharmacy I had not previously used; and while such an attempt to curry my favor was obvious in the extreme, it had the benefit of making my life easier, a development very much welcome in the wake of the distresses of recent days.

33

I have long maintained that unburdening oneself of one's cares and troubles in the presence of a mental health professional is the surest way to a more fully integrated psyche. For modern life has fractured us all into a million little pieces, to borrow a term from that controversial fauxtobiography of recent years; and to reintegrate ourselves with the *coeur* of humanity, we must focus on that which brings us together rather than that which keeps us apart, in our own separate little cells like Al Qaeda operatives waiting to attack our relationships, joys, and self-esteem.

For me personally, however, the benefits of therapy are much wider reaching; for in addition to helping me re-achieve the emotional equilibrium that I present to the sometimes misunderstanding world, a good session at Dr. R's sets me on the path to clarity of thought. It is almost as if talking with the doctor stimulates my neurons to reconnect in new and exciting ways, thus allowing me to make all manner of connections among various phenomena that previously seemed unrelated.

Thus, as I walked home from that atrocious post-war building in which Dr. Rosenthal has shrunk ten thousand heads, I began re-examining the several odd developments that had so perplexed me in recent days. At the heart of all these mysterious matters lay the sudden and tragic deaths of Pat and Lee. In a very real sense, they were the ones who set these balls in motion, most likely having no idea that their night of animalistic coupling three decades earlier would lead to the present state of danger and unexplained occurrences.

I have never been one to experience that unsettling mental disorder commonly called paranoia. For, as you know, paranoia is a disease that envelops the self-obsessed, the dramatic, the solipsistic; and as one who has rarely fallen prey to any to *idée fixe*, I have been spared the crazed ravings of the delusional mind. This time, however, thoughts of a very disturbing nature began pounding at my consciousness, shaken free from their shackles by virtue of my conversation with Dr. R.

As to Pat's mental state and physical health, I cared not a whit; for Pat was nothing but a stranger, a shadowy form on the fringes of my life. Lee was quite a different story, however.

While the late Lee Harris could keep a secret like no other being on this planet, I could not imagine that my ex would never have mentioned any heart difficulties to me. For many years we'd been treated by the same general practitioner, Dr. Larribee, who'd always kept me aware of Lee's physical state, and Lee aware of mine. For this is a courtesy accorded to life partners by doctors, who understand that remaining healthy is easier when it is a team effort. I distinctly remember Lee returning from semiannual physicals in which Dr. Larribee had pronounced Lee "healthy as a horse." And the more I thought about the situation, the more I realized that I had never seen Lee take any of those precautions urged upon patients with problematic tickers. Indeed, Lee had continued to eat fatty, grease-laden foods and to get no exercise whatsoever.

And here is where I get back to that ominous word *paranoia*. As a very trusting person who has always taken the world at face value (for, as Dr. Freud said, a cigar is sometimes just a cigar), I never think to question the findings of those in authority. Someone, somewhere, had declared that Lee had died of a heart attack, and I had accepted this without question, for the unsuspecting drop dead each and every day of undiagnosed maladies.

And yet, do not those of us who work in a sleuthing capacity often tell ourselves to *cherchez la femme*? Such advice may work in cities where love is the driving force behind human motivation, such as Rome or Paris; but this is not the case in cities like Hong Kong or New York, where the driving force is money. *Cherchez la femme*? No. *Cherchez les billets*? Yes. Because the conventional wisdom had been that Lee was worth quite a hefty little sum, though few besides myself knew that Lee's monetary reserves were not quite what they had once been; and even I was not supposed to have been privy to that information, which is where a bit of harmless snooping in one's partner's private papers does come in handy, which is one's right when one has had one's money drained in unexpected ways by a larcenous partner.

Could it be that Lee had not died of a heart attack, but rather through some other maleficent means? This was a question I had asked myself previously; and the time had come to re-open that line of inquiry.

To the paranoid mind, murder would have been a foregone conclusion; but as a person who has always looked before leaping, I did not want to rush to judgment; for, as the saying goes, fools rush in where angels fear to tread. Earlier in my investigation, you may recall, I had been suspicious of Alex, who benefited the most directly from both Lee and Pat's deaths; but the handwriting comparison had shown me that Alex couldn't possibly have written Pat's suicide letter, and hadn't Alex also been nearly victimized on the Empire State? Though that had turned out to be nothing more than an unfortunate coincidence, with Alex sharing that odd prematurely gray hair color and slender build with that much older female victim.

Still, answers were needed, and I realized I could go right to the source. Thus, rather than going home to enjoy a light repast, I continued walking directly to the office of Dr. Larribee. As always, the waiting room was crowded and the receptionists looked harried.

I marched up to the elder stateswoman who presides over the office staff like Queen Elizabeth presided over her court.

"I need to see Dr. Larribee immediately."

But Queen Elizabeth proved quite uncooperative.

"Do you have an appointment?"

"No, I do not. But this is an urgent matter."

"Everyone in this waiting room has an urgent matter. Valentina will make an appointment for you."

Always a person of utmost patience, I felt every last ounce of that virtue draining from my body.

"Now, listen to me carefully. This is not a request. You will summon Dr. Larribee this minute."

In *The Rape of the Lock*, that eighteenth-century mock epic, the dwarflike Alexander Pope (a distant relative of mine on my mother's side) wrote:

> *Then flashed the living lightning from her eyes,*
> *And screams of horror rend th' affrighted skies.*
> *Not louder shrieks to pitying Heaven are cast,*
> *When husbands, or when lap-dogs breathe their last;*
> *Or when rich China vessels, fallen from high,*
> *In glittering dust and painted fragments lie!*

Such was the look worn by Queen Elizabeth, who opened her mouth to begin some sort of verbal assault on me; an attack I was more than ready for, as I'd already begun stockpiling my verbal arsenal in order to grind her into dust at my feet. For I am truly capable of such when I am crossed; and while I rarely resort to such desperate measures, I was not about to brook any opposition in my continued quest for Truth.

But before the Queen could sputter out even a sentence (such are the effects of rage, which clouds the minds and ties the tongues of the inarticulate), Dr. Larribee entered the reception area from a side door.

"Dr. Larribee, I must have a word with you. Your—woman—here seems intent on preventing me from talking with you, but I can assure you it is a matter of great import."

By this time Dr. L's many patients were watching the exchange with great interest, tapping away on their Blackberries, most likely to send emails to Page Six of *The*

New York Post, where I have occasionally been featured in not the most flattering of lights.

"Robin, I apologize. Do come in." Then a bit of living lightning flashed from the eyes of the clearly displeased Dr. Larribee directly toward Queen Elizabeth herself, who gulped and turned aside, in a rather futile effort to maintain face in the wake of a most humiliating incident in which she'd revealed her transparent desire for power to an entire roomful of patients, who would never look at her the same way again. For this is the price to be paid when one crosses Robin Anders; and while I take no enjoyment in such matters, perhaps it is not unuseful for the less experienced to learn a valuable lesson from the public humiliation of a senior staff member.

"Now, what's all this, Robin?" asked Dr. Larribee, no doubt quite terrified that the incident might lead me to rescind those box seats at Lincoln Center that I procure for her each season, in return for her immediate attentions to me and mine when they are required.

"I'm sorry to barge in like this, Doctor, but I am still a bit overwrought after Lee's death. I wanted to ask you a question that has been pressing on me. As you know, Lee died of an unexpected heart attack. But I never remember hearing about any heart problems; and I admit this has been bothering me. Lee was careless about many things, but health was not one of them, and I find it odd that my ex-lover would have a heart condition but not make any adjustments to compensate for this, such as an altered diet or heavier exercise regimen."

"Well, Robin, I will admit it came as a surprise to me, too, when Terry told me about it. Lee's heart was indeed strong, always had been. But that does not mean an unexpected heart attack is impossible. It happens more often than you would think. And you know Lee was a somewhat anxious person. The hearts of such people tend to absorb much of that stress, weakening them in ways that are very real but that don't necessarily show up on medical scans. But what about you, Robin? How are you holding up?"

"Surviving, Doctor. Surviving. The last couple of weeks have been a very intense time of rumination for me. As you may know, Lee and I had our ups and downs, but we were very committed to each other's happiness; and I do feel a bit rudderless. But I have just been to see Doctor Rosenthal, and that has helped."

"Do you need anything while you're here?"

"No, no, I'm quite set up with everything I need. Dr. R took care of all that."

Dr. L looked at her watch. "Well, you know to call me if you need me. Unless you need anything else, I really should get going. You know how demanding these terminal patients can be. They behave as though their time is more valuable than everyone else's."

And out Dr. Larribee went, but not without shaking my hand and apologizing once again for the beastly behavior of Queen Elizabeth, who, unless I missed my guess, would soon be demoted to lady in waiting.

Not that the wretch's impending demotion could even begin to outweigh the emotional upset I was beginning to feel. For it had become glaringly obvious that someone had lied to me. Dr. Rosenthal had said that Lee admitted to the diagnosis of a heart problem, and had assumed that Dr. Larribee had it under control. But Dr. Larribee had made no such diagnosis. This could mean any one of three things: Lee had lied to Dr. R, making up some fraudulent malady as part of a ploy for Dr. R's sympathy. Or Dr. Larribee had diagnosed Lee with a heart problem, but had just lied to me about it. Or Dr. Rosenthal had lied to me when I asked if Lee had ever talked about *problemas del corazón*. Or some combination of these.

Oh, the mendacity of humanity! To be lied to by those whom one trusts most on this mortal coil! I fear my thoughts took me in a downward spiral of depression, as I walked home, dejected and emotionally disjointed; but remembering the prescription in my pocket, I took a detour to Town and Country Pharmacy, where a dowdy and unappealing young person of indeterminate gender filled it quickly, removing two of the new 'banana pills' from the bottle so that I might take them before I left the apothecary's counter.

34

Because neither Dr. Rosenthal nor Dr. Larribee had any history of dissembling to me, at least so far as I knew, I had to assume that Lee, teller of tall tales and two-timer extraordinaire, had extended that web of deception into therapeutic sessions for some sort of perceived gain known only to Lee. This explanation made the most sense, given the results of my investigation thus far; but many years of service to the Goode Foundation have taught me that one must always double-check one's hunches. For that appealing young artist may instead be a honey-tongued but derivative charmer; and that gifted singer may be a crone using a harp and lyre to fool the senses rather than delight them.

Thus it behooved me to go to the single source of information that had no financial or emotional stake in the situation: the medical examiner who'd autopsied Lee. Fortunately, the identity of this municipal employee is a matter of public record; and my oft-underutilized assistant was able to track down a name in just a few phone calls. It seemed that a

"Septimus McAllister" had been the lucky one to examine Lee's innards. Another call produced a fax of Mr. McAllister's report, which was filled with all manner of medical jargon but did seem to indicate "massive coronary" in the final analysis as the primary cause of death.

Lesser minds would have been satisfied with this report and concluded that my ex had indeed died of an unexpected heart attack; but, as one who has engaged in more than the average share of critical thinking, I was loath to trust several faxed sheets of paper. For what goes on behind the scenes is always more telling than a final "report" produced for public consumption; and as any savvy New Yorker can tell you, many a glowing report has been based on the most abysmal of findings.

No; a report would not be enough. I would need to confront Septimus McAllister face to face in this regard, to shake loose any information that was not included in that final bit of paperwork. But before I took the trouble to hunt down Mr. McAllister, I thought it best to place a few more phone calls, not only to follow up on a further hunch but also to ensure Mr. McAllister's complete cooperation.

* * *

In a filthy taxi on the way to the Office of the Chief Medical Examiner—located in an utterly uninteresting part of town, First Avenue in the 30s, just south of that architecturally undistinguished edifice in which the members of the United Nations meet to accomplish nothing of value—I pondered what seemed to be a rather unsettling coincidence. However, this strange alignment might be just a matter of procedure for these overpaid city employees, who drain our tax dollars into their generous pension funds while doing very little else; and perhaps my interview with "Septimus

McAllister" would shed some light on the ways of the New York City Medical Examiner's Office.

As I entered that moribund building on First Avenue, I was nearly overwhelmed by the smells of chloroform and formaldehyde, or at least scents that I assumed were those two unsavory chemicals; and I had to fight maintain consciousness, for my olfactory senses have always been among my most sensitive, and I had not adequately prepared myself for such an assault. Fortunately, I was able to slide two of the quickly dissolvable 'papaya pills' under my tongue, thus maintaining blessed consciousness while pulling a fine silk handkerchief from my jacket pocket with which to cover my sputtering mouth and twitching nose. I fear this behavior did not endear me to the staff, which looked upon me with great misunderstanding, even scorn; however, one cannot expect those who cavort with cadavers for a living to understand their effects upon those of more refined sensibilities; and thus I ignored their glares of impatience as I announced myself at the visitors' desk.

"Robin Anders for Septimus McAllister," I wheezed through the handkerchief, as the receptionist's eyes rolled upward in an entirely inappropriate gesture of disrespect. I made a mental note of her name—"Serena Vocci"—so that I might deal with her behavior more appropriately at a later date, when breathable oxygen was not in such short supply.

I watched "Serena Vocci" punch some numbers into a germ- and microbe-laden phone, then announce flatly, "Robin Anders is here to see you." The cretin then nodded at a door facing her. "Through that door, up the stairs, to the right, Room 216."

Without a word I went to the door, from which was emanating a loud buzzing noise initiated by "Serena Vocci." But the door might as well have been the Cretan maze with the Minotaur at its center, for all the difficulty it caused me. For there was no way on God's earth I was going to touch that disease-ridden doorknob, which had probably been rubbed up against by a surfeit of pus-filled corpses in recent hours. Thus I tried pushing on the door handle with my elbow, which was doubly protected by my shirt and jacket, but each time the lock disengaged, the handle slipped off my elbow, causing the door to lock again, and "Serena Vocci" to re-commence that hideous buzzing that was threatening to bring on the full fury of a migraine in record time.

I have never been one to demand the assistance or attentions of others; for I have always been a highly independent individual who proceeds through life without calling undue attention to myself. But in this case, my normally unassuming nature went into rapid recession as a more assertive Robin emerged.

"You, there," I snapped, pointing my finger toward an orderly of some sort who was emptying wastebaskets in the lobby. "Is it too much to ask for some help in opening this door? Clearly, you can see I am struggling; and, clearly, you do not care. I only hope you treat your cadavers with more concern than you treat living people in this house of horrors."

"James Washington"—whose nametag read thus—looked at me lazily, then at "Serena Vocci," who made an unpleasant face while nodding her head in my direction. After what seemed an eon of continued buzzing, "James Washington" grabbed the door handle—with his bare hand—and held the door open so that I might pass through.

Upon arriving at Room 216, I stuck my head in the doorway to announce myself. A smallish, fattish, bespectacled, sweating man sat at a messy desk littered with papers and computer equipment. Despite my having been announced several minutes earlier, he still looked distinctly surprised to see a live human being in his office, so I reminded him of my identity.

"Hello. I am Robin Anders."

"Septimus McAllister," said the unimpressive piece of humanity in a rather nasal tone.

"Yes, I see that from the name on your door."

Septimus rose and extended his hand but quickly retracted it when I shrank back with a distinct glare of disapproval.

"Do you want to sit down? The office may be messy, but it's clean. You have nothing to worry about."

"Perhaps, but I prefer to err on the side of caution. You understand, of course."

"Well, I suppose. There's a bit of superstition surrounding what we do, you know. I guess we pretend to get used to it, but you never get used to people thinking you're some sort of ghoul. Which we aren't, we have intense medical training...."

"Mr. McAllister, I'm sorry to interrupt your self-pitying diatribe, but I'm afraid I am on a tight schedule; and despite your assurances to the contrary, I cannot see the benefit of remaining any longer in a house of death than absolutely necessary. Rest assured I will crack no jokes at your expense, nor dismiss your profession as one practiced only by those with a twisted taste for the macabre. But in return I would like us to conduct our business efficiently, so that we may both go our separate ways, me to embrace the light, you to continue in pursuits of darkness. Are we agreed?"

"Well, um, you know, that's not quite..."

"I'll take your nonsensical sputtering as agreement, Mr. McAllister. Now, as I mentioned on the phone, I understand you were the person to conduct the post-death examination of Lee Harris. Lee's death was a shock to everyone, particularly to me. But I will admit that I am quite perplexed regarding the cause of death. Lee's doctor told me that Lee had never shown any signs of heart disease whatsoever. And yet your report clearly indicates a 'coronary' as the cause of death."

"Well, yes, that was the cause of death for Lee Harris. You know, we get a lot of bodies in here, I don't remember them all, they all sort of run together, but I pulled the report after we talked on the phone, and I did conduct the examination, and yes, a coronary was the cause of death, so there you have it."

"But could you have been wrong about this? Is that at least possible?"

"No. This one was an open and shut case."

"If I may say so, Mr. McAllister, you seem a bit defensive."

"Well, I'm not really used to strangers barging in here, questioning my work. And frankly, I don't like it."

"If the amount of sweat pouring from your glands is any indicator of how much you don't like it, then I would say you dislike it a great deal."

"Look, I only agreed to see you because apparently my boss's kid has some sort application in with the foundation you work for. Well, I don't care who you work for, you have no right to come barging in here, interrupting me, with unwarranted accusations."

"I don't believe I've made any accusations, Mr. McAllister. But now that you mention it, I do know of one or two bizarre coincidences. Not only did you perform a post-mortem on Lee Harris, you also performed a similar vivisection on Pat Armstrong, who predeceased Lee by only a short while."

"I've already told you, I do a lot of cases. I don't remember all of them. There are a lot of people in this City, all related by six degrees of separation."

"Let me refresh your memory. Pat Armstrong, who had Parkinson's Disease, had committed suicide. At least that was your finding, a conclusion backed up by various suicide notes written in Pat's own hand."

"Then what's the problem? You're saying all this with an accusatory tone."

"I've done my own research into Parkinson's disease, Mr. McAllister. People who suffer with Parkinson's can live long, long lives, especially with the medical care available today. Why would an otherwise healthy adult commit suicide over a disease that many people live with successfully?"

"In case you hadn't noticed, I'm not a psychologist, I'm a forensic pathologist. I don't know *why* people kill themselves. All I figure out is *how* they did it."

"And how *did* Pat do it?" I already knew the answer, but I was leading the corpulent M.E. down a very specific path and wanted to hear the answer from his own blubbery lips.

"Hold on." Septimus McAllister smashed his fingers into the cookie-crumb-encrusted keyboard on his desk, squinted his eyes, and read, "Poison. Or, more specifically, an overdose of sleeping pills. Fast, easy, cheap, effective. Works 99 times out of 100, unless someone finds the person in time."

"But how do you know that Pat took those pills voluntarily? What if they were forced on the supposed suicide victim instead?"

"Highly unlikely. Besides, as you already said, there were suicide notes. This was another open and shut case. So I opened and shut it quickly. Lots of bodies around here to deal with. And if people want to kill themselves, that's their business, not mine. Or yours."

"I see. Well, I'm afraid, Mr. McAllister, that this *is* my business. And do you know what I think? I think you're not telling me the truth."

"Oh, please. Are you one of those conspiracy theorists that likes to run around town making trouble? Get a life."

I sighed heavily. I have never been one to throw my weight around, or to engage in power plays. But this conversation was not going at all to my liking, and my normally high patience level was rapidly dwindling.

"And what type of life should I get, Mr. McAllister? Perhaps that of an anesthesiologist who has let not one, not two, but three children under the age of ten die on an operating table in Brooklyn? The life of an incompetent oaf whose inability to apply the proper dosages of epinephrine, resulting in said children's deaths, is concealed by the hospital administration, which puts gag orders on the impoverished parents from the low-income projects in the all-too-small settlements compensating them for their children's deaths? The existence of a moron who gets transferred to the psych ward of a Manhattan hospital, where he overmedicates patients to such a horrific extent that several of them have become the equivalent of human vegetables? Or perhaps the life of a rather rotund, fetid-smelling man whose father-in-law is a member of the board of trustees of that Manhattan hospital? Said father-in-law also having, of course, ties to the mayor's office, which allow him to call in favors and get his disgraced son-in-law a job in the City Medical Examiner's office, where he won't be able to kill anyone else, because his 'patients' will already be dead?"

As the blood drained from Septimus McAllister's face, I continued.

"I don't know about you, Mr. McAllister, but if that were my life, and I were talking with someone named Robin Anders right now, I would very much come clean with the truth, before Robin Anders made a few phone calls to various muckraking journalists to let them know about what goes on at that Brooklyn hospital, as well as at City Hall and the Chief Medical Examiner's Office. I would imagine the ensuing scandal would touch not only the mayor, but also my beloved and highly respected father-in-law, if I were to decide not to cooperate with Robin Anders."

Septimus McAllister stared at the pile of papers on his desk.

"How? How do you know all this?"

"Never mind how I know. I *know*. Now, Mr. McAllister, if you please, the *real* circumstances surrounding the deaths of Lee Harris and Pat Armstrong."

"This is blackmail."

"It's no such thing. It's one person agreeing to keep another person's secret, in return for a bit of information."

Septimus McAllister grimaced, took a breath, and said quietly, "Lee Harris was murdered."

I did not blink.

"Go on."

"Stabbed with a small knife directly to the heart. And perhaps the victim of an overdose as well."

"Explain, please."

"The cause of death was the stabbing. But the body held large amounts of a sleeping pill that would have been enough to cause death by overdose. Small bruises on Lee Harris' throat indicated that the pills may have been forced on the victim. The same drug killed Pat Armstrong."

"So Pat was murdered also?"

"No. That one really was a suicide. All the telltale signs of suicide were there. The sleeping pill was a long-time medication that the victim had recently had refilled, and there were enough pills in the victim's stomach to kill a rhinoceros. And of course there was the note received by the therapist."

"If it's any consolation, Mr. McAllister, you're not telling me anything I didn't already know or suspect. But there is one detail you've left out. Why did you file a false report listing Lee's cause of death as a heart attack?"

"It was a favor for a friend."

"A favor for a friend?"

"Yes, someone called and asked me for a favor. I had to do it. You know how it works. One hand washes the other."

"I'm well aware of that rule, Mr. McAllister, and abide by it myself. And who requested this favor of you?"

Silence.

"Mr. McAllister, I'm leaving in ten seconds, and calling my friends at *The New York Times* in fifteen."

"It was a friend of mine. Someone I'd worked with on the psych ward. Terry Rosenthal."

35

The educated person can easily list the great betrayals in history. We all know of Brutus' betrayal of Julius Caesar. Nor was Jesus done any great service by Judas Iscariot. Benedict Arnold betrayed an entire nascent country. But all of these paled in comparison to the betrayal of Robin Anders and Lee Harris by Dr. Rosenthal.

I will not describe the emotional agony caused by the revelations of Septimus McAllister; suffice it to say that were it not for the availability of several highly effective pharmacological agents, I may have ended up lying prostrate on my sitting room floor, engaging in profound self-pity. For to have been betrayed by Lee was one thing; as any experienced person of the world knows, lovers come and go, and betrayal at their hands is inevitable. But to be thrown to the wolves by one's therapist, the very person in whom one has confided almost everything, and to whom one has been almost 80% honest? Such betrayal is tantamount to homicide, the therapeutic equivalent of Medea killing her children.

In a world so filled with prevarications, I was tempted to discount Septimus McAllister's wild accusations as yet another series of untruths. But that carver of cadavers had no reason to lie to me, and all the reason to speak the unadulterated truth. This ability to dig up dirt on various denizens of New York City is one of the fringe benefits of working in my quasi-public capacity at the Foundation; for, as you surely realize, people are always much more cooperative when their reputations, or livelihoods, are at stake. Thus, prior to leaving for the Medical Examiner's Office, I'd made the requisite phone calls, attempting to connect the "six degrees" that, as Septimus McAllister had so accurately noted, unite everyone in this City:

1st degree: My assistant calls one of her paramours, a worker at the City Morgue with whom she is rumored to have engaged in necrophiliac experimentation;

2nd degree: The paramour pulls the coroner's report for Lee, then faxes it to my assistant, who hands it to me with that upturned nose of distaste that is one of her worst characteristics;

3rd degree: I read the report, looking up the occasional forensic term on the Internet, and in a moment of curiosity decide I need to have a look at the M.E.'s report on Pat's death as well; this report is faxed to my office, and upon reading it I note that the post-mortem work on both Lee and Pat has been performed by the same person, Septimus McAllister;

4th degree: Intrigued by the coincidence, and given the various unsolved mysteries crying out for explanation, I assume that Mr. McAllister might know more than he would readily admit to, which requires me to gain information that could be used to ensure his compliance upon my visit;

5th degree: I place a call to one of my contacts at the Mayor's office, a man who rules an important City agency with an iron fist, but who has a weakness for rock concerts by manufactured Pop Tarts, whom he makes a hobby of bedding; and to get him close to said Teen Idols, the Goode Foundation frequently arranges for backstage passes and/or private meetings, thus ensuring that when a Representative of the Foundation needs a favor from him, it is granted expeditiously. In this case, I must reassure this contact of my extreme discretion in the matter, for even he had not expected to dig up the sordid tale of Septimus McAllister's exceedingly high level of incompetence *in re* anesthetic practices and the subsequent calling in of favors that helped him both avoid litigation *and* collect a tidy little paycheck, with full City benefits and pension;

6th degree: All of which leads me to that disease-filled office on First Avenue, highly unwilling to use the information I'd garnered, but forced into doing so by Circumstance and an uncooperative mortician.

An investigation is not unlike an archaeological dig; the further one dives below the surface, the more treasures one finds. Thus, when I'd recovered from my newfound knowledge of Dr. Rosenthal's betrayal—ironically, with the aid of those wonderfully effective helpers that Dr. Rosenthal had prescribed for me—and regained my ability to think clearly and rationally, without surfeit of emotion, I had to ask myself the age-old question that is at the heart of every unexplained circumstance: *Why?*

Why would Dr. Rosenthal, one of Manhattan's pre-eminent therapists—a psychological professional with a reputation that lesser doctors would kill for—put that reputation at stake by becoming involved in an intricate tale of intrigue, deceit, and death? What could be the possible gain to a doctor already so wealthy and renowned?

The possibilities were endless, of course. Had Dr. Rosenthal bedded Pat, Lee, or both? Had the good doctor fallen on monetary hard times and hoped to take financial advantage of the terminally ill Pat and the monetarily strapped Lee, who had always made a habit of projecting a *façade* of wealth despite an underlying and distressing penury? Did Pat, or Lee, or both, possess some knowledge that could be damning to Dr. R's career? Or could Dr. Rosenthal be one of those psychopathic shrinks one reads about in the newspaper or sees featured at the cinema: the upstanding citizen, known and respected by all, in whom lurks a serial killer? This last scenario was exceedingly difficult to envision, what with Dr. R's geekish spectacles (some would call them "fashionable," but not I), slender build, and clumsy demeanor; but is it not said that the Evil among us often possess honeyed tongues that hide their True Selves?

Whatever the reason, I felt sure that Dr. Rosenthal held the key to unlock many mysterious rooms; and it was with this mendacious creature that I needed to have my next interview. Sitting in my favorite chair, an heirloom much valued by the Hohenzollerns in their heyday, I plotted my course of action on a little notepad; for I have never been one to dive headlong into shark-filled waters *sans* protective gear and a plan of attack.

Underlying my preparation was a nasty little truth that I could not move forward without properly internalizing: Dr. Rosenthal might be quite a dangerous person. And while my trip to Long Island several weeks earlier had proven that I live somewhat of a charmed life, and can usually repel the efforts of Fate, I saw no need to take unnecessary chances; for, as many a successful Wall Street exec who's tumbled to his death off a penthouse balcony while snorting cocaine has discovered, it is usually only a matter of time before one's luck runs out.

Thus I picked up the phone and placed a call or two, then had my doorman call me a cab to take me to a rather unsavory address in Brooklyn. This is a borough I have unfortunately been unable to avoid, as it is home to some second-tier artistic institutions, such as the Brooklyn Academy of Music and the Brooklyn Museum; and as a senior member of the Goode Foundation's board I must occasionally make appearances in these locales, to show the Foundation's support for those secondary and tertiary venues in which aspiring artists sometimes get their start. Fortunately, the 'pineapple pills' are quite effective on those occasions when I must venture off Manhattan Island; and I availed myself of several of these prior to leaving my apartment.

The neighborhood into which I was taken was not unlike that of Junior Makeba's Washington Heights; and I suppose this is only to be expected, for it has always been my experience that one immigrant neighborhood is very much like the next, with the sole difference being the language spoken.

My knock at the door was answered by a large man known to the street community as Charles, whom I followed to a back room loaded with all manner of firearms, from exceedingly small guns to weapons of a size and power that small nations would envy. I explained my need for an unassuming device that could be easily concealed and fired; Charles responded by grabbing a cute pistol that fit my hand quite nicely. I will admit to a bit of discomfort at touching a physical item so commonly associated with crime and the lower classes; but surely Society had nothing to worry about from the unassuming Robin Anders, who was short-circuiting the system solely for purposes of self-protection. And, while the existence of people like Charles did give one pause, I had to admit that his services were exceedingly convenient in a city renowned for its red tape and onerous waiting periods.

From this unsavory part of Brooklyn my taxi driver, who could not seem to stop eyeing me lustfully in the rear-view mirror, took me to a pistol firing range in Queens. Crossing the border into that borough, my senses were fairly assaulted by all things middle class: Chevrolets, Target department stores, beauty "salons" with names like "Eva's Nail Emporium," *et cetera*. Still, one must experience occasional discomfort to grow as a person; and, as a person who has never had an unrealistic sense of self, I knew that I needed some tutelage in the art of shooting, just in case Dr. Rosenthal should threaten me in any way.

Thus I spent several hours being instructed in the art and science of handling and shooting a firearm. The noise at the firing range was positively migraine inducing, despite a pair of goggles and earmuffs I was required to don, and which had amazingly rapid negative effects on my carefully prepared coif; and the glee with which my fellow trainees shot holes in person-shaped and –sized pieces of cardboard might be construed as yet more evidence of the inherently violent nature of the human animal. But I have always been one to see the positive in all situations; and I must admit that my teacher, a tall, well-built, recent graduate of the Academy, provided a not unpleasant amount of titillation in the environment of violence. In instructing me in proper methods of aiming and firing, "Jürgen" more than once let his hands linger just a moment too long on my waist or shoulder; and I will admit to allowing these liberties, for the white-hot passion of a man like Jürgen must be dispersed in small amounts throughout the day, lest it explode into wild, untamed lust at inopportune moments. At other times and in other circumstances, I would have dallied with Jürgen a bit more, taking the flirtation to the next level, driving him wild with a desire whose consummation I would allow at a later date; but the life of a detective is such that the pleasures of the flesh must sometimes be put aside in the interests of time and self-preservation.

Thus armed and instructed, I returned to my home to place a call to my quarry's private cell phone, to which, as I have mentioned, I am one of the fortunate few to have access.

The phone was answered almost immediately by an affectless woman.

"Doctor Rosenthal's line."

"I need to speak with the doctor."

"The doctor is not available. You've reached the answering service."

"Be that as it may, I need to talk with Doctor Rosenthal immediately."

"Name?"

It had been a stressful day—what with the enforced trek to two outer boroughs—and I had no time for games.

"Young woman, I am only going to say this once. This is a matter of the most urgent importance. Have Doctor Rosenthal call me immediately. My name is Robin Anders. And in your message tell the doctor that I've had the opportunity to speak with Septimus McAllister, who gave me intriguing information."

"Yes," said the message-taker dully. "Robin Anderson. You spoke with September McMaster. I will give the doctor your message. Thank you, and have a nice day." The phone went dead.

But it didn't stay dead. Ten minutes later, my cell phone beeped, the Caller ID displaying Dr. Rosenthal's office number.

36

I indulged in a bit of uncharacteristic self-congratulation as I walked to Dr. Rosenthal's office. For the good doctor had made a distinctly audible gulping noise as I outlined the results of my recent investigation, which put me in quite a position of power over that mendacious individual.

Over the years, the doctor and I had done a bit of a dance to establish alpha-type dominance, and after two decades we had found ourselves at a somewhat comfortable level of equality, though this state of affairs did occasionally chafe. But the tide had turned, and quite significantly at that. Several times I'd needed to shush the doctor's attempts to interrupt our phone conversation—as I was less interested in hearing excuses than in making the doctor exceedingly aware that I'd done my homework and would brook no further deception. This had the desired effect of humbling the normally haughty doctor to a gratifying degree; and it was with relish that I brandished my *coup de grâce*—a demand that we meet immediately so that I might receive a valid and enlightening explanation.

This demand was acceded to immediately, with no excuses regarding a busy schedule or suicidal patients who must be seen. Not that such excuses would have mattered; for I have always maintained that those who wish to commit suicide have the right to do so, thus freeing society of the burdens imposed by those morose people.

But the doctor did put up quite an unexpected fight, insisting that we meet in a public place, not in the office. It would have been in my interests to meet at, say, a restaurant or outdoor café—for surely no sane individual would make an attempt on my life with spectators everywhere? But the more the doctor insisted that we meet for our "chat" elsewhere, the more I dug in my heels. It was highly unlikely that the doctor would attempt to off me in broad daylight, in a place as sacrosanct as a therapist's office; and I will admit to just the tiniest bit of pleasure in being able to dictate my terms and force the doctor to assume a submissive position in the very place in which my trust had been so thoroughly betrayed.

Upon arriving at the offices labeled "T. ROSENTHAL, LICENSED PSYCHOTHERAPIST," I buzzed for entrance. Dr. Rosenthal appeared almost immediately, looking most serious and unhappy. I was surprised not to see Law smiling at me coyly from behind the receptionist's desk.

As the doctor led me to the consultation room, I inquired as to Law's whereabouts.

"Running some errands," was the distracted response.

This was an odd explanation, as it seemed unlikely that a doctor as in demand as Dr. Rosenthal would allow the phones to go unpersonned during business hours. But no matter.

I took my seat in the same chair in which I'd sat a few days previously; how much more comfortable it felt now!

"Well, Doctor," I began, "here we are."

A few beads of perspiration showed on the doctor's normally emotionless forehead: a good sign. I continued.

"And surely I need not tell you that the next hour will be very different from our usual session? Now I shall sit back and listen, while you do the talking."

The doctor, unaccustomed to being spoken to thus, looked distinctly unhappy, a frown forming about the lips.

"Robin, you and I have always maintained a respectful relationship. I feel that our time together has been mutually beneficial. Would you agree?"

This was not the conversation I had expected; this was not the Inquisition, nor was I Spanish. Nonetheless, as the doctor is sometimes facile with rhetorical questions, I decided to play along.

"Yes, I would agree, Doctor. I have sometimes questioned your methods, but I confess to slow but steady progress over the years, with regards to certain personal issues. And I daresay you have benefited, too, from your association with a complex and multi-faceted patient, who has challenged you to expand your therapeutic universe and thus your professional acumen. However, if you hope to trade on our long-standing relationship to justify your recent rape of my trust, then I must tell you that you are very much barking up the proverbially wrong tree."

"I sense, Robin, that you are planning to be a bit of a bear about this whole situation. I have understood your implied threats, and I can assure you that I will be completely forthright. But there is something you must know before I begin. If I go to prison, or something worse, you certainly will suffer; as you rely on me for many things"—here I was treated to a sideways glance hinting at certain pharmacological favors I have occasionally received as a result of the doctor's largesse—"that are not usually supplied by my colleagues with such alacrity."

"Let us not discuss my treatment at this juncture, Doctor Rosenthal. You have made your point."

"The point I am making is salient to this discussion, Robin. And it is a discussion I have had with only two other people thus far. As far as I am concerned, the situation is under control, and I had expected not to discuss it any further. But for some reason you have decided to replace your usual *laissez faire* approach to life with an atypical lugubriousness regarding your inquiries into the death of Lee, which brings us to where we are now."

"You should not be quite so surprised, Doctor. For you know I have always been tenacious in matters that are important to me."

The doctor took a breath, looking around the room nervously and keeping one eye on the door to the waiting room, which had been left ajar.

"Regardless," the doctor continued, "I will give you all the details of what has transpired over the last two months. I trust I can count on your discretion in these matters."

"I make no promises. Doctor, you surprise me. I hold all the cards in this particular game of poker, both king and queen in this game of chess. Now please, the information I seek, forthwith. My patience wears thin."

The doctor sighed. "Approximately two months ago, I was visited by an investigator from an insurance company. While I avoid taking on clients who must rely on insurance companies to pay their bills"—I nodded my head sympathetically—"it is sadly unavoidable in this day and age, especially when rents have become so astronomical.[*] It seems that the insurance company felt that I had been prescribing expensive medications with too much regularity, and they assigned the case to a particularly self-righteous and nosy senior staffer, who was quite obviously resentful of the success of my practice. Prior to his visit, he used the databases at his disposal to trace several of my patients and the medicines I prescribe for them. This led him to the conclusion that I am nothing more than a drug dealer for the wealthy."

---

[*] See *Who Gets the Apartment?*, Tales from the Back Page #1.

I said nothing; for surely there was nothing to say? The upper echelons of New York Society have always had their own ways of doing things, and access to an unlimited supply of any prescription is one of their much-deserved perks. This is surely not unreasonable, for the costs of maintaining Culture, Decency, and Respectability in New York City are very high among those who are charged with such tasks; with the result that the stresses can be very intense indeed and require the occasional, and sometimes even the regular, administration of agents to soothe the mind and calm the body. On occasion, even I have availed myself of this privilege. And it goes without saying that one does not become one of *New York* magazine's annual "Top Ten Therapists in New York City" if one is stingy with the prescription pad.

"This unsavory individual then offered me a deal. In exchange for a monthly stipend, he would look the other way, as well as eliminate perhaps incriminating information from the database. In the interests of my patients, I acceded to his request."

I continued listening. What Dr. Rosenthal had admitted to thus far really was not all that disturbing; as this is very much business as usual in Manhattan. From this perspective, the investigator was nothing more than a paid consultant; and as such, his fees could be written off as a business expense. Such expenses would of course have lowered Dr. R's overall profitability level, but everyone knows that profits are more elusive in New York these days, and most accept this fact as a reality of doing business.

"Nothing you say is overly shocking to me, Doctor, and I can't imagine you being unable to deal with the situation accordingly. But there's a big leap between an inconvenient business proposition and covering up a murder."

"That was a development I did not expect either. If the investigator and I had been left to our own devices, none of this would have happened."

I recalled a comment the doctor had made earlier in the conversation. "You mentioned you'd discussed this situation with only two other people. Clearly, the investigator was one. Who was the other?"

Once again the doctor's eyes slid nervously across the room, stopping ever so briefly on the door to the receptionist's area and waiting room.

"The other, I am extremely distressed to say, is Law."

"Law, you say?"

"Yes, Law. Your 'friend.' I'm quite aware of your ongoing 'arrangements' with my receptionist. Though I am not sure if you are aware of Law's similar 'arrangements' with others. Many, many others."

"Doctor, I will thank you not to impugn Law's character in front of me. I am not sure what you are implying, but I *can* tell you that such accusations smack not only of sour grapes, but also perhaps sexual envy."

"I am not impugning anything, Robin. But you wanted to know what has led me to the unenviable position in which I find myself, and I am telling you. Law eavesdropped on several of my negotiating sessions with the investigator and took quite good notes. So, just when I thought I'd worked out a satisfactory arrangement and could close the book on that chapter of my life, I was approached by Law with a similar proposition. In exchange for a greatly increased stipend, Law would keep my secret and not expose my private business dealings to the world at large, including Page Six."

I wish I could say I sat in shock, or horror, or disbelief, but I sat in none of these. For though I have always been inordinately fond of Law, or at least certain parts of that highly sensuous creature, I have long known that Law is a Survivor of the highest order, who is not above using a situation for personal gain. If I were as penurious as Law, I might well have followed a similar course.

"This would certainly explain why I have noticed Law becoming a bit snippy with you in recent weeks," I said, as a synapse fired. For, when one is in the enviable position of blackmailer, can one not be tempted to lord that over the blackmailee, losing any sense of deference and brandishing a bad attitude like a saber?

"Yes, that is an understatement. But I am in the horrible position of being powerless here, Robin. If I am exposed, many of my patients—who rely on me for the utmost discretion—will be thrown to the wolf pack of the media. I saw no choice but to accede to Law's demands. And, as you might guess, putting up with the daily snottiness of a power-mad receptionist is an existentialist punishment that not even the worst sinner deserves."

Another mystery solved, as I considered the extravagant sums Dr. Rosenthal must be lavishing upon Law. These payments would certainly explain the audaciously expensive timepiece and *depeche mode* I'd noticed on Long Island and during my last visit to the doctor's office, as well as the cessation of Law's usual attempts to charm financial support from me.

"There's something I don't understand here, Doctor. Given these new financial arrangements, why would Law continue working here? The freedoms of a guaranteed income are certainly more substantial than the hourly wages of working in an office patronized by neurotics and emotional wrecks."

I watched Dr. R's lips purse in distaste. "There are two likely explanations. The first, which you can surely guess, is psychological in nature. A sociopath like Law takes great pleasure in the current situation, and seeks to keep me in a constant state of submission. Every day I am faced with a new challenge in this regard; and frankly it has begun to take a toll on me. The only way I was able to get Law out of the office now, so that we could have this conversation, was to have"—here Dr. R mentioned the name of an exceedingly well known but psychopathic clothing designer—"call and ask Law to serve as a stand-in fashion model for an important photo shoot, which I can assure you is costing me quite a lot of money."

And this explains why Dr. R has achieved so much prominence in the world of New York psychotherapy. Because appealing to Law's vanity, and using it against that blackmailing demon, was a stroke of psychological genius.

"As far as the second reason goes," Dr. Rosenthal continued, "I can hazard a guess. There are certain benefits to working here, benefits that no ethical psychological professional would ever use to his or her own advantage. I would not be surprised if Law is also blackmailing several of my patients, using information gleaned via eavesdropping during their sessions."

A lightning bolt struck me. Of course an unethical receptionist could do exactly this; for, as I have commented in the past, the walls of Dr. R's office are ridiculously thin, and with the type of wailing and dramatic behavior that occurs in individual therapy sessions, a receptionist with an acute sense of hearing—or an ear to the doorjamb—could certainly become privy to the secrets of New York's Most Important. In fact, I remembered with a start, Law had eavesdropped on at least one of *my* conversations with Dr. Rosenthal! How else could that self-serving individual have known that Dr. R had recommended that I find a new pharmacy to fill one of my recent prescriptions? For Law had been kind enough to hand me the name and address of Town and Country Pharmacy on my way out of Dr. R's office during my last visit, *without Dr. R or myself having mentioned a word of it to Law directly.*

But while this was all somewhat useful information—perhaps I could use it to my own advantage with Law, though I would think more on that possibility later—I seemed to be no closer to receiving enlightenment on the one question to which I most needed an answer.

"I sympathize with your plight, Doctor Rosenthal," I said in a very unsympathetic tone, "but all of this is irrelevant to my line of inquiry. Deal with Law as you will; that is not my concern. But none of what you've said begins to explain why you placed a phone call to Septimus McAllister, requiring his complicity in your deceit regarding Lee's death."

"It has everything to do with it. Law is the person who requested—with the utmost urgency, I might add—that I get Septimus involved."

I drew back in confusion. The many layers of this poisonous cake were beginning to affect me; and while I have always been able to multi-task, to keep all my cognitive processes operating at simultaneous peak efficiency, I could not quite process this latest piece of unexpected data.

"Let me make sure I understand you, Doctor. Are you telling me that Law asked you to call in a favor at the medical examiner's office, to have them cover up the fact that Lee had been murdered?"

"That's exactly what I'm saying."

"But why? Law benefits in no way from Lee's death." I remembered the reading of Lee's will, in which Law had been quite summarily "dissed" and disinherited. Which had not shocked me in the least, for Law and Lee had never been particularly tight, and had never seemed to much enjoy each other's company. I was the connecting link between them; without me, those two rivals for my affections would not have sought each other out. But though there had been no love lost between them, I really could not see Law—a person, really, of the utmost indolence—going to the trouble of murdering Lee in retribution for some real or imagined slight.

"As you can imagine, Robin, Law does not feel any particular compunction to explain the demands now made on me. I must simply do as told, or have my practice and my patients exposed to the harsh light of the media."

"But how would Law know of your ties to Mr. McAllister?"

"I do not widely publicize this fact, but I do lose patients to suicide on an occasional basis. This office works with the Medical Examiner from time to time, and I have worked with Septimus on some cases. I assume that Law eavesdropped on my conversations with Septimus, enough, at least, to intuit that he and I had worked together at the Institute for the Mentally Challenged at"—and here Dr. Rosenthal mentioned the name of an Upper East Side hospital that the Alcohol-Soaked and Drug-Crazed Wealthy visit on occasion to buck up or dry out. "To even a casual observer, it would be clear that Septimus and I were not simply colleagues thrown together by chance, but rather quasi-friends who have known each other for a while."

"What was the exact sequence of events?"

"As you probably know, Law and a group of friends found Lee's cold cadaver after a search-and-recover mission when Lee hadn't returned any phone calls for several days and had even missed an appointment with me. Upon realizing that mortality had indeed descended upon Lee, Law called and rather peremptorily ordered me to join them at Lee's apartment. Law intercepted me at the elevator and made it clear that I was to ask no questions and conduct no investigation, and furthermore that I was to call in favors at the Medical Examiner's office to ensure that the official cause of death was listed as a coronary. Law also made it very clear that if I were to argue in the slightest, my name would be plastered all over the *Observer*, the *Sun,* the *Post,* and the *Clarion* by morning. So I used my cell to call Septimus, told him that a Lee Harris would be shipped there shortly, and that I needed him to conduct the examination and declare the death by heart attack. And there you have it."

Yes, there I had it. It was an explanation, of sorts, but entirely unsatisfactory. It did not tell me why Law had forced the doctor to commit acts of subterfuge with the New York City Medical Examiner's Office; nor did it tell me whether or not Law was Lee's murderer. For Law could have been covering up for someone else, perhaps one of those wealthy patrons to whom Law was indebted—though that explanation did not make sense, either, given Law's newfound source(s) of blackmail income.

Which meant that my investigation was far from complete, and that I might need to confront Law directly. Which would prove quite interesting, for I could only imagine that the possibility of Law's being a murderer would heighten that mysterious creature's mystique in my own mind, which could put me in a very dangerous situation indeed. Fortunately, I have never been one to flee danger. In fact, I embrace it.

37

Philosophers and various academicians sometimes conduct what they call "thought experiments"—purely internal discussions with themselves in which they propose theories, weigh evidence, and seek to develop a consistent, logical system to explain various puzzling phenomena. Economists such as Lord Keynes, a distant relative of mine, were famous for engaging in such mental gymnastics; and such application of the powers of the cerebrum have led to some of the greatest breakthroughs in history—so many, in fact, that it would be impossible to list them all here.

The time had come for me to engage in such a thought experiment. For I had gathered quite a lot of information, bits and pieces of flotsam and jetsam that might somehow reveal a more complete whole if only an incisive intellect might retrieve them from the water and fit them together properly. But before beginning my experiment, I needed to make two calls.

The first was to my new associate "Kevin Jenkins." I asked that always-helpful individual for the name of Pat's practicing physician, and he was able to supply that information in short order, but only in return for a referral that might help move his niece higher up on the list of those ambitious young people trying to secure summer internships at the Foundation.

As it turned out, I had a passing acquaintance with Pat's physician, a certain Dr. Zaditha, who is known as something of a satyr in medical circles. On more than one occasion I had been a most unwilling recipient of Dr. Zaditha's attentions; and I do recall Dr. Z being more tenacious than most, despite my clear lack of interest. As a man he was just not my type, so I did not indulge him; though I suppose I may have toyed with him just a bit, as I am sometimes known to do. Ultimately he'd moved on to seek other conquests—for a man like Dr. Zaditha, the watchword is *quantity*, not *quality*—but I knew that he'd miss no opportunity to recommence his pursuit.

I placed a call to Dr. Z's office and gave my name. Within moments Dr. Z picked up the line.

"Well, if it isn't Robin Anders. I knew you'd call eventually."

"Dr. Zaditha. I hope this is not too much of an intrusion."

"Of course not. You know you are always uppermost in my thoughts."

"Now, now, Doctor. If what I hear is true, you have had many a Robin-substitute in recent months."

"Perhaps, but artificial sweeteners are never as satisfying as real sugar."

Such hideous similes are, I'm afraid, one of the occupational hazards of dealing with Dr. Zaditha, who fancies himself quite the wordsmith. I chuckled lightly, however; for stroking the ego of a man like Dr. Zaditha can have only positive results, especially when one is looking for information.

"Your sweet tooth notwithstanding, Doctor, I wonder if I might ask you a question or two. A patient of yours who recently passed on was an acquaintance of mine. Pat Armstrong."

Dr. Z sighed. "Yes, Pat. An enigmatic and, dare I say, morose individual. Such depth of feeling can be counterproductive."

"My understanding is that Pat had been diagnosed with Parkinson's Disease. Is that correct?"

"Yes, it was a fairly recent diagnosis, as a matter of fact. As I told Pat, many people live many years with the disease; it's a matter of good treatment and developing certain coping skills. But you know Pat was always a bit dystonic. As soon as the diagnosis was delivered, off my patient went to make out a new will, get affairs in order, and so forth. I tried every reassurance trick in my repertoire, laying out a plan of treatment, but I'm afraid the prospect of it was just too much for poor Pat."

"So you thought Pat's suicide was…unnecessary?"

"That is an understatement, dear Robin. Some diagnoses are death sentences, and intense reactions to such news, while perhaps demonstrating infirmity of character, are understandable. But Parkinson's is not this type of diagnosis. I'd told Pat that we'd found the disease early enough to control it, but Pat's usual downtrodden demeanor won out. In fact, I remember Pat saying, 'I've always been free as a bird; I can't stand to have my wings clipped.' While I kept saying the diagnosis was *not* a death sentence, Pat simply would not hear it. This is a problem with doing research on the Internet. Apparently there is an article somewhere in cyberspace stating that people with Parkinson's can take unexpected falls or choke to death, and Pat was terrified of that happening. So by the follow-up visit, my patient was already telling me that a lawyer had been visited, a will had been drawn up, arrangements had been made, and amends for past wrongs were being planned."

I sighed, for as you know I have never had much patience for such dramatic behavior; and I sympathized with the plight of poor Dr. Zaditha, having to deal with the likes of patients like Pat.

"So, Doctor, you think Pat's thoughts were a sort of runaway train that ultimately led to suicide?"

"Well, that seems to be what happened, though I really thought Pat had calmed down. We'd begun a treatment regimen, and Pat was responding well after the initial panic. I'd thought we were out of the woods. But Pat obviously felt differently. I can only assume that some depression issues were involved, as they frequently are; but I will admit that in my experience, Pat's suicide was not typical. In fact, if I'd had to guess, I would have thought Pat would have received a great deal of satisfaction from milking the illness, getting the attention that goes with it, and so forth. But I was clearly wrong. It happens, occasionally."

"Thank you for the information, Doctor. This has been most helpful."

"While I have you on the phone, Robin, I thought I might invite you over for a cocktail one of these nights? Just the two of us...."

"That sounds lovely, Doctor. May I check my schedule and get…" Here I pushed the END button on my cell phone, the better to make it appear as if the call had been dropped inadvertently. For while the reliability of cellular technology is almost nonexistent, I do find that its many drawbacks make the perfect excuse when one wishes to terminate a conversation.

* * *

The conversation with the sexually aggressive Dr. Zaditha out of the way, I was ready to begin my thought experiment. I drew the curtains, lit a few candles I'd purchased from a Zanzibarian native I'd met under circumstances that need not be gone into here, and unlocked the top drawer of my heirloom rolltop desk, in which I keep a special inlaid box, a priceless item once owned by Queen Victoria and given as a gift to one of her ladies in waiting, my Great Aunt Phyllida. In this box I keep my highly limited supply of a special substance much prized by Native Americans for its ability to kick open the doors of perception and expand the consciousness. I use this supply exceedingly rarely, for the addictive properties of the stuff are well documented; in addition, it is extremely hard to come by, requiring more than the usual number of phone calls and some quite unsavory contacts whom one would normally eschew. But the mysterious matters of Pat, Lee, *et alia* were proving to be opaque in the extreme, and, while the 'apricot,' 'banana,' 'asparagus,' and other pills had served me well to a certain point, they had clearly reached the limits of their effectiveness.

I poured myself a glass of my favorite white, donned the silk robe that had been a gift from the Emperor of Japan to my paternal grandfather, and swallowed the tiny capsule that promised so much insight. I then put on a recording of the London Symphony Orchestra's early twentieth century recording of Ravel's *Bolero*, which has always succeeded in putting me into a hypnotic trance.

Sitting in my favorite chair and closing my eyes, I began to make a mental list of the inexplicable events to be explained.

1. Pat is dead. Could Pat have been murdered, despite Septimus McAllister's assurances to the contrary? If so, why and by whom?

2. Lee is murdered. Why, and by whom?

3. Pat's apartment is broken into and "tossed," quite clearly after the police have closed their all-too-brief investigation. Lee's apartment is also visited by person or persons unknown, who steal not Lee's cheap jewelry or other minor valuables, but rather a bunch of toiletries and other bathroom products.

4. Lee's belongings are removed from the safety deposit box by Alex.

5. Chris and J's apartment is broken into by someone who gains access through the fire escape.

6. Both Alex and I receive fraudulent invitations from the other to a lunch at the Empire State Building.

7. A person who resembles Alex is assaulted, and nearly killed, on the Observation Deck.

8. While Alex and I are off on our wild goose chase, my apartment is burgled, and the thieves make off with a box containing photos of the young Lee and Pat, as well as the adoption papers for Baby Jody and some inconsequential baubles.

9. Junior Makeba, who helped Pat discover the provenance and whereabouts of Baby Jody, is murdered in his apartment, sometime before I arrive.

10. Law, the most understated of our group, is blackmailing not only Dr. Rosenthal but perhaps also many others.

11. And last, but far from least, the tortoise shell hairbrush that is rightfully mine appears to be completely lost.

All of these circumstances *could* be unrelated; but they seemed to have happened too close together for all this to be coincidence. So how might these myriad mysteries be linked to unravel the shadowy motives of Lee's killer?

I felt my heartbeat accelerate ever so slightly as the Native American mind-opener began to work each point on my list.

First there was Pat, who'd received a diagnosis of non-fatal Parkinson's Disease and embarked on a search for a long-lost child. Pat's money had to be the logical motive for murder—if indeed a murder, rather than a suicide, had been committed. Because the sole beneficiary of Pat's will was Alex, it made sense that Alex would have to be the murderer, not only of Pat, but also of Lee. Oh, Alex, like a character in a Classical Greek drama committing the double sins of matricide and fratricide!

Suppose Alex *was* the murderer. Why would someone then make an attempt on the heir's life? Law's report regarding what had supposedly happened on the Empire State Building obviously could not be trusted. Whose goal had been to stab Alex on the Observation Deck, and for what reason? Who would benefit from Alex's death?

And why get me involved? Was I solely a decoy used to lure Alex to a desirable place for murder? But no—clearly someone had wanted me to be away from my home for a significant amount of time, so that it might be searched and burgled. Two birds were being killed with one stone, here: the burglary of my apartment and the attempt on Alex's life.

Would this not argue for two people working together in some sort of fiendish plot?

My eyes, made small by the incantatory effects of the consciousness expander, suddenly became wide. For right before my very eyes, right within my Inner Circle, was a monstrously inseparable duo, a two-headed beast joined at the hips, never seen or heard apart from each other. Two people who lived together, separated only when the requirements of business forced them to be apart, during which they of course kept in constant touch via cell phones and text messages.

J and Chris.

Always the more vigorous of the two, Chris could have dressed in black and made the attempt on Alex's life on the Observation Deck while J, the infinitely sneakier, could have found a way to sneak into my apartment and to remove (a) the incriminating evidence of the phony invitation to the Empire State, which I'd believed to have been written by Alex but which clearly had been written by somebody else, and (b) that green metal box I'd liberated from the storage cage in Pat's apartment building.

But why would J and Chris want to destroy any evidence of Alex's familial relationship with Pat and Lee? Were they planning to somehow steal Pat's fortune from Alex, perhaps by dispatching Alex at 86 stories above the ground? But how could they guarantee that Lee and Pat's money would pass from Alex to them?

And what of their own apartment being broken into, their meager and cheap possessions being "stolen" while they were out and about? The whole burglary could have been a set-up, a complete and utter fraud, the better for the two of them to play the victims and the better for Chris to meet eligible police officers with whom to engage in sexual excess. This could also explain why no locks had been broken or doors been smashed during the supposed "break-in."

The larcenous couple could also have double-teamed to mastermind break-ins at the apartments of the recently deceased Pat and Lee. And had they been involved somehow in the death of Junior Makeba? What could Junior have learned that would be such a threat to J and Chris's nefarious plots, the motivations for which remained perplexing?

Stumbling to my chair and grabbing my fountain pen, I furiously scribbled down all these epiphanies so that I might act upon them when released from my trancelike state of advanced insight. When I awoke the next morning, however, I found nothing but well-crafted poetic couplets where my investigative insights were supposed to have been. I suppose I had been visited somehow by the spirit of Samuel Taylor Coleridge, a distant cousin of mine who'd often experienced inspiration of the most delicious variety while indulging in various intoxicants.

I should have had more faith in myself, of course. Such important insights as I'd gained could be counted on to remain in one's mind, and while performing my morning ablutions, all my conclusions came flooding back to me. Which led me to ask myself what my next steps should be; but all that could wait, as the manicurist was due any minute, and certainly J and Chris would still be felons, and still at large, later that afternoon, after my physical needs had been tended to.

38

The great scientific minds have written about their moments of insight, those *eureka*! experiences that led them to the discoveries so important to the progress of mankind. Unfortunately, the scientific method available to my comrades in genius was not quite applicable to my situation. For in scientific experimentation, the environment is controlled to isolate the effects of this or that variable; but dealing with human nature, and all its attendant lies and deceptions, makes for much messier experimental design.

A plan of attack was needed, but I was feeling a bit at sixes and sevens, as the many loose ends of the case were swirling about in my head like the arms of a particularly unruly octopus. As luck would have it, however, I did have a small supply of 'broccoli pills' in my medicine cabinet; these I save for those rare occasions when I am unable to focus my thoughts in their usual laser-like fashion. An hour later, the pills had kicked in and I began a concerted effort to harness my creativity.

First, it seemed clear that Alex's life was in danger, that the diabolical dyad was plotting Alex's death for reasons I had not yet uncovered. Now, Alex has never been a particular favorite of mine, for reasons that I am sure have become obvious in the course of this narrative; but the fact remained that I preferred Alex alive rather than dead. Despite any feelings of rancor I might have felt for that lustful and greedy creature, the fact remained that Alex was the offspring of the person to whom I'd had the strongest of lifetime bonds, Lee's many infidelities, thefts, and deceptions notwithstanding.

Thus the most pressing point of triage at this point had to be preserving Alex's life against any imminent threats. I picked up the phone and dialed Alex's home number, which was answered after three rings by (of course) the answering machine. I hung up and placed a call to Alex's cell, which, for reasons I have elucidated previously with respect to the average Manhattanite's desire to feel exceedingly popular and in demand, would most likely be answered. But here, too, I encountered voice mail.

This worried me in the extreme. As we all know, there is no place in this City that is considered inappropriate for responding to the piercing tones of a ringing cell phone; people of my acquaintance take them everywhere, keeping them to hand even while they are showering, defecating, or making love. I supposed Alex could have been "screening" my call, though that was highly unlikely, as a call from me was rare enough to warrant immediate attention.

The situation seemed frightening enough that I overcame my loathing of voice processing technology to comply with the demand to "leave a message at the beep."

"Alex, I say, this is Robin calling. Without going into a lot of detail, I am concerned for your well-being. Some information has come to light that makes me believe you may be at risk, for something other than the usual sexually transmitted diseases. Please ring me back as soon as you can. This really is quite an emergency."

Concern for Alex's continued existence created a level of anxiety I had not quite expected, and I found myself pacing the apartment, trying to keep my mind occupied by hand-dusting some ancient Egyptian figurines a great uncle of mine had managed to remove from the Valley of the Kings on a dig there back in '18. As the hours passed, I grew ever more nervous, and while a dose of the 'kiwi pills' kept me functional, I was unable to completely repress horrific images of Alex soon joining Pat and Lee in the family plot.

Finally, I could take the stress no longer. I took ninety hurried minutes to get myself dressed, properly coiffed, and armed, then fled my building in search of a taxi. A leering Middle Eastern cabbie stopped to pick me up—why, oh why, could I never escape these swarthy and sensual types, who seem to seek me out, undressing me with their eyes as they eat their halal food?—and I barked out Alex's address. For perhaps Alex was already lying dead in bed. Until recently I would not have suspected that one could so easily be murdered in one's own home, but the deaths of Lee and Pat had quite effectively proven otherwise; and I was reminded of even my accidental mishaps on Long Island, what with the chandelier, the croquet situation, the Saab, the peacocks, and the asp.

Upon arriving at Alex's building—a hideous brick affair that, according to the current grapevine, Alex was planning to leave for much more exclusive digs, funded by Pat's accumulated wealth—I asked the doorman to buzz Alex's apartment. There was no response, and the doorman attempted to deny me access; but I innocently maintained that Alex was expecting me and was most likely in the shower, and I was waved through to the elevator.

When my knock at Alex's door went unanswered, I fell back on Plan B. I pulled from my pocket that large, clanking ring of Lee's keys that I'd secretly had duplicated all those years ago and began trying them one by one. Though Lee had always denied the *liaison* with Alex that friends had long suspected—and one really could not now dwell on the Freudian aspects of that—their behavior on Long Island had been exceedingly suspicious; and if you will recall, I had assumed right from the beginning that Lee was using the weekend getaway as an excuse to flee Pat's demands and to engage in a lighthearted affair with Alex.

All of this hinted that, due to Lee's fondness for collecting the apartment keys of various lovers and friends, the mystery keychain might hold a key to Alex's apartment as well. For who knew how long, exactly, the two of them had been carrying on? Sure enough, the twelfth key that I tried fit snugly into the lock. As I turned it, I heard the telltale click of tumblers letting go, and with a turn of the knob I was in Alex's unkempt home.

It seemed as if the rumors regarding the purchase of a more upscale piece of property in an infinitely better neighborhood were true. The floor was littered with boxes, labeled "DVDs," "CDs," "Sportswear," and the like. The walls showed rectangles of cleanliness from which inexpensively framed prints had been removed, and a large plastic bag in the center of the living room floor held the usual detritus of which one rids oneself when moving from place to place—toenail clippings, almost-empty bottles of personal lubricant, recipes that one has clipped but never cooked, mysterious and ancient plastic containers found somewhere in the refrigerator, and so on.

"Alex, are you here? Alex, it is I. Robin."

With clenched jaw and great trepidation, I pushed open the door to Alex's tiny bedroom, half expecting to find my friend sprawled out in a manner similar to Junior Makeba. But my eyes were spared such a sight; the bedroom, like the living room, kitchen, and bathroom, were unoccupied by all but moving boxes and general chaos.

Well, here was some good news at least. Alex was not dead. At least not yet, or at least not at home.

Out of the corner of my eye, I spied a stack of boxes leaning precariously, as if the slightest movement would spill their contents. These boxes, labeled "Photos," "Magazines," "Tchotchkes," and "Misc," might hold interesting treasures; or, at the very least, provide additional insight into Alex's character.

Removing the top box from the pile, I brought it to the bed and pulled open the flaps. Inside were half a dozen yellowed photo albums, as well as some of those smaller, floral photo holders that residents of public housing purchase for 99 cents at the local Duane Reade.

I pulled the top photo album from the pile and began flipping through. These were exactly the types of photos one would expect to see: old Kodachromes of a youngish and not very attractive couple at the seaside, standing in front of an old car, sitting on the steps of a small Cape Cod-style home in a place that could only have been Levittown, Long Island. The photos seemed to have a late 1970s/early 1980s feel to them, and indeed, some of them had small explanatory cards inserted near the photos: POINT LOOKOUT, June 1978. JERSEY SHORE, October 1979.

These had to be Manfred and Emily Mann, adoptive parents of Alex.

As I turned the pages, I had a surprise. A fairly thin woman in March of 1980, Emily Mann was quite rotundly pregnant by October of that same year. Manfred seemed to have captured his wife's growing belly at every stage of the process, culminating in a portrait labeled AND BABY MAKES 3, DECEMBER 14, 1980, in which the beaming Emily and Manfred are seen holding their precious bundle of joy.

Subsequent albums charted the progress of baby Alex from infant to toddler to pre-schooler, showing the youngest Mann resembling Manfred more and more with each passing day. Whether this resemblance was fortunate or not, I leave to more artistic minds to judge.

By the time I turned the final page of the album, I needed no further convincing that there was no way on earth that Alex could have been adopted from that Upstate orphanage.

I pulled some of the smaller Duane Reade photo books from the box and began flipping through them. These provided fewer surprises. There were photos of our group, along with photos of various other transient friends who'd passed into and out of Alex's life over the years, as is the norm with those who are single in Manhattan.

The smallest of the photo albums was filled with photos of Alex and Lee in all manner of diversion, arms around each other, playing checkers, lying on a couch in some unknown locale, legs casually intermingled. The date imprint on the photos corresponded more or less to the time during which speculation had been rampant that the two were engaged in some sort of thing. And here was the final proof.

I looked at my timepiece. I'd been sifting through Alex's personal effects for nearly fifteen minutes, and while I was sure I could explain my presence if Alex were to arrive home, my recent discoveries had made me significantly less willing to be found out; for what if Alex were, like Lord Byron, mad, bad, and dangerous to know?

I packed up the box to the best of my ability, attempting to remember the order in which the albums had been stored. The box on which the "Photos" box had been stacked was labeled "Magazines." Before I replaced the photo albums on top of it, I thought it could not hurt to have a quick look at Alex's choice of recent reading materials. I flipped open the box to find the usual type of magazine favored by the young, single, and libidinous: all manner of magazine with many more photos than words, much more flesh than editorial content. Really, I'd known that Alex had an adventurous side in terms of physical activities—and who doesn't, in his or her own heart of hearts?—but I'd no idea regarding the wide extent of what Alex found attractive. Magazines devoted exclusively to the male form were intermingled with those devoted exclusively to the female form, answering once and for all some questions I'd always entertained regarding Alex's sexuality.

And let it not be said that Alex's tastes and preferences were anything but catholic. Some of the magazines featured models of Asian heritage, while others laid bare some very dark-skinned African natives. Where had I seen such magazines before? Yes, I remembered—at the home of Junior Makeba in Washington Heights.

I flipped through one of the African magazines, averting my eyes a bit, as it is always somewhat painful to see the female form so exploited. Toward the end of the magazine, a napkin fell out of the back pages. I retrieved this from the floor and turned it over to see a yellow, green, and black logo for SONNY'S JAMAICAN JERK CHICKEN.

Where had I seen this logo before?

In the same neighborhood where Junior Makeba had lived.

Until he'd been murdered by Alex Mann.

I quickly packed up the magazine box—except for that particular issue of *Nubian Delights* and its damning napkin—stacked the box of photos on top of it, and ran out of Alex's murderous apartment as quickly as my legs would carry me. Fortunately, I have always been as swift of foot as I am of mind.

39

Back at my blissfully quiet apartment, I poured myself a glass of eighty-five-year-old scotch. I have never been one to indulge in intoxicants, but Father always said that nothing clears the mind like a good stiff drink. And indeed, as the first sip of that charcoal-like *aqua regia* burned down my throat, I felt myself relax enough to ruminate on the various inconsistencies and puzzles under consideration.

The problem with my investigation thus far, I decided, had been my piecemeal attempts to make sense of the situation. I'd succeeded in discovering interesting tidbits here and there, but clearly there was a larger *gestalt* at work; and only by fitting all the pieces into one consistent whole would I be able discover who, ultimately, had killed whom, and why.

The best way to proceed, I concluded, was to write down the unassailable facts, on a person-by-person basis, solidifying my queries as I went along.

ALEX

*Alex had inherited all of Pat and Lee's money by posing as their heir. But Alex was not Pat and Lee's love child. Rather, Alex Mann had been born with that name, to two rather nondescript parents, on Long Island.

Pat had hired Junior Makeba to find the long-lost child. Clearly, Junior had found baby Jody somewhere—and Alex somehow knew this. To make sure that Junior told no one else the baby's identity or whereabouts, Alex had gone on a murderous junket to Washington Heights to dispatch the unfortunate Mr. Makeba, eating Jamaican jerk chicken for lunch and picking up a few pornographic souvenirs during the process.

QUESTION #1: If Alex was not baby Jody, then who was?

PAT

*Junior Makeba had discovered the whereabouts of baby Jody, and he must have delivered this information to Pat, who'd recently been diagnosed with a disturbing but not highly terrible case of Parkinson's.

The murderer, or murderers, would have plotted Pat's death, forging not only the suicide note to Dr. Rosenthal but also the letter to Lee identifying Alex as their love child.

QUESTION #2: Did this mean that Alex had killed three people: Junior, Pat, and Lee? Such a conclusion was logical, given Alex's intense greed and burning desire to receive dual inheritances sooner rather than later. BUT...

J AND CHRIS

*While one of these codependents had attempted to stab Alex on the Empire State Building, the other had been burgling my apartment.

QUESTION #3: Why would these two have attempted to kill Alex, and why would they want the contents of Pat's green metallic box?

LAW

*Like a moth fluttering around a lightbulb, Law seemed to be flitting around these events while ostensibly taking part in none of them. But Law had blackmailed Dr. Rosenthal into having Septimus McAllister cite a heart attack as the cause of Lee's death, rather than murder.

QUESTION #4: How did Law fit into all these events? Was Law involved in Pat's death as well as Lee's? How would Law profit from the situation?

I believed I saw a pattern forming. And the longer I pondered the shapes of the pieces composing that pattern, the more perfectly they seemed to fit together.

My mind flashed to my memories of Lee, all frowzy red hair and chunky physicality, as well as to the photos of Pat I'd seen strewn about the apartment floor, after I'd gained access and found that some villain or villains had been there before me, ripping the place apart. Pat had been unremarkable looking, but I did recall the photos of Pat and Lee side by side, Pat's green eyes and pale flaxen head next to Lee's raging red hair and crazed hazel eyes.

How could anyone have believed that Alex—brown-sloe-eyed, wispy, lanky, brunette-turned-prematurely gray Alex—could be the result of Pat and Lee's commingling? Alex looked nothing like either of them. But someone in our circle did share Lee's blocky build, Pat's fair coloring, and the green eyes of both parents.

J.

J, whose true hair color—which no one had ever seen—might match the red of Lee's head or the yellow of Pat's. J, whose real name I'd never bothered to ask, as I really had not cared all that much. Until now. For couldn't "J" be a truncation of "Jody"?

There was an easy way to find out. I picked up the phone and called one of my contacts from the Foundation, asking her to please find out the names of the leaseholders on Chris and J's apartment. Such records are easy to locate, what with the Internet and all, and I waited patiently for a call back, as I didn't wish to go too far down this road of speculation until I had the facts. In less than an hour I had a call back from my colleague, informing me that the lease had two names on it: Chris Blackheart and Jody Crewe.

I sat back and closed my eyes, not only congratulating myself on my perspicacity but also feeling moderately overwhelmed by all the new possibilities opened up by this latest morsel of information. Suddenly, many of the unexplainable scenarios became much more explicable.

J's position as rightful heir would explain why Chris and

J had made the attempt on Alex's life. Alex had killed Junior to prevent him from divulging the name of Pat and Lee's child, but somehow J and Chris had discovered what Alex had been up to. As the true progeny of Lee and Pat's loins, J/Jody would certainly be next in the inheritance line, especially after J's provenance had been proven. Eliminating Alex—who had no apparent heirs—could only cause Pat's riches to revert to J.

And how could J prove any claim to be the child of Lee and Pat? Well, certainly there would be the adoption papers, which might be traced with some effort; for surely if Junior Makeba had succeeded in doing so, so could Chris and J. But a court of law might want further evidence, easily provided by modern biotechnology. For a bit of DNA from J's living body could easily be matched with Lee and Pat's DNA to prove the genetic link.

I bolted upright from my chair. For not only did this theory explain why J had broken into my apartment to steal Pat's green metallic box—which contained information about the birth and adoption—it also explained the whereabouts of the tortoise shell hairbrush I had been seeking since the beginning of my investigation. When I'd visited Lee's apartment after receiving the awful news, I'd been puzzled by the fact that Lee's bathrooms had been completely cleaned out of all personal effects, including my hairbrush. And now I realized why: that hairbrush would surely contains strands of Lee's coarse, frizzy hair, from which DNA samples might be extracted. The same was true of Pat's apartment, which had been "tossed" rather mercilessly in a crazed attempt to find personal items that could be used as sources of Pat's DNA, the better to establish the genetic link with J—all without exhuming any bodies, which might have caused the authorities to begin making uncomfortable inquiries.

But all of this begged a very important question. How would J know in the first place that a guilt-ridden parent had begun the process of searching for a long-lost child? This seemed to be a secret that Pat had guarded quite closely, confiding in few people about the guilt and sorrow of giving up that child so many years earlier. Even Lee, the other parent, hadn't seemed to know much about the search. Or could this have been the source of Lee's upset upon arriving at my house on Long Island all those weeks ago? Lee had alluded to an unpleasant "something" with Pat, but, in typical fashion, had refused to go into details. Could Pat have confided in Lee that a private investigator had been hired to search for the child's whereabouts? Certainly such a conversation would have upset *me*; I could only imagine what it would have done to the psyche of Lee, who was always much more susceptible to an onset of nerves than I.

Had Lee known of J's true identity prior to that weekend on Long Island? If so, had Lee shared that knowledge with J during our vacation weekend? And might Lee have also confided in Alex during the same trip, providing that paramour with all the details of the long-ago tryst with Pat and the ramifications of their lust thirty years later? Ever an opportunist, Alex might have begun plotting the deaths of Pat and Lee at that very moment.

But if Lee had confided in J on Long Island, why hadn't J come forward immediately to declare Alex a fake? Why, instead, would J and Chris go to such lengths to search Lee and Pat's respective apartments for DNA evidence, and then to make an attempt on Alex's life on the Observation Deck?

And yet none of these questions even began to address the role of Law in all these goings-on—Law, in whose flickering presence I perpetually found myself: on Long Island, in Dr. Rosenthal's office, at the reading of the will, everywhere. Nor did they bring me any closer to the reason why Law would blackmail poor Dr. Rosenthal into helping cover up Lee's murder.

But I was beginning to formulate a theory about that, too.

40

A brief *tête-à-tête* with Law was going to be necessary at some point, and I decided not to postpone the inevitable. Thus I picked up my phone and punched in Law's number, only to encounter Law's slightly breathy voice mail greeting simultaneously titillating me and encouraging me to leave a message. I requested an audience with all the humility I was able to muster, suggesting that the matter was somewhat urgent and asking for a prompt response.

To my surprise, the call was returned only a few minutes later.

"Robin, you'll forgive me for not answering your call, I hope? Doctor Rosenthal has been simply unbearable about allowing me to take 'personal' calls at the office, which has necessitated switching the phone over to that atrocious vibrating mode. As a result, calls are sometimes missed."

Now, of course I knew that Dr. Rosenthal would not have dared impose any such condition on Law, who very much had the upper hand in that relationship at this juncture. However, I decided to simply play along.

"Dear Law, I understand completely. The good doctor, while a very competent therapist, can sometimes be a bit inflexible and unreasonable. As I have long said, the flexible person is the happy person; but Dr. R does not always seem to take my words to heart, or put them into practice."

Law clucked in agreement, and I got to the matter at hand.

"Say, Law, I hope this will not be too much of an imposition, but I'm hoping to have a brief discussion with you regarding some matters I don't feel quite comfortable discussing on the phone." In the past, this phraseology has been a euphemism for my request for certain types of favors that Law bestows in a very satisfactory but not inexpensive manner, so I hastened to elaborate. "What I mean is that I have an issue or two that I cannot discuss with Doctor Rosenthal, but that I believe you will have some insight into. Is it possible for us to meet sometime this evening for an hour or so?"

The question was, of course, whether Law would toy with me—and if so, for how long—or accede to my request with alacrity. In the past, the answer would have been dictated by the state of Law's finances at the moment; however, I thought it a safe bet that Law's newfound arrangement with Dr. Rosenthal—and, perhaps, with the doctor's Park Avenue clientele—rendered Law rather financially independent.

"Your timing is actually quite fortuitous, Robin. I'm planning to work late this evening and wouldn't mind a stroll and a chat afterwards. Would you be able to stop by the office sometime around, say, 9 p.m.?"

Several alarm bells went off in my head. For everyone knows that Law, always averse to work in any form, certainly would never voluntarily "work late," especially now that substantial income was being earned via blackmailing activities. In addition, the very thought of a stroll was usually anathema to Law, who has been known to take a taxicab for a three-block journey rather than walk the grimy streets of Manhattan, which might soil one's clothes or negatively affect one's coif.

Though perhaps there was an easy explanation. It certainly seemed possible that Law had taken to staying in the office late to dig through Dr. Rosenthal's files, the better to find new sources of blackmailing income. But no matter; I readily agreed to meet Law at Dr. Rosenthal's office at the appointed time and rang off, delighted that I might soon have the answers to all my questions, after receiving which I could recommence living a somewhat normal life.

* * *

In the meantime, though, quite a number of questions remained, and I thought it might be helpful to arrive to my chat with Law armed with some additional answers. So once again I picked up that instrument of the Devil and placed a call to my new friend "Kevin Jenkins."

The attorney's delight upon hearing from me was all too obvious, and I wondered if I would have to fend off yet another series of unwanted advances from yet another unwanted suitor. For, as delightful as the man was, and as helpful as he'd been, I really could not see myself dallying with him, for reasons too numerous to go into here; suffice it to say that we are of different backgrounds and move in different circles, which could lead only to misunderstandings and hurt feelings over the longer run, no matter how interesting and fulfilling the physical side of our relationship might be.

I have never been one to amass large numbers of photographs, as I find they tend to reek of both self-love and insecurity. There are those who feel a sense of personal validation by seeing photographs of themselves, arm in arm or hand in hand with friends and loved ones, the better to prove to oneself that one is socially attractive, worthy of love, *et cetera*. In addition, the vast majority of photographs have always struck me as simply too unnatural—with posed photographs appearing artificial and stiff, and the so-called "candid shots" all too frequently displaying flaws in hair, teeth, or physique, and rarely showing the subjects in a manner presentable to future generations.

Nonetheless, photos have been pressed upon me by various friends and colleagues over the years, and these I keep in a small, tasteful tin box in a closet, not unlike the picture of Dorian Gray, away from prying eyes who might use them as evidence to document the disturbing effects of the aging process. In the box I was able to find photos of various members of my circle, either individual portraits of the type sent to casting directors or in group shots. Included among the photos were several of Lee in younger days, looking porcine yet alluring and—I was shocked to notice—quite a bit like poor J, who seemed to have inherited most of the unflattering aspects of both parents. A shot of Lee and myself, taken at the house on Long Island more than two decades earlier, showed us in one of our more agreeable moments, both of us smiling impishly at the camera, full of the energy and enthusiasm that go with youth.

The pain my heart felt was quite real, and I found myself welling up unexpectedly. It was only by running to the bathroom cabinet and retrieving a healthy dose of the 'orange pills' that I was able to restore my equilibrium. For this was no time to engage in maudlin flights of sentimentality. Like the Romantic poets, I could experience that spontaneous overflow of emotion later, and then reflect upon it in tranquility. For now, though, there were appointments to be kept.

"Kevin Jenkins" was as welcoming as ever, inviting me to sit and expressing his delight at seeing me again. Underhanded and self-serving though he might be, I had to admit there was something alluring about the man. Perhaps it was his self-confidence, or the way he filled out his suit. Or, perhaps, it was the portrait of himself with his wife and two broad-faced children that attracted my interest. For, as I always admit, Robin Anders does enjoy a challenge.

"Kevin, I realize I am taking a bit too much of your time these days, but I wonder if you might aid me once again?"

"Robin, I have enjoyed trading favors with you so far. Very mutually beneficial. And I hope we'll continue trading favors long into the future."

Was this last statement made with a *soupçon* of flirtation? I could not help but think it was, and my pulse quickened just a little, as it often does when the game has begun.

"What I'm wondering, Kevin, is if you recommended the services of Junior Makeba to other clients besides Pat?"

"It's sad about Junior. You've heard?"

I nodded. "Yes. Very tragic indeed."

"Junior may have flown just under the line of legality sometimes, but he wouldn't have hurt a fly. But in his business you get mixed up with some rough people. I have an office and a suit and tie to protect me from the lowlifes. He dealt with them directly."

Again I nodded and tried to bring Kevin back to my original question. "But did you use his services regularly? Did you often recommend him to your clients?"

"Well, I wouldn't say I used him *regularly*, but I did sometimes. He was good for missing-persons-type stuff and for catching cheating husbands. For a while we did quite a bit of that—he'd find them cheating, and I'd draw up the divorce papers and get a big settlement for the wife. But those are cases for a younger man. I like wills a lot better now. Less drama, less aggravation. Usually."

"I'm wondering—if I showed you some photographs, would you be able to tell me if you recommended Junior to any of them?"

"I could try. I mean, I've had a lot of clients over the years. My memory's good, but it's far from perfect."

"This would have been fairly recently, say within the last month or so."

"That should make it easier. Let's give it a try." He sat next to me on his office couch—perhaps a bit too closely, it might be argued, which I found a bit of a distraction at a time when intense focus would have been preferable.

First I showed him a head shot of J, which had been taken in those days when J was attempting a more legitimate career on the stage. Kevin shook his head: "Doesn't ring a bell." I followed this with a similar head shot of Chris; again no recognition. Ditto for Law and Lee. I then pulled a picture of Alex from the envelope, at which Kevin narrowed his eyes.

"Hmmm, that face is familiar." He took the photo from me and examined it more closely. "Yes. Definitely. And I remember. A friend of Pat's, yes?"

"Yes. Please go on."

"I can't remember the name—Al, maybe? An androgynous name, I seem to recall. Only came in once, using Pat's name as a referral. Said that before dying, Pat had mentioned how a P.I. that I'd recommended had helped find a long-lost child. Al—or whoever—was looking for a long-lost brother, or sister, and thought the P.I. might be able to help. So I recommended Junior."

And what more evidence did I need that Alex was Junior's murderer? But how did that homicidal individual know about Pat's investigation? In fact, how did Alex even know about *Pat* or Pat's existence? Certainly not from me, and certainly not from J, the rightful heir. Not from Law, who was too busy blackmailing Dr. R; and not from Chris, who would greatly benefit from J's newfound wealth as Pat's legal heir.

That left only one avenue of communication: Lee.
And suddenly it all made sense.

41

L et me go on record as saying that I take no pleasure in
unraveling the misfortunes of others or immersing myself
in their sordid lives. *Schadenfreude* is not a vice to which I have
ever been susceptible, as it is the province of small, petty minds
whose guts twist with envy, jealousy, and other base emotions.

However, there is a certain intellectual joy that goes with
solving an extremely intricate puzzle, and I will admit to a
purely academic sense of satisfaction regarding the conclusions I had drawn as a result of my investigation. I imagine
Watson and Crick felt a similar smugness upon discovering
the double helix of the DNA molecule, and Einstein feeling a
similar delighted exhaustion after hitting upon that simple
yet enlightening equation $E = mc^2$.

For one thing is clear: This case certainly would have baf-
fled, and perhaps even defeated, the greats. Jane Marple would
likely have thrown her arms up in defeat, and Nero Wolfe
would have found his bluster to be quite a disadvantage in
the subtle lines of inquiry required to "crack" such a case. Lord
Peter Wimsey, satyr that he was, would have been too busy
fending off the advances of Harriet Vane to pay much attention to the subtleties of the plot; and that insufferable Hilary
Tamar would have been too focused on the legal intricacies to
see the bigger picture. Perhaps Hercule Poirot, fresh off the
Orient Express, *might* have been perspicacious enough to determine that the deaths of Lee and Pat were not simply two mur-

ders, but rather the effects of an intricate web of crimes, lies, and betrayals—but I really do not like to compare myself to M. Poirot, for reasons that should be obvious.

But let me not get ahead of myself. At present I needed one or two final details clarified; and I was sure that all would be illuminated following my meeting with Law. In the meantime, though, I had to admit to my own *naïveté* with regard to that particular character. For I believe I have been completely honest in admitting over the course of this narrative that my heart has always had rather a soft spot for that sensuous but (as recently revealed) nefarious individual. For too long I had thought of Law as a sybarite of the highest order, a languid individual who relied on God-given physical attributes to ensure a life of leisure and comfort. But recent events had shown Law in a less than flattering light, and for this reason, it behooved me to take precautions. For years I had underestimated Law, as had others. This had ultimately led to their undoing, and I did not wish it to lead to mine.

Fortunately, I had recently acquired a rather potent item of self-defense—the compact Saturday Night Special for which I'd ventured into Brooklyn and consorted with that red-tape-cutting arms dealer. The firearm might prove handy at Dr. Rosenthal's office if the situation got out of hand.

From an upper shelf in my parlor, I retrieved the 12th century Chinese box in which I had stored the handgun and the additional ammunition I'd purchased at what I assume was a highly inflated price. The man at the pistol range—what was his name? Jürgen; yes, that was it—had shown me how to load the ammo, and had admonished me to make sure the firearm was always loaded, as one never knew when a miscreant would break into one's home while one was snuggled in bed; and one did not want to be caught with an unloaded gun when it came time to shoot the intruder dead.

So I proceeded to open the chamber, which was three bullets short of a full ammunition load, perhaps the result of forgetting to reload after target practice. Adding the bullets should have been an easy matter, but the plastic box in which they were stored proved exceedingly difficult to open, as it contained many rough edges that would have wreaked havoc with my manicure. Insult was added to injury when I did finally manage to use my right elbow to slide the box top open, only to have the box slide crazily off the table and pour its contents all over my parlor floor in a cacophonous racket.

This was annoying in the extreme, but one could not leave a floorful of bullets for the cleaning lady to pick up, as questions were bound to arise. So I found myself in the most indecorous position of kneeling on the floor and picking up the bullets one at a time, retrieving them from the far corners of the room, into which they'd spread like so many illegal immigrants who enter the country and then scatter in all directions to prevent their capture and repatriation.

As I reached under the couch in search of errant bullets, my hand happened upon a smooth round object. Curious, I pulled the item out for a closer inspection. It was a bauble of some sort, certainly not of a texture or design that I would have acquired or inherited. But I knew I had seen it before— and it took only a few minutes of intense thought (aided by the 'plum pills')—to remember where. The bauble was the peridot that had adorned the pendant in the tin box I'd retrieved from Pat's storage cage.

But the tin box had been stolen from my apartment during the break-in. So how could the peridot have found its way to the floor beneath my couch? Why would the thief—in other words, J—have removed the bauble from the box and placed it under the couch? Or would J have been rooting about in the box while in my home, not realizing that the bauble had dropped to the floor and rolled away?

Clearly this chunk of peridot was of some significance, and I tried to remember the other contexts in which I'd seen that less-than-precious stone. And suddenly it came to me. I retrieved the photos I'd brought to the office of "Kevin Jenkins" and closely examined each of the portraits.

And there it was, in not one but two of the photographs. It dangled from J's neck in a headshot, catching the light in a way that was surely added by a retoucher during the photographic production process. But there it was, too, around Lee's neck in the photo of the two of us from twenty years earlier.

That made three baubles—one for Lee, one for Pat, and one for Baby Jody, a touching if tacky physical reminder of their familial bond.

And also an explanation for the break-in at Chris and J's apartment.

42

Olympic athletes are well known for the mental and physical preparations they undergo, as well as the personal rituals in which they engage, prior to competition. For it cannot be denied that in an arena of equals, preparation is essential to successful execution. Now, certainly it is not appropriate to suggest that Law was my equal; and yet Law had proven to be a person of more ingenuity than I had expected. Thus I took several hours not only to ensure that I would look my best for the encounter at Dr. Rosenthal's office but also to ensure that I was able to lay out my case to Law in the most brilliant, flawless manner possible.

As I believe I have mentioned, in their eternal quest for the proper image, Manhattanites make it a point to be late to every appointment, believing that such a lack of punctuality makes them appear busy, important, socially desirable, or some combination of the three. Yet too strong an adherence to such a policy can backfire; and the young rarely take the time to consider the benefits of arriving early. Of course, such a daring social stunt requires the greatest of finesse; and perhaps it will not surprise you to know that I perfected the art of the early arrival several decades ago, though I have used it sparingly, as its effects can be quite diluted if the technique is implemented too often.

In this case, I felt that I might greatly benefit from the element of surprise in my appointment with Law, as I needed to stack the deck in my favor as much as possible. Thus, despite our appointed 9 p.m. meeting time, I decided to arrive closer to 8:45. The frosted glass doors that separate Dr. Rosenthal's office from the elevators may be opaque, but they are not soundproof, and I might be able to listen in on any phone calls Law might be making, which might prove enlightening in the extreme. Though Law might be able to discern a shadowy presence on the other side of the doors, I felt confident that my balletic ability to move about undetected would serve me well in that regard, allowing me to blend in with the hallway shadows in an unassuming way.

I was silently rehearsing my opening volley with Law as I rounded the corner to Dr. Rosenthal's building, having decided to walk rather than take a cab as a way of keeping my mind clear. As I approached the building, I saw a rather tall form hurriedly entering through the front doors. As the personage signed the guest book silently gestured at by a highly uninterested security guard, I caught a glimpse of the visitor's *visage*. I will admit to some surprise upon recognizing that agitated-looking individual as Chris.

Now why on earth would Chris Blackheart be at this particular office building at this particular time, and why would that same individual walk, head down, toward the elevators, as if to avoid the security cameras? Was it possible that Law had summoned Chris here, as well? I looked at my timepiece, a pocketwatch given by Queen Elizabeth II early in her reign to a cousin of mine, and noted the time: 8:48.

I hung back and allowed Chris to disappear into the elevators before I entered the building, announced my destination, and was pointed to that same guest book. I looked at Chris's signature and found a hastily-scrawled pseudonym: G. Rodriguez.

As the security guard continued to stare at a black-and-white TV broadcast of *The Golden Girls*, I more closely scrutinized Chris's signature. While I could not be sure of my conclusion based on a first initial and a last name, it did strike me that the style of penmanship was very similar to that of the note I'd received summoning me to the Empire State Building.

Elevators in New York City are highly unpredictable; one may push a button and have the doors open, only to reveal persons who had entered that same car two, five, or ten minutes earlier. If I were going to eavesdrop on the encounter between Law and Chris—Good heavens, could it be a tryst?—it would be unfortunate indeed for either of them to become aware of my presence before I decided to reveal myself. Thus I made the decision that any self-respecting sleuth would make: I proceeded past the elevators and made a sharp right turn to the staircase. For God knows both Law and Chris are much too lazy to ever *not* use an elevator.

This decision necessitated my climbing five flights of rather shallow stairs; and though I consider myself in excellent shape, these stairs were particularly challenging and caused a shortness of breath by the third flight. I used my inhaler and braved onward, taking a rest at the fourth story and, upon arriving at the fifth, resting for a good five minutes so that my slightly labored breathing would not be detected.

In my pantherlike way, I crept from the staircase to the opaque glass entryway to Dr. Rosenthal's office. Law was not at the receptionist's desk, but I did hear what sounded like an angry muttering from the confines of the doctor's inner office, the room in which I'd unburdened myself of so many cares.

I tried the doors, which usually require one to be buzzed in. To my delight, they were unlocked, and I was granted ingress with no ado. Hugging the wall, I approached the inner office, where Law and Chris appeared to be engaged in a very heated exchange.

"So that's it?" Chris spat. "Just like that?"

"Please do not become hysterical, Chris," Law responded languidly. "We have given it our best try, but I think you will agree, if you look at the situation objectively, that it was not meant to be."

"Not meant to be? After I went along with every plot you've hatched?"

Law sighed. "You act as though I am the only one to benefit from these so-called 'plots.' You'll benefit, too, if you play your cards right."

"That debacle on Long Island was bad enough, a comedy of errors, though I'm not laughing. And I still don't have a dime. But you seem to be doing quite well for yourself."

"Look at it this way, Chris. Instead of three people being dead, there are only two. And they were getting on in years anyway, and didn't have much quality time left."

"That's not my point. My point is that I want things the way we planned them. I don't want to be stuck with J just for the money."

"So then feel free to execute our plan, and dispatch your partner as soon as the rightful inheritance has been received and you've been made heir to the fortune. But you'll need to do it without my help, as I have taken quite enough chances in recent months, and I'm out of the accelerated-inheritance business."

"You mean you're out of the killing people for money business."

"Semantics, Chris, semantics."

"How can you be so callous? It's not only the money I want. We have something special. The only reason I went along with these get-rich-quick schemes was to be with you."

"I know, Chris, and it did seem to be a good idea at the time. But we have grown in different directions, and I do reserve the right to change my mind when circumstances evolve in unexpected ways. You're still young and reasonably attractive. Wait a few months, get rid of J, then buy yourself a fabulous condo in South Beach. You'll have new paramours lined up at your door within a month, and you'll forget all about me."

"You know what, Law? Everyone is right about you. Everyone else sees what I was never able to see."

"There's no need to be melodramatic, Chris. All of us have done what we needed to do to survive. Our older friends have always known they are playing a dangerous game. They thought they could outsmart us, but they couldn't. No one's the wiser, and it shouldn't take too long for J to get the inheritance back from Alex. Doctor Rosenthal and I fixed it so that no one will ever find the deaths suspicious. So J will get the money, you'll stay with J or take care of that situation however you see fit, and I'll get on with my life. Lee had some regrets about the many botched attempts on Long Island, but as we both know Lee is out of the way, so as long as you keep your mouth shut, no one will be the wiser about that, either. If J ever has a qualm or desire to confess, you may have to do some cajoling and so forth, but when the two of you are living it up on Pat and Lee's money, why would J give a second thought to that awful weekend? So everything works out. Not exactly the way we planned it, but in the final analysis we're all much better off."

There was a momentary silence as Chris (and I) took in the full import of Law's words. I'd suspected that not one, but two, dyads were involved in the mysterious deaths of Lee and Pat (for reasons that I will get into later on, at a more appropriate time), but to hear my suspicions confirmed was somewhat gratifying, and created in me a feeling of humility that stood in stark contrast to Nadine Gordimer's ungraceful acceptance of her Nobel Prize.

"Well, Law, you do seem to have it all figured out, as always. I suppose it was one of the things I loved about you. Note the use of the past tense."

In an emotive move highly uncharacteristic of Law, I heard that selfsame individual draw an unexpectedly sharp breath. But Law, being Law, seemed to return to the usual state of *ennui* rather quickly.

"Please put the gun away, Chris. It will do no one any good to splatter my brains about Doctor Rosenthal's office."

"It'll do *me* some good. To see you get what you deserve. Let's see how *you* like being murdered."

"And I suppose you'll enjoy spending the rest of your life in jail, taking care of the needs of fellow inmates? For someone of your delicate features is sure to be quite popular among the ruffians who comprise the modern prison population."

"But you taught me well, Law. No one's caught me so far, and no one will catch me now. I'm sure you've made more than a few enemies during your stay here in the City, what with the blackmailing tendencies and the like. There'll be so many suspects, the police will never be able to interview them all."

"Have it your way, Chris. Robin will be here any minute. Yes, you heard me. Robin and I have an appointment here at 9 p.m., which is what—three minutes from now? If we're lucky, there'll be an eyewitness who'll see you leaving the building with a smoking pistol. I suppose you might try killing our friend, too, to cover your tracks, though Lord knows Robin does know how to escape sudden death at every turn."

Now this situation simply would not do: a jilted ex-lover waving a gun in the face of the jilter, and Law using my impending arrival to prevent a murder by the jiltee. And although in different circumstances I might have needed to pop two or three of those miraculous 'coconut pills' to buck up my self-confidence and bravura, I was enraged enough at the exposure of these various manipulations to take action without them.

I dug into my pocket, grasped the gun, pulled it out of my pocket, and emerged from the shadows into the doorway of Dr. Rosenthal's office.

"And speaking of Robin," said I, pointing the gun directly at Chris, "I've had enough deaths in the last several weeks to last me a lifetime. So, Chris, kindly put that ridiculous instrument down and take a seat. The three of us need to have a long overdue discussion."

43

As countless killers have realized in their quest for media attention, nothing makes as much of an impression as a crazed lunatic waving a gun about. Certainly I was neither crazed nor a lunatic, but the waving gun (actually, more of a graceful motion from side to side, in emulation of those unflappable gumshoes of yesteryear) did stop the attempted homicide in its tracks. But while Chris did not pull the trigger, nor did that spurned lover sit as I had instructed.

Law was the first to speak.

"Robin, thank heavens you've arrived. As you can see, Chris is behaving in a most inappropriate fashion."

I looked Chris up and down while keeping the gun trained squarely at a vulnerable point.

"Chris," I said slowly, as if speaking to a child of below-average intelligence, "are you aware that you are in a rather significant amount of danger at this point? Now, please place your gun down on Doctor Rosenthal's ugly coffee table, and take a seat in that chair there." I motioned with the gun toward the patient's chair, as Law was firmly seated in the doctor's chair.

"No, I don't think I will, Robin. If you go ahead and shoot me, I'll have enough time to pull the trigger. And I doubt you want your little favorite dead."

"I don't want *anyone* dead, Chris. As I mentioned, I've become quite satiated with murder these last few weeks."

"But some people deserve to die, don't they? I think if you knew what Law has been up to the last few months, you might reconsider letting your 'innocent' plaything meet a fitting end."

"I have a good sense of what Law's been up to, as well as what you have, Chris. And I must say, while I have always thought of both of you as opportunistic in the extreme, I would never have thought you capable of two murders."

"Three, if all had gone according to plan; but then again, if all had gone according to plan, you wouldn't be standing here, now would you?"

I confess that these words threw me into a momentary state of confusion. "Are you referring to that incident at the top of the Empire State?" I asked, wondering if perhaps I, and not Alex, had been the intended victim.

Law hurriedly interrupted. "Robin, pay no heed to the ramblings of this madperson. Surely a gun-toting maniac is not to be taken at face value. By which I do not mean you, Robin, of course."

"Shut up, Law," Chris said through gritted teeth in a tone that I don't believe I'd ever quite heard before from that set of lips. "Robin, I'm serious. Why don't you just leave and forget what you've seen here? No one will ever know what's happened. I'll be rid of a two-timing lover, and you'll no longer have a bloodsucking leech to drain away your money. And you'll be much, much safer moving forward. Because if you knew Law like I know Law, you'd know that you'll be in quite a bit of peril if Law's sorry existence is allowed to continue."

Amazing how a simpleton wielding a firearm could underestimate the indefatigable Robin Anders! But Chris seemed to be forgetting that I have weathered much, much worse than the homicide of my ex-lover and that series of unfortunate accidents on Long Island. If one can survive a decades-long relationship with Lee, including all its attendant deceptions and prevarications, as well as maintain a long-term position in a highly profitable nonprofit organization like The Goode Foundation, one certainly has the tenacity to wait out any given situation until a satisfactory conclusion is reached.

"Well, Chris, we seem to have reached a Mexican standoff here. I won't sit idly by while a bit of jealousy puts you temporarily off your nut. So while we're all just standing around waiting for something to happen, perhaps you can both answer a few questions for me."

Neither responded immediately. Law seemed too busy looking about the office nonchalantly for a way out of the dire situation, but options did seem limited indeed. I blocked the egress with my form, and I held a gun that might have accidentally gone off if Law tried to rush past me. Behind Chris was Dr. Rosenthal's washroom, which I knew from experience had no window or other method of escape, unless one counts the toilet; and, lissome though Law may be, I doubted that the sewer pipes could comfortably accommodate that method of exit.

"When exactly did you two take up?" I continued, addressing the question to both. "It took me a while to figure it out, but when I did, I began to understand recent events much better."

"So you knew before tonight?" Law asked, humbled at being bested by someone perhaps no longer youthful, but still quite intellectually agile.

"All of this seems to go back to that fateful weekend at my house on Long Island," I responded. "Chris, as you may recall, you and J showed up in quite a state of rancor. Your tiff lasted throughout the weekend. And as anyone who has spent time in the company of you and J can attest to, these types of prolonged arguments are usually founded on accusations of infidelity. I hadn't given the situation much thought at the time; as you may recall, a series of mishaps befell me that particular weekend and distracted my attention. Besides, I have never been one to interfere in domestic matters that do not concern me."

Both Law and Chris seemed to be listening intently; or perhaps they were both looking for an opportunity to distract me, or each other, and make a break for it. At any rate, I continued uninterrupted.

"But as I became suspicious regarding the circumstances surrounding Pat and Lee's deaths, and as I began my private investigation, I started to realize that my preoccupation on Long Island had caused me to neglect several rather obvious interpersonal interactions that might shed light on recent matters. Now, the young always do think that they've outsmarted the rest of the world; but, my friends, allow me to assure you that the slightly older but infinitely more experienced have done everything you have done, and we are savvy indeed at seeing our previous actions repeated by those younger than us.

"When the attempt was made on Alex's life at the Empire State—and my apartment was simultaneously burgled—it became clear to me that two people must be working together; and Chris, due to your inseparability from J, the two of you seemed the ideal choice for the diabolical duo. But that did not quite square with the fact that your apartment, too, had been broken into. You and J could have set that up yourselves to cast the bright light of suspicion elsewhere, but J really did seem distraught; and, as we know, J is not a very good actor, which is why the poor thing has ended up in films that do not require much speaking, or acting.

"So, even if the burglary on your apartment were an 'inside job,' it seemed clear to me that it could have been masterminded only by you, Chris. But all the links of the chain didn't quite come together. If you and J had worked together in some regards, why would you choose to break into your own apartment without J's consent? That led to one real possibility: That you were working with someone else as well—that you were the proverbial apex of the criminal triangle.

"Ironically, I know you didn't have anything to do with the break-in...."

Chris took this moment to interrupt, words bursting through my brilliant soliloquy and breaking my dramatic delivery.

"You know who broke into our place?"

I sighed, perhaps a bit condescendingly. "Of course I know, Chris. It was Alex. And that was yet another love triangle in our curious geometry, where everyone seems to have bedded or been infatuated with everyone else at some point. That break-in through the window simply did not seem plausible to me, as the window showed no signs of criminal activity. No, the thief had to be someone who got access to the apartment through more legitimate means, by which I mean the front door. And who would have a key so easily available? Well, Lee would, of course—Lee always kept the keys to the domiciles of former and current lovers, in case they should ever come in handy. Chris, I know you're not so naïve as to be unaware that J and Lee had a dalliance several years ago, which is how Lee would have come by the key to your apartment, in which J had been living for several years before the two of you met, began cohabiting, and renewed the lease. And as much as it pains me to admit this"—here my voice caught and I had to blink back a tear, and indeed I would have reached for the 'pineapple pills' if my arm had not been engaged with keeping the pistol trained on Chris's torso—"in recent years Lee had taken up an on-again, off-again thing with Alex, who, as Lee's recent lover and fraudulent heir, had access to all Lee's worldly possessions, including that oh-so-useful keychain.

"But this insight presented me with an odd dilemma. If you were working with someone, Chris, surely you could have given a copy of the key to your partner in crime; thus Alex would not have needed to use Lee's copy of the key. And, if the burglary had indeed been your own doing, I was sure you would not have allowed your highly personalized and difficult-to-replace iPods and iMacs to be stolen.

"In my purely speculative world, Chris, this meant that you could not be dallying with Alex. But it did not mean that you were *not* dallying with someone else instead, and it did *not* mean that Alex had not been the one to break into your apartment in search of evidence that would establish J's genetic link to Lee and Pat. I have a fair idea of what it was that Alex was looking for, and which was indeed stolen from your apartment, but there's no need to go into that now.

"In the meantime, if you *were* conspiring with someone against poor J—who, it had become obvious to me, was the rightful heir—I wondered who a likely suspect might be. And, Chris, despite your acquaintance with others in your— industry, shall we say—the more I thought about it, the more I really could not imagine you having any social, or any other type of, intercourse with an unknown party without J's knowledge, given your highly symbiotic relationship. Which meant that your partner in crime had to be one of our little circle. Pat and Lee were dead; we know it wasn't poor unaware J, who has never been particularly quick on the uptake; I'd eliminated Alex from consideration for reasons I've already mentioned; and it certainly wasn't me.

"This left only one candidate—you, Law. And once again I found myself thinking about all those ominous undertones and interpersonal oddities that marked our weekend on Long Island. As I looked back, I realized that I had not seen you and Chris interact or speak on even one occasion. At meals you sat as far apart as possible; in the kitchen and living areas you studiously avoided one another; even during that unpleasant game of croquet you had as little interaction as possible. When two people go out of their way to avoid one another in public, it can mean one of only two things: They either intensely dislike each other, or they are engaged in a surreptitious romance. As your lack of interaction did not at all seem based on hostility, I could only conclude that it was based completely on the latter. And, as usual, my intuitions regarding matters of the flesh have been borne out."

Law, always somewhat pale, did seem more translucent than usual, which I found just the tiniest bit gratifying.

"As for *you*, Law—once I began to suspect that Lee's death was not natural, it was exceedingly easy to get accurate information from the corpulent medical examiner who'd autopsied dear Lee—which of course led me to question Doctor Rosenthal, who really had no choice other than to expose you. And because I'd determined that you and Chris must be somehow working together, both in and out of the bedroom, I began to think about the other ways you might be involved in recent events. I'd long since learned to pretend that the walls of these offices aren't very thin indeed—but I was reminded very forcibly of how easy it is to eavesdrop when one has underhanded motives. Of course, you'd used the information you'd gleaned from your eavesdropping sessions to blackmail this practice's patients, and to torture poor Doctor Rosenthal at the same time; you'd even eavesdropped on at least one of *my* sessions, Law, making the mistake of writing down the name and address of Town & Country Pharmacy, which Doctor Rosenthal had recommended to me behind closed doors! For that I shall never forgive you, Law; and as God is my witness, if it should ever come back to me that you have repeated even one word of my private conversations with the doctor, so help me I will make you regret you ever set foot on this island."

An icy fire burned behind Law's languid lids—cold, unrepentant, vengeful. Unintimidated, I continue to unravel Law's sordid tale of lust, treason, and greed.

"And certainly you'd eavesdropped on Pat's sessions, as well, as that unfortunate victim of Parkinson's Disease unburdened a heavy soul of a tale of a love child conceived decades ago and given up for adoption. Yes, I can picture it, Law—you sitting with one ear glued to the door as Pat told the doctor about a recent meeting with Junior Makeba, a private detective who'd told Pat that he'd found the precious baby, who was living here in the City and whose grown-up name was Jody Crewe, known to friends and loved ones as J! What a wonderful coincidence—the lover of your lover was heir to a fortune that could make both of you rich at a fairly young age! But how to get that money when its owner was in the unfortunate position of being alive?

"The answer was easy—simply eliminate those who stood between you and the money. Given Pat's recent diagnosis of a serious but not terminal disease, as well as Pat's emotional history as a morose and dystonic individual—it would be easy to commit a murder and write a phony suicide note. Pat, of course, had told Doctor Rosenthal that all the money would be left to Jody as a means of expiation for past wrongs—and Law's willing ear would have taken in all this information with alacrity. You both expected J to inherit quickly and easily…and, after a few months, poor J would meet with some sort of unexpected and tragic accident, but of course only after you made sure you'd be sole inheritor, Chris. Then you and Law could go off together and enjoy spending every dollar of your ill-gotten gains. But there was one thing you didn't count on—Pat putting Lee in charge of the money, instead of leaving it directly to J. Pat of course hadn't planned suicide, but *had* taken the precaution of leaving the estate to Lee for safekeeping, just in case something happened before Pat could figure out a way to meet and bond with the long-lost Jody. But by leaving the money with Lee, Pat inadvertently signed Lee's death warrant. For, to face the ineluctable facts, we all know that Lee could not necessarily be trusted to ensure that all of J's money would not be quickly drained into (shall we say) other accounts that would have benefited Lee quite a bit more than they would have benefited J. Thus Lee needed to be dispatched as well."

Law sat back, a grimace crossing that flawless face, while Chris kept Law locked in the gun's crosshairs. In truth, my own arm was getting tired, but this was hardly the time to engage in any sort of laziness in that regard, as I was in no rush to join Lee and Pat behind the pearly gates.

"Well, you do seem to have everything figured out, Robin," Law commented snidely. "So perhaps you can enlighten us on a small matter we have been unable to puzzle out. How, exactly, did Alex manage to steal J's inheritance? Of course, we all know *that* Alex did it. We just don't know *how*."

"As much as I would like to enlighten you, Law, I am afraid that my throat is getting a bit parched." I eyed those tantalizing bottles of water on Dr. R's desk, so near and yet so out of reach. "As you know, I usually prefer to listen and observe rather than monopolize any given conversation. This evening, I have unfortunately found myself in the latter category, and I fear that my vocal cords are becoming harmed due to my inability to simultaneously drink a bottle of water and protect you from Chris's maleficent intentions. But I will make the proverbial 'deal with the devil' with you. I'll tell you how I rather ingeniously pieced together Alex's involvement in this entire sordid tale, if you'll help sate my curiosity in one particular area."

"I agree to no such conditions," responded the very impertinent Law peremptorily, "without first knowing the question you wish answered."

"Law, you may like to see yourself as an island, as a completely independent entity who needs and relies on no one. But I know all too well that the opposite is true, as I am just one of the many with whose affections you have so callously toyed. You rarely leave one fawning admirer unless there is another waiting in the wings. And yet this very evening I eavesdropped as you declared an end to your felonious relationship with Chris. So who, may I ask, is the new recipient of your favors? Anyone I know?"

"Of course you know me," said a voice from behind Chris's shoulder.

And out of the bathroom walked Dr. Rosenthal, pointing a very large handgun—at me.

44

A technique in modern cinema and literature that I find banal in the extreme is the "plot twist." As we all know, such unexpected turns of event are usually highly unlikely, pushing the boundaries of reality to unacceptable levels. In addition to being the mark of incompetent writers or *auteurs*, they are also insulting to the consumer of that particular form of entertainment, whether on film or paper. And yet there are those rare times when such unexpected events prove to be completely congruent with the unfolding of the tale. Such was the case at this particular juncture, as I shall now explain.

Needless to say, the appearance of Dr. Rosenthal from the water closet was quite shocking to me, as well as to Chris, I daresay. As my brain took in the circumstances, I recriminated with myself quite bitterly. How could I have missed this? I consoled myself with the knowledge that the details of my investigation were complex and varied; and I supposed that I'd made the unforgivable mistake of focusing solely on my circle of friends when I should also have been investigating those lines tangent to the circle.

"Well, Doctor Rosenthal," I said calmly. "I see you have decided to emulate your patients and partake in some sociopathic histrionics. Kindly point that gun away from me, if you please."

"I'll do no such thing, Robin. But I would like both you and this other interloper—Chris, you are nothing like what I expected—to set your firearms on the floor, immediately. As you can see, my pistol is larger than both of yours."

Chris certainly is no genius, but that betrayed individual at least had the sense to know that relinquishing the gun was not likely to result in any positive outcome—for Chris, at least. I, of course, knew the same, and continued to grip my weapon. The scene if viewed from above must have been quite comical: Dr. Rosenthal pointing a gun at me, as I pointed mine at Chris, who pointed at Law. A chain reaction would leave all of us dead, except for Dr. Rosenthal; and I couldn't help but think that two-thirds of such an outcome might not be at all displeasing to that theatrical therapist.

I shook my head in pity. "Don't tell me you've been taken in by Law's charms, Doctor? One would think that one so experienced with the inner workings of the psyche would see through Law a mile away. Or have your loins gotten the better of you?" Based on my own experience, the latter seemed the more likely explanation.

"The problem with the two of you," Dr. Rosenthal began, in that professorial tone of voice I find so grating, "is that neither of you has the depth of human knowledge to fully understand Law. Robin—you've always seen Law as a plaything, nothing more. And you, Chris, simply aren't intelligent enough for someone as brilliant as Law to make a life with. No, it was only inevitable that Law and I should find each other, drawn to each other like moths to the flame."

I pursed my lips in distaste. Had Dr. Rosenthal, dispenser of tranquilizers to the rich and deserving, gone completely insane with lust? Perhaps it was not in my best interests to recriminate with the doctor when a handgun was trained squarely on me, but I could not help myself.

"Shoot me if you must, Doctor," I challenged brazenly, "but kindly give me the courtesy of an explanation first. Am I to understand now that Law was *not* blackmailing your patients, that you fabricated the entire story?"

"Without going into excessive detail, my patients were indeed being blackmailed—but Law was not the mastermind of that plot. I was. Law, of course, helped me implement the plan."

"I fear I do not understand, Doctor."

"Let me spell it out for you, Robin, so that you may learn once and for all that you are not the smartest person in the room." Yes, the doctor did have the effrontery to say exactly those words; and whether or not they proved true you will discover in the succeeding pages.

"I am listening," I responded, biding my time and wishing I could look at my watch.

"Law and I have been a couple for more than a year now. We of course have kept it quiet, as private loves should not be a topic of public discussion. As you can imagine, when one finds one's soul mate, everything else recedes into unimportance, and as our relationship progressed, we both realized that remaining here, on the island of Manhattan, could only drain our very souls out of us. We wished to live a simpler life, which meant stockpiling our money so that we could move to Provence and enjoy a life of quiet tranquility.

"But, you see, money has been increasingly hard to come by, as my accounts have been drained by the demands of that highly avaricious insurance company investigator. There would be no way to escape from that mongrel if we were to remain in New York; therefore, we decided to leave, but first we needed a large sum in order to establish ourselves a world away."

I looked at Law, who sat quietly as the doctor continued.

"It made sense to try to get moneys from various sources. By virtue of the mere fact that you are standing here, Robin, you can see that one of our sources of income proved more resilient than we had expected."

I blinked, as those sentences made no sense to me; which I found surprising, given my demonstrated ability to juggle the many strange strands of this murderous saga. But I had little time to dwell on the doctor's enigmatic statement if I were to continue paying attention to the details of the revelations that seemed to be dropping fast and furious from the doctor's lips.

"Another possible source of income revealed itself during Pat's therapy sessions, when we learned that Pat was quite wealthy indeed, as well as sick and prepared to leave a substantial fortune to a young, recently found heir. Of course, this required Law to take up with Chris so as to move things along in this regard; and, Robin, I think you know the rest of that part of the story, so I won't dwell on the details."

Chris gasped. Could that naïve fool really have believed that Law would have entered into a relationship with *anyone* on an honest, nonmonetary basis?

"So Law didn't really force you to call in any favors with that grotesque creature, Septimus McAllister," I declared with disapproval. "You did it all willingly."

"It did seem the best way to ensure that Pat's money made it into J's hands, and then into Chris's, and then Law's and mine, with a minimum of fuss. Of course, we hadn't quite expected that Pat would leave the money with Lee for safekeeping. That was an annoying fly in the ointment. But we got around it."

I snorted in disgust. "Yes, by doing away with Lee, who you knew could not be trusted to keep the money safely. So then, Law, that snippy attitude you displayed toward Doctor Rosenthal in my presence was all an act to hide the true nature of your relationship?"

Law smiled smugly, as if to bask in the glow of an Oscar®-worthy performance.

"And your final source of income was your patients—am I correct, Doctor? It makes complete sense to me now. You were able to feed all the most prurient bits of your patients' sordid lives to Law, who then began the blackmailing process. In this way you seemed to remain above it all, as much a victim as everyone else. And when you'd amassed enough money, you planned to flee the country. In the meantime, the insurance company blackmailer would be completely unaware of this income flow, as it was being amassed by Law, not you."

"A good therapist is also a good businessperson," retorted the doctor snippily. "Having someone else collect the money and keep it in his or her name requires no more thought than the refusal to validate parking."

"So now that your shrewd business practices have paid off so handsomely," I continued, "you and your paramour have decided to leave for Europe sooner rather than later? But what of J's inheritance? It's still a lush fruit, ripe for the picking."

"There's such a thing as too much riches, Robin. Besides, it's not worth waiting two years for. Law has proven extremely adept at cajoling large sums from some Fifth Avenue magnates and mavens, so we don't really need Pat's relatively meager estate any longer."

I felt my heart burn with cold fury. "How convenient for you, Doctor. So, in the end, the deaths of Pat and Lee really don't matter to you. They were for nought."

"You are becoming hysterical, Robin. As you know, Pat didn't have long to live anyway, maybe another ten or fifteen years at most. As for Lee—well, you know as well as I do that Lee was not one of the earth's most upstanding or trustworthy citizens."

"So tonight is to be your last night in New York?"

"Yes, it is," replied Dr. R. "You seemed to be asking just a few too many questions of a few too many people, and there's no time like the present to make a change."

"But why all this pomp and circumstance?" I asked. "Law, you could have simply left without saying a word to Chris; and if you'd done so, you wouldn't now be sitting here with a gun in your face."

"You are right, Robin. But I do feel an affection for Chris, and I wanted to end things on a positive note, not just leave the country without saying goodbye. I'm not made of stone, you know. Or that's what I told the doctor, at least. And speaking of the doctor: Chris, why don't you point your gun in that direction, instead?"

As ordered, Chris swung the pistol 180 degrees and aimed it squarely at the doctor.

"Well, Doctor," I said, with a degree of grudging admiration for one so fiendishly clever as Law, "you certainly seem to have covered all your bases. Except for one."

45

In my younger days, I had given serious thought to treading the boards as a career. Throughout my youth it had been acknowledged that I was a master mimic and mime, as well as second to none in conveying the broad-based yet subtle emotions that are required of stage actors. I mention this tidbit because I wish it to be known that, as a thespian of some talent, I have long prided myself on being able to see through the techniques of other fine actors at work, to critique them silently while also appreciating specific parts of their method.

Now, based on the revelations of the last several minutes—as my arm ached from holding that small pistol and my parched mouth begged for one of those grandiosely packaged plastic bottles of water on Dr. R's desk—it would seem that I shared the room, and its attendant doorways, with some of the finest actors in New York City. Everyone in the room had played a series of roles for the last several months, with greater or lesser degrees of success.

In the doorway of the loo, Dr. Rosenthal looked extremely puzzled. Until this point our gun pointings had formed a linear function, sort of a domino effect where one gunshot would lead on down the line and end at Law. Now the geometry had shifted to a triangle, with me aiming at Chris, Chris aiming at Dr. Rosenthal, and the recently betrayed doctor aiming at me.

"Is this a joke, Law?" Dr. Rosenthal asked, bewildered, and inwardly I questioned the many tens of thousands of dollars I'd wasted in that office over the last several decades. For the doctor's lack of comprehension seemed to indicate an almost unbelievable lack of intelligence.

"If it is," I said with some satisfaction, "it seems as though the joke is on you. For shame, Doctor! You should have seen it coming."

An exceedingly puzzled look remained on the doctor's face, so I explained.

"Don't you see what's happened? All along you thought you had the upper hand. Your dear Law, you thought, would gladly betray Chris—not to mention myself and Lee—so that the two of you could enjoy mushroom omelettes in Provence for the remainder of your days. But, don't you see, that was never the plan? You thought you were using Law, but in fact quite the opposite was true. Law used *you* to amass a fortune in blackmail dollars from your clients, but the plan was never to run away with you. It was, and still is, to get rid of you and keep the money. I assume this cash is locked in a box somewhere, and that Law of course knows its whereabouts and how to access it? And Chris is here to help Law dispatch you. Don't you see this was the plan from the beginning?

"Now, Chris—and I say this with the utmost affection—don't you see that you're next? When J comes into the inheritance and you're made the heir, of course poor J will meet with an accident. Soon thereafter, you too will be pushing up daisies."

"Don't be ridiculous, Robin," Chris sneered angrily. "You don't know what you're talking about."

"No, I begin to see Robin's point exactly," Dr. Rosenthal said, turning to Law while keeping the gun pointed at me. "You! You pretended that you wanted to break it off with Chris gently and asked me to hide in the bathroom just in case things got out of hand. Then you proceeded to play-act your little scene, expecting me to charge in to save you. And then Chris could have shot me in self-defense, and you'd have your happy little testimony all wrapped up."

"I see that you have not *completely* lost your clinical ability to analyze a situation," I said dryly to the doctor. "What none of you counted on was my early arrival. Am I correct about that? You are all so used to Robin Anders arriving fashionably late that you thought I would arrive after the deed had been done, and after you'd arranged the crime scene in such a way as to suggest that a crazed Doctor Rosenthal had attacked the two of you. I'd provide the perfect cover story." And, without missing a beat, I swung my gun from the chest of Chris—whose gun remained pointing at the doctor—to that of Law. Keeping the gun trained on Law would, I hoped, give me some leverage until a satisfactory conclusion could be reached.

Dr. Rosenthal's eyes narrowed and a smile began to spread across those lizardlike lips. "Yes, Robin, but there's one thing these two didn't count on. What's to stop me from now shooting this gun twice? I have a bullet with your name on it, Law, and one for you, too, Chris. Robin, you see I am the aggrieved party here. If you back out of the room and pull the door shut behind you, you won't be witness to any of the succeeding events, and you have my word that you won't be pulled into any subsequent legal or mortuarial proceedings. One phone call will have Septimus McAllister here quickly, and two very vile bodies disposed of before any forensic evidence may be collected. Or better yet, I'll shoot Chris while you shoot Law. That could be fun, as you have been as grievously wronged as I."

Once again I was disappointed in what appeared to be the doctor's ever-decreasing analytical skills.

"Doctor, you really do not seem to be getting the point. Do you think that this understated criminal mastermind"—I nodded in Law's direction—"could have come this far and missed such an obvious detail? If you pull the trigger of your firearm, I expect you'll find it devoid of ammunition. In other words, the barrel will be as empty as your professional ethics and your moral structure."

"Then why don't we test out your theory, Robin?" asked the doctor, then did something that I expect I will be chatting about with my new therapist for years to come. With gun still facing me, Dr. Rosenthal pulled the trigger six times. Each pull of the trigger was followed by a loud click. At the end of the process I remained standing erect, mercifully bullet-free.

"You disappoint me, doctor," I said, struggling to retain equanimity. Oh, to simply reach into my pocket and retrieve two of the 'eggplant pills' that sat so tantalizingly out of reach! "Would Law really have allowed you access to a loaded gun if the plan was to murder you in your own office? I'm sure Law handed the gun to you in some sort of box or other packaging as you took up your position in the toilet there. Of course, the bullets would have been removed first—along with Law's fingerprints."

Law sighed. Rarely have I seen that foul murderer display any level of impatience, or indeed any emotion whatsoever. But Law hadn't become quite wealthy by being a person of inaction, and I watched and listened as that betraying beast took charge of the situation.

"I am sorry it has come to this, Robin. And, Terry, I admit there were times when I found you interesting. But really— anyone who would do to patients what you have done to yours really does not deserve continued existence." Normally a person of great composure, Law appeared to be squirming a bit as these words were delivered, and presently I understood why—While calmly delivering death sentences for me and the doctor, Law had reached under the cushions of the therapist's chair and pulled out yet another firearm, which was now pointed at me. Thus, once again, the deathly configuration of gun pointing had changed: Chris aiming at the doctor, Law aiming at me, and me aiming at Law.

The situation was tenuous in the extreme, and from the look in Law's eye I could see that the order to "shoot" was imminent. I was prepared to go down with a fight—as shooting Law would have proven quite satisfying—but Providence had decreed that I was to prove as resilient as I had on Long Island a few weeks earlier. For just as I began tightening my cramped index finger to pull the trigger, ready to react as soon as Law made the first murderous move, I heard a loud crashing sound come from the lobby, as of shattering glass. As the others took just a split second to wonder what was happening, I dropped to my knees and crawled as fast as humanly possible out of the doorway, almost getting trampled by twelve feet in the process.

The deafening noise was quickly followed by an equally deafening silence, which I took in from my vantage point under the receptionist's desk. The situation seemed to get under control very rapidly, and before I knew it, a friendly hand was reaching under the desk, and I heard a welcome voice saying, "Robin, I'm so glad you're not hurt." And that masculine hand pulled me into a standing position so that I could meet the adoring eyes of my savior, "Kevin Jennings."

46

I may, or may not, have mentioned in the course of this narrative that I have always had a talent for games of strategy. Back in my halcyon days at university, I was the undisputed champion at the games *du jour*, easily besting my opponents at Go, Mah Jongg, Mancala, bridge, and all those other *divertissements* in which the young partake. Victory always came easily to me during such tournaments, and I suppose for that reason I have grown accustomed to winning when I participate in a game of any type. The arrival of "Kevin Jennings" should therefore not be a surprise to you, as the unraveling of the identities of the murderers of Lee and Pat was not unlike a game of chess played between two masters. Here, as in all areas of life, I had remained several steps ahead of my competitors and foes, granting me the ultimate victory of watching Chris, Law, and Dr. Rosenthal drop their guns when ordered to do so by Kevin and his posse of gross, yet curiously attractive, thugs, who clearly outnumbered them.

I looked Kevin up and down, my admiration for the man growing. For, truth be told, I had always found him inexplicably fetching, and his rushing in to remedy the situation had a titillating Eliot Ness-like quality to it. No matter that I had been the one to request such backup in my earlier phone call to him, suggesting that he bring along a suitably imposing group of his street associates, of which he seemed to have many, to help me bring the matter to a resolution once and for all. For, as you know, I had suspected that Law's invitation to meet at Dr. R's office might be a set-up, and that I might find myself in peril.

I looked at my watch to distract myself from the effect of Kevin's square jaw. "Well, Kevin, you are at least a few minutes later than I had expected. We had quite a bit of excitement here before you arrived."

Kevin smiled indulgently. Oh dear. Was this to be the beginning of one of those long, drawn-out affairs, the type in which I have overindulged, in the past?

"But no matter," I continued lightly. "You and your friends have saved the day, and for that I thank you. In future, however, we must synchronize our watches, so that I do not end up dead."

Over my shoulder, I could hear Law and Chris muttering something, to themselves or to each other, about my "indestructibility." This comment I ignored, as I'd already paid more than enough attention to the crazed ravings of those two homicidal maniacs.

I took a step into the room and gazed upon the hangdog expressions of the three would-be assassins.

"All," I began, "I would like you to meet a new friend and associate of mine, Kevin Jennings. In addition to being a savvy man of the streets, as just demonstrated, he is also a man of letters and the law. In other words, in addition to understanding how the human mind works, he also understands legal processes and systems. And he's here to help us bring satisfactory resolution to the events of the last several weeks."

The assembled masses looked at one another confusedly.

"I will explain," I continued. "Murder and blackmail may seem like fun and games to you, but I can assure you that they are quite serious matters. The proceedings of late must not be allowed to continue, and I fear that if I do not take immediate action, they will. I suppose if I thought more like the lot of you, I'd simply have Kevin and his associates shoot all of you, then call Septimus McAllister to dispose of everyone properly—isn't that would you would do if you were in my shoes, Doctor?

"But, alas, I am not a devotee of murder. I may investigate death, and look for suitably poetic justice for the perpetrators, but I am not a murderer myself. No, as you all know, I am much too gentle and kind-spirited to even consider such a horrific idea. And this is why Kevin is going to draw up airtight legal contracts, right now, in which you all agree to certain terms and conditions. Kevin, I trust one of your people here has powers as a notary?"

Kevin cocked his head toward a tough-looking person who could have been a man or a woman to indicate that he or she was indeed a notary. Was this what the world was coming to—an amalgamation of the genders? Well, to each his or her own. If a person chooses to mask his or her gender inside a type of clothing or a particular manner of speech, far be it from me to argue with the person's decisions; though I cannot imagine that life would not be very difficult indeed for those who persist in such stubborn androgyny.

"Once the individual contracts are drawn up," I resumed, "you have two choices. Option number one: Each of you will sign the contract willingly and happily, and then abide by the terms in perpetuity. Option number two: Kevin and I call the police and tell them everything that has transpired. I admit that the latter option is less appealing to me, as Law, you would not last two seconds in a jail; though—Chris—I am sure you would find a codependent partner quite quickly. As for you, Doctor—despite your many flaws, I will admit that our time together has served me well over the years, and I would hate to see you spend the remainder of your days behind bars."

As I spoke, Kevin took a seat at the doctor's desk, turned on the computer, and pulled up a word processing program.

"I'm ready whenever you are, Robin," said the dear man. "Please dictate the terms."

And I did so, in great detail, as the faces of the three conspirators became progressively more pale. When all the contracts had been drafted, Kevin printed them out, and I circulated them for signature. As I did so, I once again noticed the unopened bottles of water on the doctor's desk. As you might suspect, having just dictated the terms of three contracts, I was quite parched and in need of life-giving liquid refreshment.

"Law, would you be so kind as to hand me one of those water bottles, please?" I asked. Law did so with alacrity, scooping up four bottles and handing one to me, as well as one to Dr. R, Chris, and even Kevin. Rarely had I seen Law so solicitous; perhaps the contract terms were kicking in sooner than even I would have hoped.

As I was unscrewing the plastic top of the bottle, preparing my throat for the much-needed quenching, it struck me that Law did not hold a bottle; but surely Law—who so easily became weary from any exertion—needed refreshment as much as the rest of us did? And it really was most unlike Law to go above and beyond any request. I'd asked for a bottle of water; and given my dominant position in the room, there really was no way Law could refuse to comply. But the others had not asked for water....

"Stop," I yelled, as Chris and Kevin both lifted the bottles to their lips. "Don't drink that water!"

Kevin and Chris stopped as directed, looking at me quizzically, as if I'd lost my marbles. For it is indeed rare for Robin Anders to speak in such a loud and urgent tone.

But Dr. Rosenthal had begun chug-a-lugging already, and by the time I shouted my order, half the water was gone from the bottle. An eerie silence filled the room as we heard a small gasp emanate from Dr. Rosenthal's lips, and we watched as the good doctor dropped dead at our feet.

I grimaced. It seemed that in this particular endgame, Law had yet another move that I hadn't anticipated.

47

One should never underestimate the power of a good night's sleep. Whether these slumbers are the result of natural forces or a much-needed 'blueberry pill' is immaterial; for mornings allow one to start afresh, to look at the world anew, to cast off the unpleasant memories of yesterday in favor of a brighter today.

Needless to say, I slept the sleep of angels on the Evening of Revelations and Death, or ERD as Kevin so succinctly acronymized the phrase. Of course, we'd gone through all the usual motions of ascertaining whether Dr. Rosenthal's life might be saved, but the dear doctor was indeed dead as the proverbial doornail upon hitting the floor, the victim of a quite deadly poison with which Law had had the foresight to lace all those bottles of water, just in case the evening hadn't worked out quite as planned. This, at least, was the scenario to which Law admitted; however I suspect the truth was quite different, and that Law planned to drink a celebratory toast with Chris after the doctor had been dispatched, with Chris of course quaffing the H_2O while Law drank from an untainted bottle. This would have effectively dispatched two inconvenient lovers within minutes of each other, and Law would most likely have been on the way to France with a valise full of cash, instead of signing contracts that would grant me favors of a most important variety indefinitely, as well as the large sum of ill-gotten funds that had been extorted out of Dr. Rosenthal's patients. Given the invitation I'd received to the Office of Death, I can only assume that I, too, would have been offered a poisoned water bottle, and I, too, would have ended up at that morgue on First Avenue, in which (after my visit with Septimus McAllister) I had vowed never to set foot again. The thought that someone had made an attempt on my life was disturbing in the extreme, as it certainly had never happened before; but four of the 'apricot pills' helped to calm my frayed nerves, which still had not quite recovered from my Long Island-induced PTSD.

Although events had not transpired quite as Law had expected, a phone call was still placed to Septimus McAllister. Of course, Law had been in touch with that cretinous creature earlier in the day, outlining all the illegal activities in which McAllister had been involved to date, and letting the morturian know that his services would be called on one last time to dispose of some inconvenient business. McAllister certainly hadn't expected that Dr. Rosenthal would be the one so dispatched, and he hadn't expected to have to write a report confirming the doctor's death by suicide. But what choice did the man have, really? Via the dead doctor, Law knew exactly what McAllister had been up to; and so, of course, did I. The man was at our mercy, so he did as he was told, and within a couple of days the tabloids were filled with headlines about the tragic death of one of Manhattan's most beloved therapists, whose suicide note revealed the identity of the blackmailing insurance company employee. This last, I thought, was a nice touch on my part; as anyone who engages in that sort of behavior deserves his comeuppance. No one would ever be able to claim the doctor's suicide note was forged, because we left it typed on the computer screen. Kevin had, of course, donned gloves before typing anything, so any fingerprints on the keyboard would belong to those of the doctor.

The rest of the office was arranged accordingly, with the doctor's corpse placed gently on the couch by Kevin's goons and the poisoned water bottles sent away with Kevin for safekeeping. The next morning, Law arrived for the workday, "discovered" the doctor and suicide note, and called the police; meanwhile, Septimus McAllister waited to do his part. And, indeed, all went smoothly, for the case was quickly ruled a suicide, and no inconvenient police inquiries followed. Which was, of course, quite a relief, as I'd had more than enough stress over the last month, and I had no wish to fend off the amorous advances of police officers and detectives.

Thus released from the worry of homicide investigations, I settled in for a period of nearly 24 hours rest in my featherbed. Kevin, solicitous as always, had seen me home, and had been somewhat angling for an invitation to join me in my *boudoir*; but one must make one's suitors wait a suitable amount of time, and I hinted that perhaps, just perhaps, I might be willing to entertain him some evening a fortnight hence, the office photos of his wife and children notwithstanding. For now, though, I said, Morpheus was to be my only bed partner, and Kevin Jennings—gentleman that he is—winked politely, while no doubt beginning to plot his renewed attacks on my virtue at a later date.

Three evenings later, the caterers brought several large platters of gourmet food, as well as several wines of delightful vintage, to my manse. Money really was no object, given the large sum of cash that Law had transferred to me the previous day. That Law had skimmed some off the top was absolutely certain, but I supposed I could forgive the poor creature for this moral lapse. By virtue of the contract, Law was prohibited from leaving New York City, ever again, without my expression permission; thus the loss of, say, a few tens of thousands of dollars seemed on balance a very fair deal—a consolation prize for Law, as it were.

At the appointed time, the doorman called up to say that three people had arrived to see me, and might he send them up? A few moments later, J, Chris, and Law entered my apartment, looking sour indeed. I could only imagine the conversations in which J and Chris had engaged in recent days, which must have been rancorous in the extreme. But codependents would rather be destroyed by each other than end the relationship, and here they were, looking even more bitter and unhappy than they'd looked upon their arrival at my house on Long Island. Which, I suppose, is to be their fate until the end of time.

"Cheer up, friends," I said gaily. "We're here to celebrate new beginnings. Perhaps our *visages* should be expressing joy, or relief, instead of gloom and doom. Eat! Drink! And lest any of you think of slipping a poisonous substance into my food, rest assured that in the event of my untimely death, Kevin Jennings stands ready, willing, and able to reveal the events of a few nights ago to the proper authorities."

I heard unhappy murmurs as the crowd milled about, filling their plates with assorted *amuse bouches* and their glasses with wines they did not have the palates to appreciate. Everyone had more or less settled into various chairs, couches, and divans when the doorman called to announce the arrival of the final guest. A few moments later, Alex entered the apartment, looking very put out indeed. I'd left that selfsame identity-and-inheritance-stealing thief a very pointed voice mail the previous day, outlining the facts I'd managed to piece together. I'd also suggested that attending the gathering at my home the following evening would be very much in Alex's best interests. The alternative was, of course, to call the police and give them some interesting information, particularly about a man named Junior Makeba. I'd received a surly voice mail only an hour or two after leaving my message, assuring me that Alex would, indeed, join the party.

As the guests sat chatting, I was reminded of that weekend on Long Island. It seemed so long ago; and everyone seemed so much younger then, though our little getaway had happened less than a month earlier. The key difference was, of course, that Lee was no longer a member of our close-knit party, and that epiphany sent me scrambling for one of those 'strawberry pills' that make unbearable pain more bearable. Of course, I slipped into my bedroom momentarily to down the 'strawberry,' as preserving a steely and calm *façade* was essential among this particular set of homicidal guests.

With the 'strawberry' taking effect, I took my position at the front of the parlor, clinking my glass with an appetizer fork to claim everyone's attention.

"Thank you all for agreeing to pay me a visit this evening. We have all been through some rather distressing times in recent weeks, and I hope that this evening will begin the process of putting the unpleasant memories behind us. In order to do that, however, I feel that we must all understand what exactly has happened. I've gathered you here to bring closure to some of the unanswered questions you may have, as well as to ask a few of my own. This, as you may know, is the way it is traditionally done in fiction; and as a devotee of classic crime capers, I feel it incumbent on me to maintain the tradition. Thus, without further ado, let me begin.

"Chris, on that fateful evening in Doctor Rosenthal's office, you asked me who broke into your apartment, and Law—you asked how Alex had managed the difficult task of slipping away with Pat's inheritance. These questions were of course part of my examination of the various crimes, and the time has come to reveal all. Alex, will you do me the favor of telling me whether I have the facts straight?"

The newly poor Alex nodded in a defeated manner. In my study lay Alex's unsigned contract, written a few days earlier by Kevin, and not yet signed. I expected it would be signed with great enthusiasm by the end of the evening.

"Let us not forget," I continued, "that this entire process began as a result of the quest for riches by the many personages in this room. I don't know what other plots you four have hatched to bilk money from unsuspecting innocents, but that is not my concern right now. I shall focus merely on the facts of this particular case.

"I think we all know that there was a time when Alex and our dearly departed Lee carried on quite a torrid *amour*. Needless to say, they always denied the rumors, but in fact there is quite a bit of evidence that this romantic entanglement was not a one-shot deal, but rather a protracted on-again, off-again affair. At the time of Lee's death, the affair was most assuredly back *on*.

"The exact details are unclear to me, but here are the broad strokes. We know that Pat had recently been diagnosed with Parkinson's, and that Pat had hired a detective named

Junior Makeba to find Pat and Lee's love child. Somehow, Pat found a way to convey this information to Lee, but the information must have been delivered in writing, not in person.

"Here is what I believe happened. Pat, sensing the magnitude of the situation and knowing Lee's volatility, sat down and composed a letter, which was delivered via messenger to Lee's apartment. Someway, somehow, the letter was intercepted by Alex. Lovers in this day and age have keys to each other's apartments, don't they? So perhaps Alex was just lolling about Lee's apartment when the messenger arrived. Always the opportunist, Alex would have had little compunction about steaming open the letter to find out what sorts of juicy tidbits it might contain.

"And certainly it did contain more than its share of useful information. I can imagine the shock on Alex's face upon discovering that our close friend J is the child of Lee and Pat! But how could Alex use this information for personal benefit? Well, the answer was quite simple. Why not simply rewrite the letter, picking up many of Pat's phrases while altering some of the information to Alex's advantage? Though the letter that Lee ultimately received made no specific reference to the Parkinson's diagnosis, I think it's safe to assume that the letter that Alex intercepted did. This is how Alex was able to write up a credible forgery, with spiky and shaky handwriting that did not truly resemble Pat's.

"I also think it extremely unlikely that Pat would have made reference so early in the original letter to 'not having much time left as a result of my own decision,' as I believe the phrase went. Parkinson's is not a terminal disease, so suicide should have been completely unnecessary. But Alex's plan required a credible explanation for Pat's death.

"So—Alex, correct me if I am wrong about any of this—a plan was formulated rather quickly. Alex rewrote the letter, making sure the name 'Alex Mann' was substituted for that of 'Jody Croux' as the identity of the love child, and the names 'Manfred and Emily Mann' were substituted as the names of the adoptive parents. And who, really, would be the wiser? Alex and J are about the same age, with equally shadowy provenances.

"But Alex had to move fast to make sure that Lee wouldn't be able to directly verify with Pat the information in the letter. Knowing that Lee often retained keys to lovers' apartments, Alex removed Pat's apartment key from Lee's keyring, then broke into Pat's apartment the same day on which the original letter was delivered to Lee, somehow forcing poor Pat to take an overdose of the 'blueberry pills.' But more on that in a minute.

"The next day, Alex dispatched a messenger with the rewritten letter to Lee's apartment, of course in its original envelope, which Alex had steamed open so as to preserve it. This is the letter that I saw in Lee's safety deposit box, and that Alex later retrieved as the 'heir' to the estate. And it was, of course, the letter that caused poor Lee to believe that Alex was the love child from so many years ago. Am I correct in all this, Alex?"

Alex simply nodded sullenly, while J and Chris looked at each other in confusion.

"But," Chris began, "we…"

"Yes, Chris, I know. By that point, you and J had already broken into Pat's apartment and forced the poor victim to take an overdose of those ubiquitous 'blueberry pills' for which all of us have prescriptions, including Pat. Did you do it at gunpoint? Or some other foul method?"

"Gunpoint," J admitted.

"So you see, Alex, you really committed one fewer murder than you think you did. Pat was already half dead by the time you got there. Did you ever stop to wonder why the victim didn't put up much of a struggle over being forced to take an overdose of sleeping pills?"

"I assumed it was the Parkinson's thing," Alex responded matter-of-factly.

"A question for J and Chris," I put in. "How exactly did you two get into Pat's apartment without being noticed?"

Chris looked at Law, who didn't quite make eye contact. No words were necessary, for the implication was clear: Law had granted favors to someone in exchange for access to the apartment.

"The doorman?" I asked.

"Superintendent," responded Law.

"What I don't understand," J said, speaking for the first time, "is why Pat wouldn't have just told Lee about this in person. Why did Pat have to write a letter?"

"J, as you are not a person of letters, I am sure you cannot understand that for the more literate or educated, writing—especially about one's own feelings or highly sensitive matters—is sometimes preferable to spoken language. Besides, as some of you may know, Lee arrived to the house on Long Island more than a bit agitated. I knew that Pat and Lee had recently begun a renewed acquaintance, and that it had been as fraught with conflict as it had been all those decades ago. There had clearly been some sort of blow-up prior to Lee's coming to Long Island; Lee intimated as much to me upon arrival, indicating that the past had made an unpleasant reappearance. I suspect that Pat told Lee about the plan to find the child, and that Lee had mixed or negative feelings about that. For as we know, Lee always preferred to live in the present and might have wanted the past left alone, which could have led to a rip-roaring argument with Pat.

"So, if the two paramours were not on speaking terms, it would make sense for Pat to write. Of course, when rewriting the original letter, Alex made sure to cover all the bases there, too, implying that Lee was unreachable due to being at my house, where cell phone reception is less than ideal. And, as we all know, cell service often *is* spotty in exclusive neighborhoods, so this reason made perfectly logical sense."

Alex's stony silence made it patently obvious that not a word of what I'd said thus far could be disputed.

"What Alex hadn't expected, of course, was the fact that Pat was a patient of Doctor Rosenthal, who was of course the lover of Law, who not only dallied with Chris on occasion but also eavesdropped on patients' private sessions. It was Law who heard Pat tell the doctor that the love child—adopted name Jody Crewe—had been found in New York City. Law, never one to miss any details, understood immediately that J was heir to a large fortune, and began plotting with Chris immediately to get it. Hoping to secure J's fortune quickly, J and Chris plotted Pat's death, while Law (as I have just discovered) pretended to be a friend in need and worked behind the scenes to get them access to Pat's apartment. Of course, Law and Chris had been carrying on for quite a while, but to keep Dr. R in the dark, Law pretended to take up with Chris solely for purposes of the plot.

"In the meantime, Alex had to make sure that nobody would be able to expose the identity-theft scheme. So, posing as a prospective client, Alex visited Pat's attorney—none other than the delightful Kevin Jennings, whom you all know—to try to discover the name of the private detective who'd been hired to find the love child. While Pat's original letter to Lee is lost to posterity"—here I threw a glance at Alex, who most assuredly had destroyed it long ago—"I think it is safe to assume that in it Pat made reference to having hired a P.I. recommended by an attorney, and that the P.I had found the child here in New York City. Kevin, not suspecting any foul intent, recommended to Alex the services of Junior Makeba, a streetwise detective from Washington Heights." At the mention of that less-than-desirable neighborhood, *moues* of distaste were seen around the room.

"And this is a part of the story you three may not know," I continued, nodding at Chris, Law, and J. "Very quietly, Alex paid Mr. Makeba a visit and eliminated him from the ranks of the living. A telltale napkin from a Jamaican Jerk Chicken restaurant gave me all the clues I needed to discover the identity of Mr. Makeba's killer. But let us not dwell on Junior Makeba, who is tangential to our story."

The masses murmured their assent, and I resumed my narrative.

"Even before Junior was dispatched, however, one person remained a stubborn obstacle in all of your quests for inherited treasure. You all had assumed that Pat's money would go directly to the heir, so you simply waited for your money to arrive."

Guilty glances were exchanged. I soldiered on.

"So you all sat back and waited for the phone call from an attorney's office to alert you to your newfound fortune. From Pat's original letter, Alex knew that the money was being entrusted to Lee for 'safekeeping.' Meanwhile, I can only imagine poor Lee's horror upon discovering in a phony letter from Pat that Alex, a current paramour, was also that same love child from three decades earlier!

"Law, Chris, and J had not considered the idea that Pat would ask Lee—the other parent in this equation—to hold the money and make sure it got into the heir's hands. And, as we all know, Lee could not be trusted with such a large sum. I suspect that the setting up of the trust fund was Lee's way of draining off as much of it as possible, and all of you—who I am sure have heard rumors of Lee's financial peccadilloes—needed to make sure that the inheritance happened while it still existed.

"This meant that Lee had to be dealt with. J and Chris, aided by Law, no doubt wondered why they were not notified of Pat's death and their impending riches—until Law eavesdropped on one of Lee's sessions with Doctor Rosenthal and learned that Pat's money had gone to Lee for safekeeping, and that the final heir would be Alex. One can only imagine the rage of you three upon seeing your fortune stolen out from underneath you by Alex! Still, you managed to remain calm at the reading of Lee's will, because DNA was on your side, J. With the proper personal implements, you'd easily be able to prove that you were Lee and Pat's child.

"This is why both their apartments were in such disarray when I visited them. All of you were busy looking for items that would prove J's lineage, including things that you hoped would provide hair samples. Hair is full of DNA evidence, and what could be better proof of J's parentage? With such samples, there would be no need to exhume the bodies, which would have been highly inconvenient, especially if the authorities starting looking more closely at the cadavers and the causes of death. Which reminds me, Alex, did you bring the requested item?"

Alex nodded and retrieved an obsidian box from a satchel. I opened it and caught my breath. For inside lay the item that had launched this entire sordid investigation: the much coveted, and much stolen, tortoise shell hairbrush, which Chris and J had stolen from Lee's apartment, and which Alex had stolen from theirs.

48

Let me not waste ink on describing the surfeit of emotions engendered by that stunning hairbrush. For there it sat, a reminder that no man-made instrument could ever tame Lee's shaggy locks, just as no human could ever tame Lee, that untrue, embezzling, and wandering lover. But I suppose this is my lot in life: to always be the one to give love freely and purely, and to be taken advantage of by those with baser instincts and desires.

Almost overcome by these thoughts, I excused myself momentarily so that I might place the hairbrush in its rightful place. In truth, I thought I might also find solace in one of the 'zucchini pills' that reside in my *boudoir* and that sometimes have the beneficial effect of rebalancing my emotions; and, given the circumstances, I decided to engage in this small bit of self-indulgence. I returned from my private quarters just a few minutes later, took my position at the center of the room, and picked up where I'd left off.

"Ahem. To continue. So the race was now on. Alex needed to rid the world of Lee, before Lee could do any investigation into Alex's past, and before Lee could siphon off part or all of the inheritance. J needed to do the same, as did Chris and Law by association. And so the murderous plotting continued. J, your 'blueberry pills' had proven quite effective with Pat, so why not use the same technique on Lee? I assume the scenario was very much like ours at that pretentious little café on Ninth Avenue. You met Lee for lunch, administered the dose while Lee visited the restroom, then returned to Lee's apartment to complete the nefarious act. Or did you also have your bartender friend slip mickeys into Lee's drinks, as he did with mine?"

J remained silent, an admission of guilt if ever there was one.

"This time, however, you changed your method. It would not be a problem for you if the authorities realized that Lee had been murdered. Suspicion would of course fall directly on Alex, who was the titular if fraudulent heir. So, with one fell swoop, you could get rid of two obstacles—Lee and Alex. So you put Lee into bed and stabbed that poor innocent with a small knife, directly in the heart. You and Chris assumed someone would find Lee within the next few days, Alex would be questioned, and you'd be that much closer to your fortune. Of course, you did all this without Law or Doctor Rosenthal's approval, which got you into trouble later. When the deed was done, you went on a hunt for any of Lee's personal items that might contain DNA material, including the hairbrush, so that you might that much more easily establish your identity at the proper time.

"But you didn't realize that another homicidal maniac was also hunting Lee at the same time. Of course, it was easier for Alex, who had a key to Lee's home. Alex had much more of a stake in making the death seem accidental. So, soon after you left Lee for dead, Alex crept in—during the night, I am sure, given Lee's predilection for taking those 'blueberry pills' to ensure a restful night's slumber—and murdered poor dead Lee a second time, by administering a fatal dose. Everyone knows Lee had a prescription, so an accidental overdose would raise fewer questions. As Septimus McAllister pointed out to me, pills are quite easily forced down someone's gullet, and that, I am sure, is the method Alex used, leaving some minor bruises on poor Lee's throat in the process. Thus, Alex, once again you murdered someone who was already dead. I suspect you didn't take the time to inspect

Lee's body. If you had, you might have seen the small trickle of blood from the stiletto knife wound. But you had no reason to suspect that others were stalking Lee as well, so I assume you got into the apartment, committed your foul deed as quickly as possible, and left as soon as you finished searching the apartment for items that might link the genetics of Lee and J. I'm sure you were surprised that all such items seemed to be missing. You thought you were one step ahead of everyone, but you hadn't anticipated Chris's special relationship with Law, Law's special relationship with Doctor Rosenthal, and the doctor's special relationship with Septimus, who was able to sweep the murder completely under the rug.

"In the meantime, J and Chris, I suspect the doctor and Law were quite upset with you regarding the knife wound. What you two thought would be an effective method of casting suspicion on somebody else actually pointed to a real murder as opposed to a simple overdose. But no matter—it was easy for Dr. R to call in a favor with Septimus McAllister, who coincidentally had also examined Pat's body and truly believed that Pat had committed suicide. This has always been a problem with the two of you—thinking you can match wits with your intellectual superiors." I flashed back to that scene in the garden on Long Island, when J and Chris had feebly been attempting to play Scrabble, a game as much beyond their cranial capacity as *Jeopardy*. "Then again, Chris, perhaps old habits die hard. You and J have always been of one mind, so it probably made sense for you to continue plotting with J on your own, so as not to arouse J's always-ready suspicions regarding your relationship with Law."

J glared at Alex. "Let's just say that maybe we chose to do it the way we did because Alex deserved a suitable punishment for the many sins committed."

"And this is why you didn't go to the authorities imme-diately, regarding the stolen inheritance/identity. Am I cor-rect, J? You felt you and Chris should 'take care of' Alex in your own way, to ensure the proper revenge?"

"Yes," J said proudly.

"And was this idea suggested to you by anyone in partic-ular?" I asked.

"It was Chris's idea."

"Which is to say it was Law's idea to keep an entire series of plots from being found out."

Alex nodded, taking it all in. I'd provided the brief strokes in yesterday's message to that deranged individual—just enough information to ensure Alex's cooperation, but this was the first time the would-be double murderer was hearing all the sordid details unraveled in one suspenseful and enlightening narrative.

"But our tale continues. At this point, Alex has inherited a large fortune that rightfully belongs to J. In the meantime, both sets of criminals have burgled the victims' homes: J and Chris gathering personal effects that will help establish J as the rightful heir through DNA evidence, Alex seeking to remove and destroy any such items."

I pointed at Chris and J. "And you two thought my apart-ment might hold some additional important items, didn't you? But I wonder—and I do admit that this question has puzzled me—how you knew that I had Pat's box of personal possessions here?"

J grimaced. "Well, I guess that was our one lucky break in this whole thing. We went back to Pat's apartment one last time to make sure we hadn't missed anything, and afterward we stopped at a café on the corner. You must have gotten to the apartment just after us. We were pouring cream into our coffees, looked up, and saw you leaving the building with that metal box. Where did you find it? We looked everywhere and didn't see it."

"Never you mind, J," I said, unwilling to share trade secrets. "The answer is immaterial at this point. But you assumed—rightly—that it contained important information. That's when you and Chris, with Law's able assistance I am sure, hatched the next part of your plot. You arranged to meet me for lunch, and you worked with your 'friend' the bartender to slip some 'blueberries' into my cosmos, causing me to black out for most of the afternoon. You graciously escorted me back to my apartment and put me to bed, then proceeded to snoop around the apartment until you found the box. And in it you found not only the photos but also those baubles that would help establish your provenance."

J and Chris frowned, Alex stared blank-eyed and perhaps medicated, and Law gazed off into the distance, dreamily.

"Of course you could not take the box with you that day, as it would be quite obvious to me, when I returned to consciousness, who the thief was. So you decided to work with your partners in crime to accomplish two important tasks at once. You issued the phony invitations to me and Alex to meet atop the Empire State Building. While Chris attempted to rid us of Alex once and for all, J gained access to my apartment and made off with the tin box, its photos, and its baubles. Dare I ask if Law played a role in granting favors to anyone in particular to gain J access to my home?"

"The doorman," quoth Law. Oh, the betrayal! I had suspected as much, the doorman's longstanding infatuation with me notwithstanding. For I could not deny the impossibility of anyone, even a devoted doorman, holding out long against Law's ample charms.

I forged ahead. "I admit that the baubles—or, rather, the fact that there exist three sets of them—has created a not insignificant amount of mental gymnastics for me. But, as always, logic has prevailed. J, you have long had a reputation for wearing ornate and occasionally bizarre jewelry, and I think many of us have long since stopped paying any heed to it, as it has always seemed rather a plea for attention.

"But I suspect that perhaps Alex was paying rather more attention than the rest of us, at least for a while. Having been a paramour of Lee's, and no doubt having looked through Lee's personal possessions when Lee was not present or conscious, Alex would have known that Lee owned a set of these baubles. Because Lee had stopped wearing jewelry more than a decade ago, none of us would have seen the onyx ring and peridot pendant, except perhaps for me, but I admit that I do not spend much time thinking about the jewelry of former lovers. I also suspect that somewhere in Lee's apartment Alex may have seen photos of Lee and Pat in the old days, each wearing the same pieces of jewelry, and that Alex noticed that J was the owner of identical baubles. Could these pieces of cheap costume jewelry be proof of J's blood relation to Lee, some sort of Dickensian plot device? If I were in Alex's position—i.e., the position of preventing anyone else from getting a hold of Pat and Lee's money—I would have assumed the worst, and that's exactly what Alex did, breaking into J and Chris's apartment in search of the baubles, as well as any of Lee or Pat's personal DNA-filled items. You used Lee's keys to gain access—yes, Alex?"

"Yes," responded Alex.

"To your chagrin, you didn't find the baubles, which left two sets of them unaccounted for. You had Lee's baubles; and Pat's baubles sat in the tin box in my apartment, before J stole them. Where were J's baubles? Well, as your bad luck would have it, on the day of your break-in J was wearing the onyx ring you sought. You did find the pendant, but it was missing something." I reached into my jacket pocket and pulled out the peridot. "And here it is. I found it under the couch here in my parlor purely by happenstance. J, I assume it dropped off your chain while you were bringing me to bed after drugging me with the 'blueberries,' or when you were searching my apartment for Pat's tin box."

Chris tossed an evil glance at J. "*How many times* did I tell you to get the mounting on that pendant fixed?"

I continued. "But the day at Chris and J's apartment wasn't a complete loss for Alex, who found a treasure trove of Lee's personal products, including the tortoise shell hairbrush that is now rightfully mine. And that is why J was so truly upset when I arrived to provide succour. Neither of you cared one whit about the other items that had been stolen, but those personal items were all you had to prove J's genetic link to Lee. Short of exhumation, that is—and, as I've already pointed out, an exhumation is the last thing any murderer who's gotten away with it would want.

"And that," I concluded, "is that. Really, who would ever have thought the lot of you could have conceived such complicated plots? I just feel relieved that none of you ever tried to kill *me*, for I know I discussed the terms of my will with the late Doctor Rosenthal, and at one time you were all beneficiaries."

49

I have often wondered how the world's great artists—Michelangelo, Leonardo da Vinci, Rembrandt, Monet, and their ilk—have felt upon completing a masterpiece. Did they stand back and view it with a critical eye? Or did they experience that most fulfilling sensation of knowing, intuitively, the great depths of their accomplishment? Though I have never been one to engage in excessive self-congratulation, I admit that I was feeling much more the latter than the former. Yes, I had missed a few details, and there were certain questions whose answers I'd needed to intuit—a sort of mental filling in of the blanks, more of a general understanding of how something *could* have happened rather than *specific* details of what took place—but all in all, I could look back on the case with a sense of satisfaction.

Equally, or perhaps more, satisfying was the outcome, or rather the scenario that would play itself out in the future. Of course, there was the inconvenience of having to find another therapist in a city full of psychological charlatans. Prior to dying, Dr. Rosenthal had signed a contract, agreeing to appointments at whatever time was convenient for me, as well as phone consultations with no notice; and all of these sessions were to be gratis, of course. These arrangements would have been highly convenient for me; but alas, Dr. R had gulped down the tainted water all too quickly, leaving me with a signed contract voided by death.

Still, there were other benefits to be reaped from the situation. By dint of our new contract, Law was obligated to provide me with requested favors, with zero complaint, and to turn over that previously mentioned large sum of ill-gotten blackmailing gains. Law, too, was to cease and desist all blackmailing activities immediately, for, as Kevin had pointed out while typing up the contract, "There's no better candidate for murder than a blackmailer." Indeed. And certainly I wished Law to remain alive, especially while young and attractive, and while my libido was still active.

For their part, J, Chris, and Alex all had certain responsibilities to fulfill as well. All had agreed in their contracts to serve as sort of personal amanuenses to me, running various

errands about town, chasing down certain delicacies that can
be difficult to procure, cleaning my home, and driving me
around the region, as I have come to an age where it is much
more pleasurable to be driven than to drive. Other personages
might see this as an opportunity to run those poor criminals
ragged with a series of excessive demands, but I have never
been the type of person to take advantage of others' misfortunes. No, I would exercise my power with restraint, using it
only when absolutely necessary, and certainly no more than a
few times per day.

And, should Alex, Chris, Law, and J ever decide to
improve their lot in life by banding together to take action
against me, it was understood that Kevin was under strict
orders to report the details of all previous activities to the
authorities immediately. But say what you will about this particular group of people, they are all rather devoted pragma-
tists, and I expected that within a few weeks of our new
arrangements they would have made a virtue of necessity, as
each individual contract did offer them continued freedom to
roam about Manhattan, as opposed to incarceration in a
dank, dirty jail cell.

And the time had come to bring the evening's festivities
to a close.

"Well, friends," I began, "I hope this evening's revelations
have answered some of your unanswered questions. Before
you all depart, I do want to mention one final thing. With all
the events of recent weeks, it seems that we never did have a
proper good-bye for our dear Lee. We also should take time to
celebrate the life of poor Pat, whom I did not know personally but who certainly deserved better than murder. Here is
what I propose. Let us all repair to my house on Long Island
two weeks hence for a memorial service. Such a private event
will certainly be healing for all of us."

Many glances were exchanged, and heads began nodding with great approval. And it did my heart good to see my posse coming together again as dear friends instead of monetary rivals.

"Of course," I continued, "I am in no shape to make all the arrangements, as I need to take to bed for several days to refresh my spirit and recharge my batteries, as it were. So, let us do it this way. Alex, you will arrange for the flowers and a suitable holy person to say a few words in memory of Lee and Pat. Law, you will be in charge of libations and nourishment for the weekend. Chris, your task will be to interface with my incompetent caretakers, to ensure that the house is prepared and stocked as necessary. And J, you will kindly prepare the guest list and proffer the invitations.

"Now, as you all know, I am not one for electronic communications, but I really feel that I must have a much-needed respite from the telephone and from human company for at least several days. Therefore, I will make myself available for one hour per day, from 8 to 9 p.m., to answer any questions via email. I expect that I will re-emerge into the world by this time next week, but for now—no phone calls please, and only emails with any questions. I trust all of you to make the right decisions; and God bless! May your slumbers this evening be as restful as mine."

50

"The world is too much with us," said William Wordsworth; and never in my life had I felt those words of my great-great-great-uncle more keenly than in the previous weeks. Certainly, there is only one cure for the demands of the world, and that is to lock oneself away in a state of solitary bliss for a number of days, in which the 'apple pills' and 'pomegranate pills' can work their pharmacological magic.

And work they did, for 48 hours seemed to pass in the blink of an eye. Passing through my study two evenings after the gathering, I happened to notice the time: 8:08 p.m., directly within the hour that I had promised to read email. Always true to my promises, I booted up the machine, clicked a few times, and accessed my personal email account.

Amidst the many emails from Kevin urging an evening visit, I saw a lone, quasi-illiterate electronic missive from "J Croux" titled "Invte and Geust List." I double clicked and read as follows:

hi robin,

here is what i think the invittation and geust list shoud look like, just rite back & let me kno if its ok. ill get them printed & sent out as soon as i get ur ok. lets also invite kevin?

thanks, j

A Memrial Service
in Honr of
Ms Pat Armstrong
Mr Lee Harris

We request the honor of your presents
at a memmorial serrice to honor the
memmories of these 2 dearly departed
persons, the parents of our good friend
J Croux.

Where: The house of Robin Anders,
_____, Long Isdlhand
When: The weeknd of _____
RSVP: J Croux, 917-XXX-XXXX

****

Guest list (alpha order):
Mr Alex Mann
Ms Chris Blackheart
Mr J Croux
Ms Law Lessness
Ms Robin Anders

I felt a familiar throb beginning at my right temple, the early indicator of a particularly debilitating migraine. Could nobody be trusted with even the smallest details? I had given J the easiest of tasks, the creation of an invitation and a guest list, and this is what had been sent to me—an email filled with misspellings and typographical errors, including a number of instances where *r*'s had been mistyped as *s*'s, and vice versa, thereby changing the gender of some of the invitees, as well as at least one of the deceased!

But I suppose this is what happens when one delegates tasks to a simpleton.

Disclaimer

This extravagant tale has made use of the New York City Medical Examiner's office as a completely fictional plot device. In no way should the unconscionable and purely fictional acts of Septimus McAllister be construed in any way, shape, or form as a reflection on the hard-working and underappreciated personnel of the NYCME.

And for all visitors to New York City: Rest assured that it is (nearly) impossible to push someone off the 86th floor observation deck of the Empire State Building, or to stab someone thereon.

To Renee Vincent, wherever you are: Robin wishes you all the best.

—S.R.

TALES FROM THE BACK PAGE

Have you ever wondered about the stories behind the advertisements in your local newspaper—those ads for fetish parties, discount psychotherapy, Gothic/Punk events, and lonelyhearts seeking to reestablish contact with a shipped that passed in the night?

Each book in the *Tales from the Back Page* series looks closely at an advertisement placed on the "Bulletin Board" of *The Clarion*, a community newspaper published on Manhattan's Upper West Side. In the first volume, *Who Gets the Apartment?*, a con artist dupes four young Manhattanites, renting them a luxurious penthouse condo (which he doesn't own) for $600 a month. When the four strangers attempt to move into the apartment on the same day, they realize they've been had. Which of them, if any, will get to keep the apartment? Will they band together to bring the swindler to justice, or will they connive and plot against one another to secure a piece of prime New York City real estate?

In Volume 2, *Circle of Assassins*, five disgruntled New Yorkers find themselves manipulated into murder by a criminal mastermind. Hailed as a masterpiece of suspense filled with shocking surprises, *Circle of Assassins* explores what happens when average people decide to take justice into their own hands.

Available Now:

#1
Who Gets the Apartment?
978-0-9773787-3-9

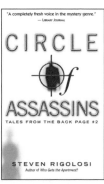

#2
Circle of Assassins
978-0-9773787-4-6

#3
Androgynous Murder House Party
978-0-9773787-6-0

About the Author

Steven Rigolosi is the director of market research and development for a Manhattan-based publisher of scientific books. *Androgynous Murder House Party* is his third novel. After years of living in Manhattan, he now lives in Northern New Jersey, where he is at work on the fourth book in the *Tales from the Back Page* series. His email address is srigolosi@yahoo.com.

About the Narrator

Robin Anders is the Associate Director of New Talent at the Goode Foundation, a Greenwich Village-based philanthropic organization founded to provide support for up-and-coming artists and performers. Robin lives on Manhattan's Upper West Side. When not writing sonnets or cooking gourmet meals, Robin enjoys arguing with receptionists and solving complicated crimes that have defeated lesser sleuths.